The Forest Bull

Terry Maggert

Cover Art: Amalia Chitulescu

Copyright © 2013 Terry Maggert
All rights reserved.

ISBN: 1484862201
ISBN 13: 9781484862209

Dedication: For Missy and Teddy, of course.

For the female of the species is more deadly than the male. - Rudyard Kipling

Contents

Chapter 1 1
Chapter 2 4
Chapter 3 9
Chapter 4 11
Chapter 5 14
Chapter 6 16
Chapter 7 17
Chapter 8 21
Chapter 9 26
Chapter 10 30
Chapter 11 33
Chapter 12 35
Chapter 13 36
Chapter 14 39
Chapter 15 40
Chapter 16 43
Chapter 17 47
Chapter 18 50
Chapter 19 53
Chapter 20 56
Chapter 21 58
Chapter 22 60
Chapter 23 61
Chapter 24 65
Chapter 25 66
Chapter 26 69
Chapter 27 71
Chapter 28 74
Chapter 29 77
Chapter 30 79
Chapter 31 86
Chapter 32 90
Chapter 33 94

Chapter 34...............99
Chapter 35...............102
Chapter 36...............104
Chapter 37...............107
Chapter 38...............109
Chapter 39...............113
Chapter 40...............117
Chapter 41...............120
Chapter 42...............123
Chapter 43...............126
Chapter 44...............129
Chapter 45...............133
Chapter 46...............145
Chapter 47...............153
Chapter 48...............156
Chapter 49...............158
Chapter 50...............160
Chapter 51...............163
Chapter 52...............167
Chapter 53...............177
Chapter 54...............181
Chapter 55...............186
Chapter 56...............188
Chapter 57...............190
Chapter 58...............195
Chapter 59...............206
Chapter 60...............207
Chapter 61...............212
Chapter 62...............214
Chapter 63...............218
Chapter 64...............223
Chapter 65...............225
Chapter 66...............227
Chapter 67...............232
Chapter 68...............233
Chapter 69...............235
Epilogue I...............238
Epilogue II...............240

I

Florida

"You may kiss me now," she stated in a voice devoid of music. The mirthless bow of her full lips betrayed her intent to me, but I knew the invitation, like my costume, was a lie. She was pretending to be human. I adopted the persona of just another lonely, awkward snowbird, my own illusion that had brought me to this intimate second with her, inviting me closer with a flicker of her brow. I bought in, leaning towards her in the alcove of a cheesy hotel that advertised in French and English. The boardwalk nearby was a haven for the Quebecois who fled the rigors of winter for the sun and crowding of Hollywood, Florida, squeezed between the fashion of Miami and the canals of Fort Lauderdale.

We were a mismatched pair because she saw what I wished: a slouching, white-bread tourist being rewarded by the gods of fate with the company of a pale, elegant woman whose body filled her sundress flawlessly. Other couples and groups passed us in a late night rush between the bars and gathering places of the beach. It was cool for November. Bursts of drunken laughter mixed with the quiet spaces surrounding lovers who walked, faces turned to the shushing metronome of the surf. A single set of footfalls clattered nearby, interrupting our moment of impending passion. It was a woman dropping her keys and swearing in lightly-accented French. With a metallic tinkling, she picked them up and moved off into the night, leaving us alone again.

Reaching out, I took the woman's thin hand tentatively as she leaned into me with beautiful but shopworn looks, tired under her makeup. A halo of dark curls was pushed back from her oval face with hair combs that were deeply burnished red, gleaming like rubbed bone. They looked regal in the careless way that beautiful women wear trinkets with quiet entitlement.

She had approached me in a bar an hour earlier as I sat alone nursing a comical umbrella drink and reading a paperback. I dress with purpose when I become someone else, leaving a riot of clues about my weaknesses and desires scattered on me. I hunch. I become meek. I mute my ego and become subservient to an affectation of absolute mediocrity. A cheap, tacky sweatshirt and garishly new deck shoes completed my identity as a visitor, unsure of my surroundings and far from home. I added moping loneliness and an aura of desperation purely for effect. With my shoulders rolled in and my body language long on failure, women ignored me. I, in turn, avoided anyone who made eye contact until she sat down, sliding into the space next to me and settling quickly. She was very still except for her eyes. They were alive, but brittle and hooded.

"Senya," she introduced herself when she calmly sat in my booth without invitation.

There was no uncertainty in her motions as she drank one glass of wine while asking a mechanical litany of questions. Where was I from? Did I have family with me? Was I staying nearby? She delivered these in a throaty accent that was purely Eastern Europe, all while flirting with me in a listless way. I played the role of the flattered rube, and, when she asked me to leave with her my eyes, went wide, the shock of my good fortune lighting my face. I fumbled awkwardly to the door with her.

And, now, here we were, in a shadowed place with the wind and water muted. Alone, or as much as you could be in public. She pulled me to her and I inhaled her scents of red wine, foreign tobacco, and the lingering grit of the ocean. She opened her mouth and circled me with her arms, warming to the moment as we kissed. I felt her body begin to flower from our contact and winced with regret as my hand whispered upwards, burying the slim knife I had silently palmed deep into her ribs. She buckled and tried to pull back, but my arms locked on her like heavy stones resting in earth. Her eyes never opened as the poisonous blade wrecked her spirit, the silvered steel shooting through her without mercy, cutting the bond to her body forever.

Immortals are always surprised when they die. She was no different, judging by her open-mouthed, hiccupping sigh as I lowered her spasmodic body, eyes fluttering, to the concrete of the hotel patio. In seconds, she began to sublime, her ashes fleeing upward with tiny blue points of moonlight that left her dress an empty outline. I stepped back, looking at the dust of Senya, and began to turn away. In that instant, two obscenely fat moths fluttered down and began to delicately scatter her remains with their feet.

I have learned that killing immortals causes changes in my body. Maybe another executioner could learn how to fly, read minds, or bend a metal rod with their hands. I tend to think that each immortal death makes us better at what we know. For me, I grow faster, more confident. I know I am something more after fourteen years of killing their kind.

I still can't fly, but one thing is certain. I'm very good with knives.

2

Arriving home, I parked, stepping through the door to find all three of my housemates spread over the living room and kitchen. Home is a single level duplex built in the 1950s. We removed the center wall years ago and tiled the floor seamlessly to match, leaving an airy feel that was classic Floridian. When one lives with people long enough in our particular dynamic, there is little need for privacy. In our unusual occupation, we also needed to be instantly available to each other at odd hours. The wall had to come down, and it turned the duplex into an open, common place for us to live and work. To the left sat Risa, her legs pulled up on a chair at the kitchen table. Her earbuds leaked music that belonged in a Lebanese nightclub. Despite a fearsome intelligence, her taste in music was on par with a cheesy disco rat. She was a compact, dusky girl with enormous black eyes and curly hair that she keeps short. Her full lips were moving slightly to the music as she pored over her laptop. A glass of wine sat next to her hand, fingers tapping lightly on the table. I could see she was scrolling through an internet message board of some sort. One browned leg hung down, her toes just touching the floor. Risa was not tall, but her intensity made her seem imposing, especially when one questioned her musical choices. I know from experience.

"How'd it go? Anything?" she looked up and spoke, reaching for her wine.

I tossed my keys on the table and opened the fridge.

"Wally bought some beer. It's in the door," she offered.

"Thanks, got it. Ale? We're moving up." I took an appreciative sip of our upgrade.

Usually, we drank like we were still on a budget in college, swilling cans of beer so foul, a person could strip paint with it. I think it was a reflection of our guilt at being financially secure after years of noodles and late rent. I glanced over at the couch before I spoke.

Wally was stretched out with a bowl of popcorn balancing precariously on her bare stomach. Her long legs were split like tanned twigs, one on the coffee table, and the other thrown across the sleeping form of our enormous Great Dane, Gyro, who had achieved the same superior state of relaxation. Both were snoring gustily. With a snort, Wally launched the popcorn bowl onto the floor and resettled, mumbling. When standing, she was a California blonde out of central casting. Her long hair hung artfully, without effort. Her green eyes and freckles were perched on a flawless face and a full mouth of perfect teeth that she flashed during her nearly constant smile. For women who looked like Wally, life was a long stretch of free food, men fighting to hold doors for her, and glares from women as their husbands walked into parking meters when she passed by. We exploited her carefree attitude and stunning looks at every turn. She was our key to even the dourest obstacles among the male population of the world. And some women, too. As Waleska Schmidt snored on the couch in a haze of popcorn burps and the aroma of a pony-sized dog, her beauty was hardly evident in that unladylike setting.

We three had met in college while I dawdled on government money after four years of self-discovery in the United States Army. With my presuppositions in hand, I had joined after the death of my parents only to find that I had rarely been so wrong about anything in my life. The army was filled with dedicated people who carried a wide range of skills abroad and within our own borders. I found that I was average at taking direction, poor with guns, good under pressure, and able to kill with little lingering introspection. Under the dedicated system that had been producing soldiers for more than two centuries, I exited the army a man, when I had entered as a skinny loner with no team-building skills. I also learned that, excepting the beaches of my home, I detested sand and heat equally. When my four year sojourn into the world of the martial sciences was at end, I returned to begin a relationship with the two women who would be my partners for what I hoped would be the remainder of my life. I am 6'3". I left the army at two hundred pounds of muscle, and I had the good fortune to inherit my mother's Norwegian looks and blue eyes with my father's crop of black hair. After serving, one could call me an adult, yet even my innate fearlessness made the physical and intellectual attractions of Wally and Risa stretch the very limits of my masculine confidence. They challenged me with their thoughts, their bodies, and their simple presence.

"Ring, you smell like salt. Beach?" Risa brought me back to our discussion.

"Yeah. I camped at a booth in Vince's and read. I didn't wait long. You were right about the place. I think your idea to read the missing persons reports from Canada will pay off big."

Vince's is the bar that tourists frequent most on Hollywood Beach, as it offers the requisite cheesy nautical décor and ice cold beer. Risa had combed French-language newspapers from Canada in hopes of finding a lead on where immortals were working in our area. We simply look for the unusual. Missing persons, sudden divorces where one partner never returns home, anything that seemed off. We followed it all. Since tourists were a moveable feast to immortals, we spread our search accordingly. We read every major online news site from the northern United States, Canada, Germany, and the United Kingdom. Our sources included translations of news from the heart of Europe to the coast of Africa, and they never failed to yield a story that was both sad and enraging. In the news, we read of broken lives and loneliness that called for vengeance, which we provided with increasing efficiency.

Risa had drawn the short straw and learned French, since it was her idea to comb the Quebecois media for tips. We all learned a second and third language in order to make collecting information that much faster, but Risa had a true gift. To her, there was a rhythm to speech and a pattern to writing. Riffing on her linguistic skills, she built on her knowledge of different languages with each passing year. Risa was a translator, a thinker, and an analyst who knew that the pitch and timbre of words could yield secrets that we needed. Some immortals refused to speak English, angry and repulsed by finding themselves at our scant mercy. Their arrogance usually held until the bitter end. Risa, Wally and I have been cursed in so many tongues we've lost track. It doesn't make it any less sweet to see a predator give in to the fear that they have visited upon humanity for years, or, in some cases, centuries. I think about the final minutes of terror that mothers, fathers, children, and lovers have felt at the hands of the supernatural. I don't know if all immortals are bad, but the ones we kill certainly pass that test.

I settled on the chair in what Risa called my debriefing pose as she began to add to her running compilation of files, which ranged from readily available sources to items she acquired less honestly. She was not above hacking an email system or server in order to get at information we needed. I looked straight ahead and told her of the beautiful East European and her odd accent. Risa stopped me occasionally, asking for an additional detail.

"Senya?" she asked, her hands poised over the laptop's keyboard.

She typed what facts we knew of the woman I had met and dispatched. And, so, our personal database grew with each encounter among the undying.

"East European. Pretty. Pale complexion. She wasn't from peasant stock," I paused, considering. "She was a bit more highborn. Turned in the last century, I think. I saved her hair combs because they look like heirlooms."

I fished them from my pocket and set them carefully in front of Risa on the table. She stopped typing and made an appreciative noise.

"These are very old. They look like . . . red jade?" she questioned me, turning one comb to see every angle in the light.

"It's carnelian," Wally announced. She had risen from her nap and stood with her head cocked at the edge of the kitchen floor, considering the rich red material of the combs. Her hair was mussed from sleep, and she yawned hugely while absently scratching her stomach. Wally knew jewelry. She plucked one from the table and examined it intently.

"Hand-worked. Very old. Look how smooth it is, yes? The more I see, I think it is very, very old. Maybe even late Roman."

Her Argentine syntax was always more pronounced when she was sleepy, drunk, or angry. On occasion, she was all three simultaneously, usually during the World Cup soccer tournament, during which she would drink beer and curse lustily at the television screen during all hours of the day or night. While Wally continued to coo over the loot, a slight tremor shook my hands as the inertia of my night's success wore off. Risa looked at me gently, knowing that the shock and effect of the immortal dying was coming home to roost. To dispatch an immortal is not without cost. I leaned over a bit, feeling a wave of unease. Sometimes, after a kill, we would feel invigorated, chatty to the point of being a pest, or aroused, but, after some more violent, personal kills, needy and awash with depression. It depended on exactly what we had contacted. Tonight, I felt an intense mixture of uncertainty and loneliness.

Risa held out her hand to me, saying to Wally, "We're going to sleep this off for a while," in a soft tone.

For all her intensity, Risa had always shown Wally and me the highest compassion when we were left with the emotional wreckage of killing an immortal. Her gentle side was freely given to us when we were most vulnerable, a sometimes hidden vein of ore in a mind that was deep and prone to cool reason. Wally patted my shoulder and gave me a one-armed hug as she turned to reclaim her part of the couch from Gyro. I followed Risa closely enough to smell the rosewater perfume she wore and decided that the comfort of her room was exactly what I needed to rid myself of the veil that Senya had left behind. She closed the door and turned off the lamp in one motion, moving through the darkness with a certainty that the kill had left me wanting. Her arms welcomed me on the bed and, very shortly, I couldn't even remember what the waves had sounded like an hour before.

3

It was late morning when I woke up, feeling good for many reasons, not the least of which was the soft tangle of Risa the night before. The buzz from the immortal had gone to work on me immediately, received seamlessly into my muscles. I felt clear-headed and quick. It had been worth the ugliness of an act of murder, although that may sound crass. It helps to stay focused on what immortals do to humans and how, in many cases, they willingly left their original body behind. Some turned for vanity, others for power, and many from sheer vindictiveness. Sociopaths all too often found the lure of a long life of wanton sin to be irresistible.

I opened the back door and walked outside, Gyro right beside me. The grapefruit and orange trees groaned with their load of dark green unripe fruits, and I could smell the distinct musty salt of low tide. We lived on a canal that eventually connected to Port Everglades and then through the jetties, where the immensity of the Atlantic Ocean rolled. Our seawall was hemmed by a wooden dock with pilings that were covered in oysters. Two davits held our modest boat in the air, away from the briny water that rose and fell twice daily with the moody tides. A grill, table, and chairs completed the yard that was bordered in a riot of hibiscus and one lone banana tree that peeped defiantly above the hedge. Gyro stretched out and drooled on my bare foot, his enormous paws raking grass as I scratched his deep chest. I straightened and looked out over the canal at the ducks preening on a neighbor's dock, swinging my arms experimentally to see how I felt. It was good. Beyond good, actually. Senya must have been older than I had judged, and the benefits of dispatching her were quite welcomed by my body.

From Risa's Files:

For Sale: 2004 Ford F-150 4x4. Loaded, low miles, babied by owner who was last seen leaving work with some Goth tramp half his age. Since he left his wife and daughters without a word or warning, I'm selling his truck the same way. First 6,000 takes it. Reply to this email to see truck. If you're my husband, don't reply at all!

4

Immortality is a strange and inconsistent curse. Risa sees it as a type of disease that mutates from body to body, with the results being wildly divergent but rarely positive. Where Risa is analytical, Wally is emotional, judging the undying as criminals based on their sins. Between the clinical and sensory, we stitch together a name, a species, and a history for each new immortal. We have seen people who match the descriptions of nearly every mythical creature from recorded history. Some defy classification, their grotesque needs beyond any bogeyman from the sum of human fears. Their bodies change in ways that are subtle or shocking depending on what their new body craves. They adapt, and quickly, to the new, base wants that compel them to hunt and kill. Even in the blackest visions of Church cynics, human imagination placed limits on what could be described. Left to run free in the world, the effects of immortality easily surpassed those Church warnings of demons and beasts whose purpose was vile and fatal. What the supposition of mankind could not capture was the elegance of these predators. From our close vantage point, we were continuously stunned by the forms that death could take. We all agreed, regardless of the killer's beauty, they could not be left to winnow the ranks of innocents. Looking at the massive sprawl of Gyro's deep blue black frame, I was amazed once again at how some beauty could be benign and some lethal beyond belief. I was desperately proud of the fact that we three held life in such high esteem, even after years of hunting. It was a trait that I hoped would never fade, lest we become far too similar to our prey to continue calling ourselves human. I ended my musings in the bright sun and walked back inside, as it was nearing lunchtime, and that meant a visit to Hardigan Center.

When my favorite uncle and namesake, Hring, passed on, he left me more than one thing of value. Along with his friendship and advice, he left me the duplex where we lived that was half of my real estate inheritance. The other address was a small but well-tended strip mall built in the 1950s, less than a mile from home. With room for six businesses, Hardigan Center was many things to me. It was a source of legitimate income. It was a place to see friends. It was also a direct connection to my past and the memory of a man who cared deeply for me when I was detached and disinterested in adulthood. The low, block building was full of tenants at all times, with the exception of the corner space, where my uncle's television repair shop lay as it had the day he closed it in 1981. With faded Zenith and Curtis Mathis signs, the paneled counter and worn interior was a time capsule. The smell of the shag carpet in front and the lingering hints of electric grease and tools still hung in the motionless air, roasted by the Floridian sun for all these years. A Formica countertop was spalled with the use of three decades, where heavy televisions and awkward customers left a record of my Uncle's success. It was a sort of church for me, so I left it untouched, the small office a sacrosanct part of my own history. Though this corner remained still, the other spaces in the Center were alive and humming with energy, and one of them smelled delicious. It was time for lunch.

On the far left of the Center was the Butterfly, a Thai kitchen run by a family that had become an extension of my own. Panit and Boonsri were second generation restaurateurs whose parents had moved to Virginia in the 1960s. Panit was four inches shorter than his willowy wife and spent the majority of his time in the kitchen or at markets when time allowed. He had the whipcord frame of a frenetic chef and the confidence of a successful cook who knew his food was great. Boon had a brilliant smile and long black hair that fell to her waist in an ebony curtain. She ran the front dining area with a graceful touch and a demand for cleanliness that kept the Butterfly filled during lunch and dinner. Bright aromas of pepper and Thai basil, with hints of peanut, wafted through the eatery. Gold and red trim accented the dark wooden tables and padded chairs that sat on a cream tile floor. The inviting space was crowned by a collection of elephants and tapestries that were exotic but friendly in tone. I smiled at Boon as I walked in and inhaled the smell, mouthwatering to my grumbling, impolite stomach. She hugged me and started towards the kitchen in a smooth loop, her gold bracelets happily jingling with each step.

"I was wondering if you would turn up. Panit has lots of little snapper to cook. Want one?" Boon asked, with a warm smile on her beautiful face.

Few people could make me feel as welcome as she. I nodded and sat down at an open table, the other patrons turning to me with a little jealousy at my preferential treatment. Panit was a wizard with the succulent little fish, frying them whole with red chilies and coriander and then topping them with cucumbers, key lime sections and tomatoes. It was heaven on a plate. I leaned into the chair and settled in to wait.

5

Beauty is indeed a good gift of God; but that the good may not think it a great good, God dispenses it even to the wicked. - Saint Augustine

France

Elizabeth stood with her elegant silhouette backlit by the city at night. One hand absently held an empty champagne flute; the other toyed with the heavy curtains that framed a view of the heart of Paris. Her brown eyes lingered over the city as she stretched her sculpted body in a feline motion that sent black hair falling down her snowy back in a silken rush. Over her shoulder, on the edge of the tangled bed, the girl dressed, pulling boots on her long legs. She was tall, young, and radiant, possibly Czech, a honey blonde in her late teens. Her looks were natural and fresh, but unfinished, where Elizabeth was a classic dark beauty with a commanding presence that only breeding and maturity could grant. Money could buy the appearance of wealth but not the assurance to wear it like a second skin. The girl's beauty would command the eyes of men wherever she went, but Elizabeth's would bend their will even as she entered a room. Even a fool could see that the blood of kings flowed in her veins. Standing in heels, the girl met Elizabeth's height, eye to eye. Around the women, furniture of rich wood gleamed with the luster of wealth. Upholstery, flawless from disuse, covered the beautifully framed items that were tastefully scattered across the rooms. Each room of the suite spoke of money and taste. Even the single lamp that threw muted light from the corner was a model of understated style. The immediate area was in the disarray of harried intimacy. An empty wine bottle, berries on a bone china tray, and the scent of perfume and damp linen testified to the activity of the previous night. At least some Europeans still respected a Do Not Disturb sign, regardless of noise. The sign had also allowed them to sleep the day away, a dreamless sleep of joyous exhaustion. She looked at the girl, who now had her luggage near the door.

"Before you go, are you ready? Do you need anything?"

In the girl's purse rested a first class ticket to Miami and credit cards, all with no limit. Elizabeth's tone was light but warm. The girl reddened slightly from the remembrance of the previous week and the life that she was about to begin. She was also flushed from her internal struggle as her body began to change.

"No, I have everything. Thank you. Thank you a thousand times. This is . . . ," she trailed off as Elizabeth gave the smallest of frowns.

"Something is missing. Here. This." She held the girl's hand and slipped a delicate ring on her finger. The diamond was framed on either side by a strange stone deeper than oxblood. Light swirls of silky color danced in the gems. The antique platinum setting was graceful and worn, like an heirloom.

"I cannot—," the girl started.

Elizabeth shook her head slowly. "It was my daughter's. Wear it, and, when you have a daughter you love, give it to her."

To a girl of such youth and beauty, children were far away where she was going.

"But what if I have no daughter?" she asked. Elizabeth looked briefly at the window.

"Petra, your life will be one of gifts, giving. And receiving. Men will want you. They will try to own you. All of them, drunk with lust, an endless line of their eyes shining with greed," Elizabeth gave a wintry smile. "You will appeal to their vanity even as they feed you. Savor it. There is no other feeling like it."

She kissed the girl on the cheek in dismissal and turned to the champagne bottle settling in the silver urn. "Whether you want to or not, you will be a mother of sorts. Many daughters, I think. And when you find one who meets your mettle, you will give her the ring as a gift. In the meantime, the gift you will give is yourself."

6

The Forest

His hands posed, considering the delicate square of amber that he had polished until luminous, its angles catching the mellowed light of his work area in a buttery hue. His long but sturdy artisan fingers held a tiny ball-peen hammer that was tapping delicately along a border of brilliant silver. Within the hem of the metal was a deep red beryl gem, cut in a square. It was seemingly lit from within, a design that caught the radiance and mystery within the stone. He hesitated for a second and then seemed satisfied with the rhythmic stippling that gave the ring a worldly elegance. Framed by the squares of amber, he considered: Another accent stone? A leaf shape of beryl tailing away, adding fluidity and a graceful curve to the setting? Perhaps a pair of them. That was it, he decided. His hands moved deliberately to carry out the delicate work. Spring was only a short time away, and one could never be unprepared for the season of gifts. He bent with extra care and began to form the next tiny frame for the stone. This ring would be given in the spirit of desire, and he wanted its beauty to match the purpose.

7

Florida

The Tradewinds Steak House is an artifact where one can dine. Built in the early 1950s, it is a time capsule, lovingly maintained by Sid Blume, Jr., whose father opened what was an upscale eatery in the halcyon days of the first Florida Boom. Serving small charred steaks, good wine, and a requisite array of seafood, the Tradewinds was the last place anyone under the age of 40 or even 50 might be found, on most nights. That was exactly why Risa and Wally and I loved it. I wore a navy blazer over a linen shirt, and the women were wrapped in mildly garish cocktail dresses far too old for their calendar age. We wanted to blend in. In the valet area, a deluge of Cadillacs, Lincolns, and other testaments to a successful life disgorged couples dressed much the same as we were, although these were men and women who had built lives over decades. They hailed from the North, the Midwest, and Canada, and they stood next to each other in their dinner dress with the comfort and familiarity of a long life together. The men had silver hair if they had any at all, and the women had style that melded every era since the Korean War into an unofficial look that signaled We Made It. The entire atmosphere celebrated the dream of Rockwell in a gentle manner fueled by years of hard work. I reveled in it. With my loafers squeaking perfectly, the three of us made our way into the lounge and ordered cocktails from Danny, a 60-year-old professional bartender who had left the chill of Rhode Island in 1988 and never looked back. At the piano, a bony Brit in a blonde pompadour coaxed "Canadian Sunset" from the faux baby grand, his silk banner proclaiming behind him that Sir Barry Lyle had entertained diners nightly since 1967. The entire lounge was comfortably full.

We were led to our table in the midst of the main dining room. Our waiter was a taller, thinner version of Tony Orlando, who synthesized New York and Floridian charm into his entire persona.

With wine on the way and a basket of crispy rye bread on the table, we began to really relax and let the room envelop us. Risa smiled into her menu and pinched Wally's forearm.

"If I order the filet will you get the lamb?" she offered as the table negotiations began in earnest. They had to share, so they could not willingly order the same item at the risk of depriving themselves of anything. I decided on Florida lobster and clams casino with a double anchovy Caesar salad. While we slathered the rye with whipped butter, we drank in the room and tried not to talk shop, but we failed.

"Why don't they hunt here?" Wally asked, looking around. "It seems odd that we've never even caught whiff of anyone unusual in the years we've been here."

"No singles. Everyone here is married or has lifelong friends," Risa answered around a mouthful of warm bread. "These people have real families. Too many ties. Too many smart people here who have just enough city sense to be passed over."

She was right. This would be a challenging place to peel someone away from a group. Why take the risk? It made grim sense. I ordered another bottle of wine as our dinner arrived. The plates were decadently beautiful and sizzled invitingly. We dove in, and, for a while, we were the quietest table in the restaurant.

After a dessert of Key Lime pie, we made our way to the valet at a sedate amble, laden with the meal and wine. The night was a touch cool, the breeze perfect. The beauty of it all made us smile with content as cars were brought up in a line for departing diners. Wally gave the ticket to the young valet, who returned a breathless moment later with her black Toyota Highlander. She rarely waited for anything, and tonight was no exception. It's an excellent reason to let her drive, despite her constant stream of profanity in even the most manageable traffic.

"Here you are, ladies," the valet said, as he opened the door with a gallant flourish, studiously ignoring me. We all turned at a sharp bark of anger behind us. Two women were being separated by their husbands and shooed to their respective cars. They had argued over something important enough to disrupt the afterglow of dinner. The other valet, a tall kid with blond hair, watched them go their ways and shook his head ruefully while smirking. *Old people*, his expression read.

The couple closest to us hurried past to their waiting car.

"She just reached out and touched my earring and pulled at it!" The indignant victim told her husband. He took a diplomatic tone and tried to soothe her.

"Maybe she just wanted to feel it. They *are* unusual. It wouldn't be the first time someone admired them."

The effect on her was immediate as she touched her earrings while waiting by the open car door.

"True. I do love them. Even your sister mentioned how they look on me, and she never wears jewelry at all," she said, her tone thick with pride.

As I got in the passenger side of Wally's SUV, I noticed the glimmer on her earlobe. It was a gold teardrop stone, deep and rich. I knew that gem. *Carnelian.*

From Risa's Files

Dear Parent of Camper,

Here at Camp Tamiami, we take pride in our safety and commitment to the children. Unfortunately, due to the continued vandalism and attacks on the horses, we can no longer include riding lessons or trail excursions as part of our curriculum this summer. We will gladly refund the extra stipend paid for this activity and substitute another fun time on the camp property. We apologize for any inconvenience this may cause and look forward to your visit on Family Day.

Sincerely,
Director Margorie Lewis

P.S. If you have any information about who has been harming the horses, or the whereabouts of former employee James Bath, please do not hesitate to call us or the Florida State Police.

8

Monday mornings were as close as we ever came to an official company function. All four members of our unusual family drifted to the kitchen after sleeping late. Gathered over breakfast to discuss any ideas or plans we had for the coming week, we hatched plans, discarded them, and came to life gradually with coffee. Our unusual occupation was dangerous but profitable. A certain moral flexibility was required when it came to liberating the belongings of thieves who stole far more than simple material goods. We three possessed that quality in spades, although I must admit that it was somewhat of an acquired stance.

The more we shared the less risk we were exposed to, either from citizens or our adversaries. Risa idly stirred her coffee as Wally sipped orange juice while opening her laptop.

"I think we should look into a new club on Las Olas in Ft. Lauderdale. It's been open for three weeks, and there hasn't been a single crime reported within two blocks."

Risa arched her brow at that, knowing full well that a late-night club crowd fueled on alcohol and sexual tension would be highly unlikely to remain on the good side of the law.

"Nothing?" I asked, thinking. "That is . . . unusual." In our experience, a bubble of calm meant that *something* was causing criminals to look elsewhere for their prey, perhaps using a close, personal method of persuasion.

We were quiet for a moment, ruminating on the tedium of loud nights at a club filled with the self-absorbed, drunk, or desperate.

"What's the hot night?" Wally asked Risa.

"There are two. Thursday and Sunday. We could all go at once. The place holds over 500 people. Big. It's on the water, so we could drive or water taxi in at different times and meet in the middle. The music is supposed to be killer. It might even be fun."

Risa was oddly optimistic about this place, but, then, she loved standing by the water at night in Fort Lauderdale. We were nodding together now, so it seemed like this was the focus of our week.

I broke the silence. "Gyro has to get his nails clipped today. I'll take him."

I volunteered to chauffeur the beast often because I always took him for ice cream, which then gave me an excellent excuse to have ice cream. Ours was a mutually beneficial relationship in this respect.

Wally piped up, "We got a message board contact from Hayseed last night."

Message boards were our link to others like us who were careful about not revealing too much of their identity. I had always surmised that anyone who sensed they were being hunted could use the very same tools we did to discover who or what was threatening them. It seemed that discretion could only enhance our ability to harry the ranks of the immortal. Over the years, we had obliquely built a network of contacts who shared our rare occupation. Hayseed was one such compatriot, operating in the American heartland. We knew he was a male, a bit older, and that he had spent the better part of a decade chasing one particularly vile creature that he would only describe as a Feeder.

When he got drunk one night after discovering the remains of a pair of teen girls, he sent us a picture of the crime scene. It was a charnel house on the edge of a wheat field. Blood and tissue hung from cut stalks, and there was so little of the girls left that the next rain would wash them into the thirsty soil, lost forever to their grieving families. Light indentations of shoeless female feet dotted the site, where a splash of rusty blood indicated the killer had planted her feet to lunge and tear. Hayseed had written of the stench, old and sour, a scent that stitched death and gore with the violating tone of ammonia. *A ghoul,* I thought instantly, looking at the hideous images. Only a ghoul would rend a human in such a gleeful and desperate manner, skipping birdlike around the victim as it bit and slashed, mumbling and tittering around a prize of warm flesh. Ghouls were the last stop on the train of immortality, often even being killed by their own brethren, who reviled their less cultured cousins. Their descent was often marked by hysterical violence and a complete loss of control. It was easy to see why their indiscretions could lead to other parties taking an interest in eliminating them from the world. Crudely put, they were bad for business and brought the one thing to immortals that they would not brook: visibility. They were not always alone, often paired with a human we branded *helper* or *friend*, both terms used as a slur to describe a truly puerile, complicit being devoid of morality. Often, a helper would act as a traitorous assistant in hopes of gaining inroads to her own immortality. Helpers became indentured servants, slaved to an amoral beast that used them for as long as they could. Rewards were never free, as even the sexual pleasure showered on them inexorably turned them into shadows. Their lives with their masters ended as they began: with deception and lust. And then death. Always with death.

We thought of Hayseed as the Captain Ahab of the plains, but he was far from myopic in his practices. He had, over the years, passed us information about the panoply of beings that traveled and stalked the highways and cities of Kansas, Nebraska, and points east. The sea of grain that stretched under the stars was a dangerous place. Commerce demanded that trucks and trains traverse the yawning spaces of the plains, and, with these, came lonely men who were exactly the type of souls that immortals found irresistible. Hayseed stayed busy. Abandoned trucks and cars and luggage led him through a skein of hints that would end in the same scene, with Hayseed moving on and the ashes of an immortal committed to the relentless wind of the prairie. He was, in his own way, as lethal as we were, but far lonelier.

"What did he say?" Risa, brow raised, was curious.

So was I. Hayseed did not contact us often, but his messages usually had some punch to them. His economy of words was offset by his discerning eye for information that was germane to us in an immediate way. The newest message was no different.

Wally got serious. "A local auctioneer was settling an estate that should have meant nothing to anyone. It was a clapboard house on a lot that belonged to a dowager who had died three years earlier. The market was so weak that there was no reason to press for a sale, but, eventually, not one, but three, relatives came forward demanding the entire estate," she said. She paused and glanced at her laptop again. "The house was empty except for out-of-date furniture that didn't even have kitsch value. The land is piss-poor and too far from town to matter, and she had a monthly check of less than nine hundred dollars, most of which went to bills, a kid who cut her lawn, and the local animal shelter."

Risa was deep in thought, and I was nowhere near a guess as to what the hook could be. We waited for Wally to continue.

"Two of the relatives seem like ghosts. No ties to the area, no discernible relation to the woman. The third has the ring of truth, and his statements are so guileless that I think he might be real. He said he was the son of her sister's first husband and that he had spent the Christmas season there for three straight years while his father served in the Marines."

I interrupted, "Why only Christmas?"

Risa followed with several questions, all focused on the reason for the dustup over the estate. "Where was the mother? Was she missing? Did they have money or . . . were they special? Who was the boy, other than a holiday guest?"

She tapped her nail against her teeth and became quiet. I knew a pensive Risa meant that I was missing some of the obvious questions, let alone the hidden ones.

Wally spoke, her tone soft and thoughtful, "Hayseed wrote almost nothing about the family. I think he only wrote about the place at all because of one detail. The attorney who handled the estate asked Ethan, the now-grown boy, if he had enjoyed Christmas on the plains. He said no, he wouldn't have even known which day Christmas fell on since they didn't have a television or a tree or presents."

Risa laughed, "You're telling me there was a single old Jewish Luddite in the middle of five states of wheat?"

I smiled, too, until Wally finished with a flourish.

"No. She wasn't anything like that at all. Ethan says she was spooky as hell, rarely spoke to him, and wore an old necklace that she would take off and shake at thunderstorms as they rolled towards the house. He was a kid, so he didn't really grasp what she was doing; he just thought she was insane. If you ask me, the old lady was a witch."

We all recognized the necklace as the only bright point in an otherwise unremarkable story, although an old woman confronting a wall of lightning on the prairie made for good imagery. Witches came in all types. A solitary woman bereft of a large family wasn't newsworthy to us. I couldn't imagine what Hayseed had thought we would find compelling about this tale, until I remembered that our information flowed both ways.

"When was our last message to him? Before or after I met Senya at the bar?"

Wally was certain. "After. And I was thorough, many details."

We all thought that, no matter how small, the details always gave insight into finding what or who was just out of our reach and how to make our grasp that much longer.

Risa finally spoke. "Since we know about Ethan, and a lone weather witch who seems to have had no impact on anyone or anything that we know of, we need to know two things. What necklace was she wearing, and who else wanted it?"

Wally nodded and said, "Yes, and one more thing, too. Who else came to claim the estate? What was the excuse they gave to travel to a place where a solitary woman presided over an unwanted scrap of ground? Was there anything interesting about them, other than the simple fact that they were even aware of her death? I'll message him again and ask him what we're missing."

Breakfast was over with that, and I had a giant dog to get into my car. Ice cream—and Gyro—could not wait.

9

On Route 441 in Hollywood is a group of saints operating as veterinarians. The Castle Animal Clinic is a modest building between a paint store and an auto shop that specializes in electrical issues and horrendous outbursts of screaming in Greek. I had made the terrifying mistake of taking my car there years earlier, where a pair of cousins had an argument in front of me that escalated to an impromptu wrestling match on the floor. I had arrived to pick up my vehicle, and, after separating from each other with ominous threats, the shorter cousin demanded sixty dollars from me for "fixing short in goddamn no good cheap cheap wiring harness." I paid without a word and have not visited the Screaming Greek Electrical Wizards since.

The staff at Castle was another story entirely. Gyro loped in through the glass door ahead of me to an enthusiastic greeting from Sandra and Lena, who ran the front of the house. Both women were in their late forties, motherly, and had a deft hand with the patrons, regardless of whether they had hands, paws, or claws. Sandra, a blonde, favored skin-tight scrubs in garish colors to augment her makeup, which appeared to have been applied with a paint gun. Her blue eyes swam in an array of eye liners and shadows that gave her a vaguely surprised look at all times. Lena was no shrinking violet, either, although her taste in makeup was more subdued. Jewelry was another matter entirely. Her straight brown hair rarely covered her trademark earrings, which ranged from spoon-like appendages covered in sequins to hoops that a parrot could roost in. Today, she had selected a demure pair of feathers plucked from some species of bird that took mating rituals very seriously, as no fewer than ten shades of greens and blues created a pattern that could cause a seizure disorder if one stared at them too long.

The women had worked there for the entirety of Gyro's life and several years before, lending a familiar comfort to the clinic that made animals and owners just a little less nervous. For me, it made all the difference. In one step, Gyro had approached the counter and rested his enormous head on it for what he knew would be a generous scratch and fuss over his presence, both of which agreed with him immensely.

"Big boy! What are we doing today?" Lena asked, as Sandra continued to fuss over him.

"Just nails today, and thanks for seeing the big goof without much warning. He's tearing up the new couch, and I lose every argument with him about staying off of the furniture."

Risa and Wally selected new couches every six months, it seemed, as a result of the cumulative damages of a giant dog and a slovenly Argentine who spilled food on the cushions each time she ate.

"Gotcha, Ring. Let me take him back and we'll have him out in a jiff," Sandra said as she walked around the counter and opened the door to the grooming area.

Gyro immediately walked in, knowing that every trip to the Castle resulted in ice cream. He may have looked the part, but he was no dummy. I sat on a squeaky pleather chair for the ten-minute wait and thought about ice cream while looking out over the blizzard of traffic. It was these normal moments that I found myself craving from time to time, a sort of clearing of my psychological palate, and I know Risa and Wally felt the same way. Sitting in that fake leather chair with my legs sticking to the cushion was the closest I would come to ordinary for some time, and I knew it.

I had gotten a text message that Liz Brenneman's lock was malfunctioning, so I dropped Gyro at home and headed for Hardigan Center. Liz, an attorney, had rented from me for six years, two of which were lost in a haze of wine and the crashing avalanche of an ugly divorce. Her ex-husband Lewis made my skin crawl. Wally and Risa had lobbied quite seriously for disposing of him in the Everglades after they had discovered just how foul a human being he had been throughout the marriage. Liz had drunk herself to the brink of disbarment, but then had managed to dig in and wrest some degree of normalcy from the ashes of a commitment she had taken very seriously. She occupied the spot to the right of the Butterfly and was a fixture in the front window, pacing back and forth in a harried rhythm with a phone held to her ear. At thirty-eight, she fought tenaciously to maintain a healthy body, especially since becoming sober and finding that life indeed continued, regardless of her previous desire to freeze time. Liz had the desperate beauty of a fancy guest soap that had been used too often but whose original features still stubbornly remained. With curly brown hair and blue eyes, she was an engaging face that fronted a bright mind. After the divorce and her rebirth, she had transformed from a ragged woman with an aura of sadness into something far more hopeful, and we were all thankful for the change, since we genuinely liked her.

I arrived at the Center, parked, and got my toolbox out of the trunk. Liz's neighbor to the right, Glen Ferloch, made eye contact with me and gave an awkward wave with his spindly arm, but, then, everything Glen did was awkward. A blonde Ichabod Crane twin with thinning hair, he stood two inches taller than my six foot three and weighed roughly half as much. With large teeth and a spastic manner, he moved about his office space and life with the rhythm of a twitchy stork, but was so earnest that he was impossible to dislike. Glen had located his business in the Center two years earlier and paid the rent one day early without fail. He owned a small niche service that transported and transplanted highly desirable trees, an unusual job that found some purchase in the newly moneyed of the area. People purchased fully grown oaks, screw pines, and palms of all varieties at exorbitant prices in order to make new homes seem more established. His work attire never varied, much like his routine. Blocky brown work boot hybrids exacerbated the enormous length of his feet, and his impeccably-pressed chinos were always belted far too tightly and pulled to just north of his navel. A celery green polo shirt emblazoned with the *Glen 2 Glen Trees* logo crowned the entire ensemble.

"Ring! Morning!" Glen called as he reached out from his partially opened door and pumped my hand vigorously, his other holding a phone. "Just wanted to say hey!"

I nodded, and, before I could respond, he ducked his tangle of limbs back into his office and walked towards the back.

Liz was not at her desk, so I knelt at the lock and pushed gently against the center cylinder. There was a small amount of give but nothing that would merit me taking the mechanism apart without one critical test being done. I leaned forward and inhaled deeply, directly in front of the lock. Liz, who had been approaching me from the back of her office, stopped in her tracks with an abashed look. She raised her hands in a gesture of supplication and grinned. Citrus. The lock, of course, smelled like oranges, which meant that Liz had been using her key to stab her daily snack in order to begin peeling the resistant rind of the delicious fruit. The buildup of pulp and dust had, in turn, fouled the mechanism of the door, causing me to squat in the increasingly hot sun while spraying graphite into the lock in order to undo her wanton disregard for technology, in general. I gave her a menacing smile and drew in a lungful of air for a sound berating only to hear her phone ring through the glass at the perfect moment for her to affect an escape. She gave me a smile of apology and turned to her laptop, assuming a facial expression that meant the call was business of the paying kind. I opted to find her innocent of the offense at hand and walked back to my car. Looking the Center over, I knew that my landlord duties were concluded for the day and, likely, the week, which meant that it was time to relax until later, when Risa and Wally would determine what I was to wear for our club foray.

I could be many things around them, but being poorly dressed was not an option.

10

The Forest

To call Europe a continent is to agree, in principle, that there is a clear distinction between the East and West, as the land itself runs in an unbroken bulk from the Atlantic to Pacific oceans. From the salty pans of the southern French coast to the enormity of the undulating Pacific, the stones of the Eurasian continent are ancient and varied. Following the land eastward, the grip of European culture attenuates with distance. Massive plains and forests curl sinuously around the ancient spines of mountains thrust upwards from the basins and plains in a series of rigid divisions, defining and delineating the cultures of humans for millennia. Mountains give way to passes and valleys only to sweep forward in vast flatlands that have harbored every human habitation from the primitive to the sublime. At various locations, the hand of man rose and fell with the ages, sometimes lingering on in hidden cave grottos or lake bottoms well past their natural existence. Antiquities were commonplace, with seemingly every spadeful of earth revealing bits and bobs of human influence. For every forgotten stone foundation, steeple, or slumping barn, there was a subterranean equivalent, where commerce, spirituality, or greed had driven human hands to prize ore from shafts and deposits wherever possible. Talus and scree announced the search for this bounty in grittily splintered piles, some covered with the dust of centuries, others fresh with the disruption of current use. Profit could be heard across the continent in the form of trucks carting masses of ore. Underneath the land, vast amounts of wealth inspired the same lust as the more obvious gifts on the surface. It simply required a different means of acquisition, and mankind was only too willing to break mountains in search of wealth.

But just as the earth had been probed, settled, and trodden upon, there were pockets of inaccessibility. Select craggy mountain passes soared above the timberline in a haze of ice and fog, impassable to everyone except the few who used them long ago to traverse the continent. These paths, dangerous and secretive, eventually fell into disfavor and were then covered by the drifts of time as other forms of travel superseded their practicality. Rarer still, tracts of immense primary forest survived in varying states of existence. Virulent nationalism protected some of these hidden groves as parks, bulwarks standing against the advance of modernity on a crowded landscape. The imbalance between social classes created others in the form of game reserves intended to keep the starving masses away from the lush bounties the land had to offer. In the geographic middle of one such fragment of time-lost woods, a small lodge, its stones green with age, rested in a cathedral of enormous oaks. Desperate maple, ash and spruce jostled for position under the roaming canopy of the oaks, which had been the undisputed masters since they began to spread upward and outward. Birch shed their bark in strips as they angled towards the panes of light of the diluted sun, low and timid on the horizon.

Within this rich tangle sat the home, with walls of flat stone blending seamlessly into wooden arches. A slate roof of dramatic pitch rested on sturdy timbers. Narrow, high windows interrupted the rocky outline of the main walls in glassine strips, bordered with dark wood inlaid into mortar that wept with age. The close bulk of the forest threatened the huddling Alpine outpost with dancing shadows.

At the main entrance, a tall woman with striking cheekbones swung open a sturdy wooden door, panels shaded with a patina of age and shyly reflecting the day's last light. A thick grey sweater clung to her muscular frame, hanging over dark green pants that were tucked into the boots of a hunter, made shiny from years of care. Her plaited blonde hair swung in rhythm as she hurried in long strides to a slate enclosure, where firewood lay in obedient rows. Selecting several, she stacked them in a leather thong, cinching it tight and hoisting it over her broad shoulder in one smooth motion. Pausing, she held her hand angled above her eyes, squinting into the forest at a raucous birdcall, and then turned briskly as if summoned. In seconds, she had returned to the interior of the lodge as the door swung soundlessly shut behind her. Above the door, a small bull's head carved from dark wood watched over, the painted accents faded to the barest of hints at the original splendor. The bull, laughing, stared sightlessly to the west with one horn chipped and splitting. Age had taken a point from the horn, but the humorous twist to the mouth endured.

II

Florida

The metronome of club music began to leak into my car as I parked on a discreet side street a solid block from the front entrance. Risa and Wally had left some time earlier, opting to go in as a pair simply because the club was large enough to provide instant anonymity once they were through the gauntlet of hired muscle out front. They anticipated no problems getting in without delay. Neither did I, given my willingness to hand out cash as needed to facilitate a speedier welcome; standing with the unwashed, albeit beautiful masses was not conducive to my plans. After a casual, quiet word with the doorman, I was fifty dollars poorer but richer in time and sanity. I detest waiting, unless I'm fishing. Then, the Zen of the activity infuses me with rare patience, something that the club atmosphere caused my mind to purge in an instant.

Every nightclub, when distilled, is the same. The Roman dog and pony show is populated by the same players; only the location and music changes. Some women come to dance. Some come to gloat or to reinforce their stature within their social circles. There are decisive women who fully intend on getting laid even as they leave their homes, just as there are women who allow alcohol, drugs, or opportunity to propel them into a liaison that they may or may not regret. Men come for the women. The camaraderie and bonding with friends are just window dressing for the real show. Rarely, there are men among them whose purpose does not revolve around finding a woman, although, in this club, I couldn't sense a single one of this rare species. The grandiose display between the sexes was in full swing, surrounding me and forcing even the most tin-eared fool to realize that the atmosphere had a purpose. Looking at the strutting crowd, that intent was easy to discern.

I pushed through the crowd to the left end of the main bar. The décor was dark and minimalist, although, to the credit of the owners, the furniture was of high quality and looked comfortable. Low circular tables of black glass sat inside concentric rings of curved couches that reeked of colognes; even from here I could detect the residual glitter from women's makeup that spattered the cushions in a gaudy accent. Bottle service areas attracted those who could pay, as well as those who could not but had something to offer. It's a complex, cynical form of social whoring that everyone understood but no one would verbalize, at least not early in the night.

I caught the bartender as she was mixing and said simply, "Bourbon. Please."

She looked up, a pretty woman under the heavy makeup and tan of someone used to late nights and late mornings. Her dyed blonde hair was pulled back severely into a ponytail and a single, trailing curl that shined red in the lights along the bar.

"Sure. Ice?" she asked. I liked her instantly, as she was an economy of words and motion.

I had my drink in a minute, the small glass resting comfortably against my palm. I felt like I could operate now, so I began to scan for Wally's face first. I knew Risa would be next to her but invisible among the taller crowd. I found them quickly, dancing together on the main floor not twenty feet away, clearly having fun without reserve. Wally danced with abandon, smiling genuinely and laughing as she threw her head left to right in rhythm with the music. Risa was far shorter but moved with a sinuous athleticism that was watery and erotic. Both were being watched by men and women, alike, but I knew that their fun could only mean one thing. There was an immortal here, and they had identified it. Since they were dancing, it meant that they thought I needed to be here to kill it. One of us is strong, two are powerful and crafty. The three of us together are something entirely different. I sensed nothing, smelled nothing; there was no fear or menace anywhere, and that meant that they had found something new.

Or something very, very old.

12

Bern, Switzerland

The mark of an excellent banker is discretion. The mark of a Swiss banker is a marriage of that same quality with an intense desire to maintain the privacy of special clients. In a room of muted earth tones, one such customer opened a steel safe deposit box, which had been placed carefully on a black wood table that gleamed from polishing. A substantial lid flipped back without a sound, revealing a green velvet lining. The box was completely empty. Without a word, the customer replaced the lid and pushed the single hasp lock back into its original position with a *snick*, leaving the box on the table before rising and leaving the private room. Herr Krieger, the manager, waited discreetly outside, and he inquired as to whether his prized customer had completed the day's business. The mellow voice was neither excited nor reserved but perfectly mannered.

"My business is finished for today. Thank you for your service. I shall require the continued use of the box for the foreseeable future. I've authorized an additional signatory for the account; please see that it is recorded promptly. She will be fully authorized in all of my monetary concerns henceforth."

Herr Kreiger was delighted at this news but exhibited the enthusiasm of a man who was paid to be unobtrusive. In a moment, his client was gone, and, as he re-entered the room and replaced the steel box, his thoughts moved to the next appointment in his busy schedule.

13

Florida

I didn't approach Wally or Risa in the club. It was ill-advised, given the unknowns. When my phone pinged a message, I knew that it was time to act. *Long hair. Brunette. Tall. Black skirt. W/ single male blue shirt. To front door. Meet outside.* I began shifting through the crowd, neither hurried nor allowing myself to be held up or have my view occluded. *There she is.* With the target in sight, my path to the door became less passive. I saw Wally's head to my right, which meant that Risa was approaching the door behind me, as well. The target slid out the door with her selection from the herd, a male of medium height. From behind, he was predictably average and alone. His arm was possessively draped around her waist, and he walked with the blissful myopia of a man who was, in that moment, working well above his pay grade. They turned left outside only steps ahead of me, but the crowd had not thinned enough to allow discrete action. I couldn't get a bead on what exactly was happening. The immortal had body language that was hardly predatory. She turned in profile to me, and I saw a woman in her thirties with fine features and skin bronzed by the sun. She was pretty in a blue-blooded way. I could imagine her in equestrian gear. In a moment of coquetry, she allowed her bland partner to kiss her lightly on the lips. It was brief and chaste, but for her teeth nipping playfully at his lip. I heard her low voice tell him she would see him in a few moments as the jangle of car keys in her hand signaled her peeling off to the dark of the parking lot.

Hold back I motioned behind me. I sensed something different was at play here. Risa and Wally came forward to stand with me, silent but watching with the same curiosity. Our forgettable but charmed target staggered slightly, his balance decaying with each step as he wound his way into the darkening street.

"Is he drained? Wounded?" Wally hissed, voicing our collective confusion. Contact with the immortal had been minimal, but the man was swooning and, after a series of choppy steps, crashed headlong into an alcove. His spastic fall left him on his knees. Risa rushed ahead but pulled up cautiously when he turned to face us, his face a rictus of pain in the sickly yellow of the street's sodium lights. I took his elbow and helped him to his feet, but a spasm slammed him into a bent position as he coughed in agony, a deep-chested heave that took him onto his toes. The pace of his demise was hideous. With one massive wracking act, he vomited and slipped from my grasp, stone dead, and his body folding in defeat at the base of the building we stood near. I felt pain that this man would be forgotten by the world shortly, an innocent who would be totally erased with the fullness of time. It was enraging.

"What is that? What came out of him? Look. *Look*."

We were all staring even as Wally shone her keychain penlight at the wetness on the concrete. In the middle of the repulsive discharge lay three obscenely large acorns, glistening with his blood.

"Acorns? Giant acorns? How did they get in him? Did she force him somehow?" Wally's litany of questions was a running dialogue of her confusion.

Risa said quietly after a moment, "She bit him. Or put something in his mouth. He was a medium for her—that's why she said she would be back. She used him as a vessel. And she knew it would only be a matter of minutes before he had served his purpose."

It made sense. It meant that she had been watching us but was gone. She had been careful. Discreet.

"I know what she is." We turned to Risa as she spoke. "Acorns. In a human host. This is bedtime story shit, but darker. Far more dangerous, because she must keep seeding her marks. It's a neverending cycle. She's a feeder, just not one that we hear much of. She's a druid, I think? Remember, two years ago, when we were trading info with that nutjob from Ireland? He was tracking the genealogy of incredibly old family lines that had migrated here to the States, but we could never really grasp what he was describing. He kept calling them Keepers and Tenders. I think we've met our first. And, judging by how casual she was, old. Old and as wanton about death as anything we can imagine."

I thought about it for a minute, chewing on the idea of acorns, oaks, and ancient Celts who spread death through germinating seeds inside a victim. I thought we would start with the obvious. I held out my arms to link up for the walk back to the car, away from the body and the scene, but not before putting the enormous seeds into a napkin that lay on the street, then into my pocket. They were still grotesquely warm against my thigh.

"Let's answer a question. Where do giant acorns come from? Presumably, giant oaks. So . . . where are the giant oaks? And who tends them?"

14

I sat on the dock with Gyro, listening to traffic across the canal. Lights of different colors smeared the dark water lapping at the pilings, ever in motion, even during the quiet hour, when the tide went slack and the wind was still. After seeing such a gruesome death, we all retreated to our safe harbor to digest the bitter rage that sickened us. Risa would sit in the shower, each stinging minute of spray focusing her hatred of immortals ever more pointedly. Wally would run until she threw up or dissolve into quiet sobs on her bed, clutching her sheets in hands that went white with hate. I chose to sit here, by the water, trying to spare the world my disgust and brittle temper, until the sun began to rise and the first ducks began their endless patrol of the seawall. These were the moments when we were weakest, when our humanity and desire for vengeance subsumed our years of experience.

Defining my existence is difficult. My morality is even less easy to describe, although I like to think that, despite the chaos that removing immortals causes, it is, in fact, serving the greater good. Liberating the personal effects and holdings of our targets may be construed as theft, but those gains are largely applied to continuing our efforts. Beyond the simple removal of evil, we were all personally motivated by loss. For Wally, it was a friend of the family who had been as close as blood. For Risa, it was an uncle she loved so much that the story was something I had heard exactly once in the fifteen years I'd known her. Three murders, three people, miles and years apart. At the time, the crimes only had one thing in common.

Each death turned us into hunters.

15

Risa

There is never a good day for a funeral, yet the light wind through the bottle brush and palm trees made it bearable, but only just. The early summer Floridian heat had not begun in earnest. It was March, 1991, and the sadness surrounding the open grave of my aunt Ruth had remained intense but studied. We loved her quiet strength and, out of respect for her, we kept our grief as contained as was possible, although, inside, I felt like crying so hard that I would shatter.

For my whole life, she had been near, kind, a presence so dignified that I didn't know how well any of us would find life without her smiles and caring touch. Ruth was a healer in every sense. She brought unity to the family during arguments that shook the walls, and not once did we feel reproved by her, even though she made us all want to be kinder merely by watching her live. Her husband, my uncle Lev, was her perfect compliment. Wiry, energetic and giving, he found in Ruth the fulcrum upon which he brought his will to bear on the orange grove they had planted by hand, after immigrating to Florida from Israel. His boundless enthusiasm and drive built a sea of trees where, before, there had been scrub palmetto and abandoned pasture. For forty years, he had paced the rows of trees, his dusty chinos stained with the perspiration rings of a man who knew every inch of his farm. When I was sixteen, Ruth felt a twinge in her back while loading oranges onto a scale, and, three months later, she was in an austere medical office being told that the cancer was in her bone and that she might not see another birthday. Lev had nearly broken right there, weeping into his hat outside the room in a crouch while we watched from down the hall. I knew that the wall was the only thing holding him up at that moment, but this was a man who had fought in the Sinai with broken bones in his shoulder from a crashing artillery shell. We watched him gather himself and duck into her room to tell her to fight and live.

And live she did, for six more years. She lost some ribs and her hair, twice, to the chemo, but Lev held her hand while she vomited into steel pans during the grim cycles of near death that we call treatment. Finally, she told Lev that she could not go on, and he sat heavy on her bed with the breath crushed out of him by five decades of memories.

So we streamed out of the graveyard, all sifting our own memories and worrying about Lev, and in a few minutes, Rabbi Frank was led away, his steps tottering and his eyes brown and sad. From within the crush of our family, my cousins, Rebekah and Beth, were holding Lev's jacket like he would fly away. I caught his eye, and he gave me a smile that made me realize he would again walk his grove. We would have him still. It was something I could cling to, and, for the first time that week, I saw a hint that his life would go on.

Lev announced that he needed a moment as we began to scatter towards the cars parked along the main pathway. He veered off towards the oasis in the middle of the graveyard, where, under a gazebo, a water fountain sat discreetly between planters filled with small gardenia bushes. I stayed back to watch him go, a small man who seemed whittled by grief, his face all planes and hard angles. Only his tears made him seem soft. When he reached the fountain, a silver car slid quietly up the path, its windows tinted nearly black. The door opened and released a woman dressed for grief, her lithe elegance apparent even from my vantage point. What she said to Lev I do not know, but she walked to him and embraced him, perhaps offering words of consolation to a man who had lost everything moments before.

I did not know what I was seeing that day. I do now. Her grace branded her as a Pranic or Sylph, and, had I known that, I would have run at her with murderous intent. But I knew nothing of her world and stood mute as they embraced. She enclosed him in long arms, her bearing one of compassion. Under the shadow of the gazebo, a messenger tendril of light and air emerged from her chest, shimmering so faintly that I could barely see it. The diaphanous probe wrapped sinuously around him, pausing for a hesitant second before plunging soundlessly into his back. Lev stiffened, and his knuckles went white on her sleeves. This was how she fed, his grief and his will being siphoned away while he sagged in her grasp. The appendage swelled slightly with dark sparks and motes, memory and soul all splintered into chaff that she greedily stole. I knew Lev was being consumed; I just could not logically fathom how it could be happening. At a visceral level, I recognized this as murder of the most egregious sort. With a chaste kiss on his cheek, she broke contact and stepped briskly away to the waiting car, all semblance of caring gone in a shift from mourning friend to sated predator. Her car door closed, and, by the time Lev had walked four steps towards me, he fell dead, the screams of my family threatening to obliterate any memory of the woman I had just watched consume seven decades of my uncle's spirit with the grace of a viper.

I knew in that instant that I could see her, and that meant I could find her. I also knew in my bones that I would never again be an observer, not when parasites like the unknown woman walked among my world.

From that minute, I would hunt. And I had an excellent idea of where to begin.

16

Florida

Morning found me ragged and needing some separation. Wally and Risa were still in bed when I left to go to the beach, where the water would be painfully bright in the winter sun. It was the type of jolt that I could build upon in order to process what we had seen the previous night. The implacability of the ocean is an excellent base to revive my belief that I can, in fact, defend myself from the rigors of my life. The sea can forget and persevere, regardless of the severity of the storms. I seek that same type of renewal each time I walk the sand, stomach churning at the recurring visions of death that color my memory. It would be capricious to fully dismiss the experiences that I have, and my conscience would not allow it even if I had the availability to drink from the river Lethe. It is this growing hall of impressions that I turn to in order to shift the fantastic into the ordinary. Or at least ordinary to a select few who realize that the wall between civilization and entropy is a thin barrier indeed. The sand, revised with each wave, felt hard-packed and moist under my feet. I thudded with heavy heels, using my steps to purge my body of the fear that I had for the unknown. When I felt reasonably prepared to share my day with the swarm of the city, I turned toward the parking lot and walked. Gulls cried over me, aloft on the onshore wind that erased my footprints even as I dug for keys. My thoughts turned to the problem of forests and oaks and who would bring them here, and why doing so cost a man his life.

Wally and Risa were on the dock when I got home, Gyro stretched between them with a palm frond in his mouth, slobbering contently. Empty cereal bowls sat between them, along with Wally's phone. Wordlessly, Wally handed it to me. On it was a blurred picture of a tattoo. It was a snake, black and silver, position on the body unknown, but there was a liquid quality to it that was both admirable and unnerving. I raised an eyebrow in inquiry.

"What is it?"

Risa spoke first. "I think it's African. It's on the shoulder of a guy that Angel fired last week for being drunk on the job."

Angel was the last tenant in Hardigan Center, a brown bulldozer of a guy with a shock of black hair and hands like five digit bricks. He stood just over five feet tall but weighed well over two hundred pounds, slabs of muscle a testament to his years as a mason. He was an artisan, too, working river rock, corals and marble with a deft, experienced hand. He never lacked jobs, so he hired crews to do basic brick and block jobs under his supervision, which was exacting. A Cuban immigrant, Angel made the most of his skills, and he would not tolerate lazy or sloppy helpers. Being drunk on the jobsite was beyond the pale for his crew. I wouldn't have been surprised if he had thrown the guy into the street.

"Who sent the picture? Angel?" Wally nodded at me as Risa tapped the screen.

"Look closer. This isn't ink. And, once Angel calmed down, he started to think that maybe the guy wasn't drunk, but sick from the tattoo. One small problem. The guy didn't get it from any needle. Angel said they were on a site and, during a break, a friendly Haitian *Tante'* next door offered them drinks. The next day, Angel says the guy, Denis, came to work late, acting like he was hammered. He was aggressive, slurring his speech, and threw his tool belt when Angel asked him why. My question is, just what was in that drink from the kind-hearted neighbor, and are there four more guys on the crew who are going to lose it and go batshit crazy?"

Wally then handed me her phone with another picture on it. It was a serpent nearly identical to the first picture, but this was painted on a reed mat of some sort. Underneath it was the caption *From the University Collection, Benin 1989*. Risa peered closer at the screen. "You notice how that serpent seems . . . flat? Like a husk? I know what it needs. A host. And Denis was a nice warm body to be exploited."

She scrolled down slightly. There, under the university caption, was an identifier for the picture. It read simply *Parasitic Spirit: Negwenya*. Wally unlimbered, stretching as I helped Risa to her feet and picked up the bowls. Gyro padded ahead towards the sliding glass doors. Wally glanced at her phone again.

"Let's go visit our Auntie for a drink, shall we?"

We considered our visit and decided a simple reconnoiter was in order. The address was in a working class neighborhood of tidy homes that were built in the 1960s. Immigrants from the Caribbean had opened shops and restaurants in nearly every nearby strip mall. One innocuous home, painted white with teal trim, was our target. We were pleasantly surprised to see a small sign in the garage window offering psychic readings from Miss Jean, Seer. That was our ingress. Risa narrowed her eyes briefly, looking back at the house while she punched the number on the sign into her phone.

"I'll see if *Tante'* Jean is taking appointments today. Should I ask for a nighttime visit? We would have less exposure."

Risa was nothing if not careful. We usually went in two vehicles for the odd quick exit, but, if the house had anything of value that we opted to liberate, it made sense to leave as small a footprint as possible. Given that charlatans were notoriously leery of banks and taxes, it stood to reason that we would have to comb her property for her ill-gotten gains. Frauds preyed on the working class in a complicated dance. They could steal, but not to excess from one mark, opting to incrementally fleece the confused or gullible. I suspected Jean would be a textbook huckster with a stash prized from the hands of hardworking families in her very area. I intended to find those funds for our own crusade. The karmic balance would ultimately end in our favor.

Risa called and spoke briefly to the talented Jean, her voice oozing hope and a hint of desperation. She was an excellent actress on the phone, her supple voice capable of a gifted range of characters.

"Eight o'clock. I'm the last appointment of the day. I think that we're about to become quite close with Jean—close enough to know secrets, like where she learned how to place a spirit into an innocent man." Risa's tone did not bode well for her newfound psychic advisor.

"I plan on finding her loot. I could use a new purse or three for spring," Wally's tone was even less forgiving.

Wally and I waited, observing the local traffic at a convenience store two blocks away, while Risa kept her appointment with the netherworld, courtesy of Jean. Through the beauty of online real estate deeds, we found that Jean's actual name was Yohanna and that she was a native of New Jersey. Apparently, her only true otherworldly quality was the appalling concrete statuary that littered her yard. I couldn't imagine what décor she had selected, but I knew we would see it soon enough, after Risa had defanged our resident medium. We had decided that some of Yohanna's stolen funds would finance the art department at the elementary school up the street from our place. They had been hawking baked goods door to door, and their financial shortfall had infuriated Risa. So, we made a note of their teacher's name and decided an anonymous donation was in order.

The air in the car was stale with waiting, so I opened the door and asked Wally if she wanted anything from the store. I had a craving for some sort of beef jerky, but she just shook her head and leaned back, her earbuds streaming a soccer game from our satellite radio. Walking in between two cars, I saw a battered tomcat holding one paw slightly elevated. He meowed plaintively at me, and I leaned down to see if he could be picked up or if he was too skittish. I can't stand to see hungry animals, let alone injured hungry animals, and he arched his back and began to purr as soon as I laid my hand on him. I was absorbed in scratching his wide, scarred head, too absorbed, it would seem, because I felt two thin fingers brush my cheek and, instantly, my mouth and gut were awash with a burning that made my breath leave my body in a shuddering wheeze. I went to one knee, a piece of the sun searing through my ribs and stomach in a merciless wave, tears washing my sight into a curtain of smudged colors and light. A woman's voice, her tone light and mocking, was at my ear.

"Compassion is so human, and so risky. Pity, that." I heard heels echo on the concrete and collapsed against the nearest car, my head crashing against the door panel with a meaty thump as the hot metallic bile began to fill my mouth and nose. I bit my tongue as my teeth met with a hard *clack* and felt the grit of the parking lot on my face. With my hands scrabbling against the ground, I felt my strength leaving like water through sand, and in a moment, I felt nothing at all.

17

I awoke to darkness and a cool, professional touch on my forehead. A young woman spoke to me in a brisk but friendly tone.

"I have your eyes bandaged. You broke massive amounts of blood vessels in them from strain. I'm going to remove the patches and let you adjust to the light. It's nearly dark, but squint at first or the tears will make your eyes irritated all over again." Her fingers were busy on my face, carefully peeling tape from my cheek.

"Where am I? Who are you? Where are Risa and Wally? Is Gyro okay? What's today?" My questions were a flood. "Did Risa see that charlatan, Jean? What was in the house?" I finished for the moment, inhaling deeply. I felt reasonably well, if a bit weak, but disoriented, and my neck was stiff. I sensed that I had been still for some time.

"You certainly wake up inquisitive. I'll answer what I can as I clear your eyes. I am Boon's sister, Suma, and you're in their studio apartment. Your friends insisted that we move you here because of safety issues." Seeing me open my mouth to speak, she interrupted me. "And your enormous dog is fine. Risa said that would be the first thing you asked when you awoke, so be silent and let me answer your endless interrogatives." Mollified, I leaned back on the pillow as one eye was now cleared of bandages. I could see a modest bedroom with tan carpet and what seemed to be an enormous amount of medical equipment. Leaning against a wedge pillow, I stretched on a bed that had white sheets and little else. A thin blanket was drawn off the side, where Suma leaned over me. She was a slightly smaller version of Boonsri, but with shorter hair and an intense expression.

"I'm an internist in Orlando, and I was on my way to visit. Risa did not see that woman Jean, and she never will. She's dead. No, sit back and be still. I need to speak, and you need to listen. Jean was found murdered in Toronto, where she was originally from. Risa found the newspaper article while searching for her after bringing you here. Wally went by her house, and, as you can guess, it was empty. It seems she was a run-of-the-mill con artist, and her past caught up with her. But enough about that. You are still capable of suffering further harm, and I need information."

At that pronouncement, I eased back, shocked that I was still at risk. I didn't even know what I was at risk *of*, so I obeyed.

"You were poisoned in a manner well outside my experiences, and by a toxin so unusual that it caused me to pursue alternative methods to aid you in healing. What was your last sensation outside the Quikstop?" she asked, pausing to let me speak.

"I felt a thin hand, a woman's hand, or fingers, rather, brush my mouth, and then a horrible bitterness, then heat and pain. God, the pain was—it was instant, and it was so complete and violating. I heard a woman's voice mocking me, and I remember feeling the asphalt on my knees. I touched a smooth car handle, I think. Light became a blur, and then I tasted metal and bile. I felt like my whole body was melting and that my guts were leaving me. I thought I was dead." The speech exhausted me, and Suma held a glass with a straw to my lips. Even my brow twitched with the effort to stay present, but the water was cold and had a hint of something earthy in it. She pulled the straw away and stroked my forehead, compassion filling the simple gesture.

"I am a woman of science, so what I am seeing is unsettling, to say the least. I found pollen on your mouth and neck and shards of tree nuts in your teeth. You were poisoned, presumably, by the same woman who killed that man three weeks ago . . . yes, stay still. You've been here for twelve days."

My alarm was immediate. "Twelve? Days?" I asked, stunned. The enormity of what happened to me muscled into my psyche, an unwanted reality that I found frightening and humbling. I knew now that I had nearly died and that only my particular augmentations had saved me. That fact also told me something about the murderess that nearly ended my life, too. She was probably unaware of how Risa, Wally, and I had gleaned, in small doses, the very traits that made her so lethal. As Suma looked at me, I decided that I would heal. I would be a good patient, and I would have to bring Boon and Panit, as well as Suma, into our inner circle, at least in terms of trust, in order to fully explain why I was so thankful for their intervention. They deserved the truth, no matter how it disrupted their world. They needed to know how dangerous their surroundings could be.

I also decided that whoever this woman was, we were going to kill her, without remorse or hesitation. And I was going to enjoy every second of her agony.

18

It was a clear Thursday when Wally drove me home. Exhausted and a bit shaky, I wobbled to the couch as my limited reserves of strength were leeched by the simple act of riding in a car and walking ten steps. In spite of this, I felt the first glimmers of normalcy returning to my body, the weakness and betrayal of my muscles leaving me gradually. I had compiled slivers of memory from my fevered sleeps as I recovered images that were disjointed and confusing. I hoped that, from that pastiche of nightmares, we could glean a tactical edge against a threat that was near and very real indeed. In my mind's eye, I had seen a deep green landscape of soaring trees, hidden streams, and broken rocks, squat with age and covered in mosses. There was a primitive feel to these scenes; no evidence of humanity was ever present until later. In a miasma of visions, I saw a thick-necked deer pause to sniff pale green shoots that clustered around a gnarled root. Glimpses of game trails and meadows covered in a riot of flowers faded into scenes of hunters stalking through underbrush, their rough-spun clothing grey and sodden. Two beasts I had never seen before ghosted through a light fog, one a small, shaggy bison and the other a hulking steer with rippling shoulders and the gait of a king. Then came thudding hoof beats and Cavaliers with swords slapping their thighs, only to pass into the smell of diesel fumes and tracked vehicles grinding over earthen embankments, the screams of dying soldiers all asking one last time for their mothers as their lifeblood ran from wounds no sword could ever make. All the violence and stillness of a place unknown, compressed into one harried dream of a history from somewhere and some place in time I could not recognize. But I knew the taste of it all, and it was bitter in my memory.

My life had been saved by the excellent care I had received and by a helping of angry resistance that my body used to mute and disperse the assault on my organs from the poison. I was lucky, and

I knew it. It seemed that sooner was preferential to later regarding an honest discussion with Boon and Panit. I was physically reduced. I was shaken. I had the echoes of death still reverberating through my body from moment to moment, a constant reminder that my physical temple had been breached. That act had pierced the collective psyche of my household. We, as a family, were left confused and angry by the attack, and the first action would be to have a quiet dialectic that would determine how and what we would do when I recovered. Risa had been brisk and businesslike towards me as I lay on the couch and in my room, but, underneath her constant motion, I sensed real fear. Wally was processing the event differently. A sensualist at heart, she saw the assault as an augury. Our world was changing, and this period of our lives would be a stone upon which we could balance or break our purpose. I called the Butterfly and asked Boon and her family over after they closed.

I had a great deal to say, and they had a great deal to learn.

Panit and Boon sat uneasily on the couch, the kids outside with Gyro in the yard. Risa and Wally hovered, and Suma was present, as well, watching me with an accusatory stare. She intimately knew my wounds, and she was nonplussed by my choice of a serious, emotional discussion, regardless of its necessity. I turned and asked Suma a seemingly innocuous question.

"Did I speak while I was in the bed? Did I say anything that seemed even more detached from reality than you anticipated?" My tone was cautiously bland. This was new to all of us, and I was not only exposing myself to risk, but Risa and Wally as well. Boon, Panit, and Suma were about to be inculcated in an entirely different type of situation, one that could cause them harm from a quarter that they had not previously known. It was an enormous step, but my attack had removed any hope of remaining coy about exactly what and who we were.

Risa intervened as I deliberated how to begin. "You know I am a realist, yes?"

When Boon nodded her assent, Risa went on. "Ring was attacked by a woman who is not entirely a woman. She is . . . she is a person, a being, very violent and amoral. I couldn't tell you what she is, exactly, but what is important right now is that she is not alone. She is a type of killer who is or was human at one point, but something changed her body at its most basic level into a new form. This new form, or being, regards us as glorified cattle, weak and rife with love and joy and caring, and she will take from us whatever it is that she needs to fulfill the gulf where her soul used to be. Pan, every story you've heard as a child, be it a spirit or beast or something else, they are here. They have always been here, and Wally and Ring and I seek and destroy these blights in our world. No matter what shape or name they take, we've always believed that the three of us were too strong. Too clever, or fast, or even lucky, to ever be seriously harmed. It was a dalliance at first, albeit a dangerous one. In fourteen years of this life, none of us have been scared for more than a second. Until now. I can see it on Ring's face. I know him more intimately than a lover, and I can tell you know. The things that we hunt? In the night, the day? This is different in a bad way, and, simply by knowing us, we are fearful that you may come to harm." Risa paused and looked intently at their faces.

Suma had a question on her tongue, but Boon silenced her with a gentle touch on the forearm.

Boon turned to me. "Spirits, bad things from stories? They are . . . , "she waved vaguely, "all around us? And you kill them? How? Why?" It was a reality so divergent from five minutes ago that her voice was soft with shock. Pan sat mute, his eyes flicking to the yard, where the kids sat with Gyro between them.

Wally followed his gaze and spoke up. "They are safe here, Pan, just as they are when they are with you." He shook his head lightly as if to clear a fog.

Suma recovered quickest and asked me a definitive question. "Ring, if these beings are supernatural, how did you discover you could kill them?"

19

Ring

Among the many visitors to Florida are Australian pines, which line waterways and shed their needles at a rate that goes well beyond a simple nuisance. Rough limestone and coral at the water's edge is carpeted in a thick mat, hiding shell fragments and sand with a prickly coat. Crabs clamber over and through this deposit while insects root under the layer of desiccated boughs. The pines act as insulation against city and traffic noises but let the breeze through unmolested. At the edge of a quiet offshoot of the Intracoastal Waterway sits an unremarkable, single-level motel where my family stayed during their first forays into Florida in the early sixties. Faded teal and black lettering declared that the Reef Queen Motel had occupancies available at all times, not surprising given the simplistic appearance of the building. We had always found it charming in a utilitarian way. With the office in the middle, two sections of eight rooms each stretched out to both sides, ending in a bleak parking lot, dotted with crushed oyster shells and the odd bit of white conch. A concrete seawall ran the length of the building, giving way to the Aussie pines and a shoreline composed of enormous chunks of coral rock put in place by the Army Corps of Engineers years earlier. The water slapped listlessly at the seawall, chopped up by the endless parade of small boats that churned the Intracoastal year round. Still, the trees and a hedge in front of the motel lent an air of privacy, and my parents savored the feeling of peace in the midst of the tourist hordes, themselves included.

Naturally, while my folks dozed or sunbathed, I fished and swam, clambering down in a break between two exceptionally large rocks to a small but firm patch of sand that the tide rarely covered. It was a private resort of my own, and I spent countless hours browning in the sun and catching a myriad of fish, crabs, and any flotsam that looked intriguing. My gear was Spartan but effective. I carried two fishing poles, a small net, a bucket with some tackle, a knife that served as my carving tool, bait preparer, and fish removal kit. It also dissected any dead creature that I came across, satisfying the curiosity of a twelve-year-old boy, so I kept it sharp out of respect for the gift from my uncle as well as sheer practicality. The knife was seven inches long and had a rubbed wooden handle that was dark with use. The metal gleamed with a pewter hue, the blade straight but with a runnel along the spine where the maker's mark, wholly indecipherable to me, perched just near the well-worn leather wrap that covered the junction of wood and steel. Looking back, it was remarkably light and well balanced, although, at the time, I just appreciated the blade as a functional gift that appealed to my youthful masculinity.

The tide was slack, and the sun was angled in a way that meant it was late afternoon. My unspoken agreement to be back in time to clean up for our family dinners out was at hand. My parents would dress casually for dinner but were satisfied if I managed to wear shoes and be relatively free of fish scales and sand. I took vacationing quite seriously, and hygiene was among the first casualties of my routine upon arriving in the Sunshine State. I packed my bucket and bundled my rods together to climb the few feet to the parking lot and instantly knew I was being watched.

My first step toward the rocks framing the path upward was accompanied by a chill. I stopped, completely motionless, and looked at a man's face waiting above me. The wind was very still just then, and I heard little traffic. The pines were quiet. His smile was lewd and oily, grotesquely spanning his tanned face. A shock of white hair was artfully tussled, and he crouched in a linen suit that spoke of money. He appeared to be in his late 50s—impossibly old to a twelve-year-old, but radiated a venomous vigor that made me instantly brand him *dangerous*.

He waved slowly with the fingertips of his right hand and spoke, his eyes never leaving mine. "You're a bit far from home, aren't you," he questioned, moving forward slightly, with his hands spanning the two coral rocks. His fingers were long and delicate. He held his body poised like he was afraid I would bolt. He was right.

I thought of my parents and how close they were. I felt the water behind me, the sun pulsating in spots across my back, and the shards of oysters beneath my bare feet. It was 20 feet to safety and the eyes of others. It was six feet to the man whose smile faded into a triumphal leer, his lips parted slightly by his probing tongue. The tip was almost white, and there was saliva at the corners of his mouth, gummy and moving with each breath as I sensed him tense his legs to rush me.

I leapt, arm out, knife in hand, and buried the blade to the wooden hilt in his chest, the bones grating under my hand as a shock travelled up my arm and burst from the back of my shoulder like invisible confetti. He fell forward, the oleaginous smirk still on his face as inertia pulled my knife from his body and he rolled partially over, the coral raking his ear and cheek in a bloodless gash that was tan, then grey and pink in layers that looked diseased and dead. Next to the deep burnished suntan on his skin, it was gruesome and jarring. A smear of gore at his point of impact was tinged with the brown of his skin. It was makeup, covering the pallor of a dead thing gone ripe with time. He made no sound, and his body began to wilt where the salt water surged slightly forward from a passing sailboat moments before, the wake just now reaching my private little beach. He was dissolving in a cloud of decay as I gathered my things and pulled myself up to the parking lot, the knife in my left hand, still rigid with fear.

I exhaled. The pines whispered in a freshening of wind. I walked to my parents and our room, where I would bathe in scalding water, scrubbing at my skin until I felt the fear rinse down the drain, never to reappear.

I was no longer a child. I left that under the pines. But I kept my knife.

20

Florida

The room was very still when I finished, my mind and weakened body exhausted. There was no catharsis with the truth, only a realization that more good people were now painfully aware of another unseen threat to their lives and children. It was an act I reviled. I reached for my water, but Suma moved first, ever the healer, and guided the straw to my mouth. She also spoke first among the quietly stunned faces of her family. Risa and Wally sat mute, knowing that there was so much more to tell.

"Is it the knife?" Suma ventured. Her tone was pensive. "It makes some sense in that you mentioned it as an heirloom, but that doesn't explain all three of you. If it isn't a thing, a weapon, whatever, then it must be you. Or some aspect of you."

Panit asked a halting question, his eyes flicked from me to Risa to Wally, curious. "Boon, do you remember when we were robbed?" His tone was quiet, echoing the fear of a father and husband who had seen a very personal act of war come to his doorstep. Two addicts with knives had slashed at him one night, barking their anger even after he had dropped the cash deposit on the ground. He had positioned himself between the criminals and his car, where his family sat in the dark, waiting. It was a moment of sheer, unbridled terror, but he had remained calm until the robbers fled, and then had broken down in shuddering sobs against the car door, prayers of thanks gusting through his chattering teeth.

Boon caressed his shoulder. They were an inseparable team. His fear had not been for himself, but at what he might lose. It had been graven on his face for days.

Panit continued, "The fear ate at me, but I could not let it consume me. I have never been afraid like that again, but I was that night. Tell me, Ring. Have you ever been afraid?" He looked at me intently. My true nature was revealed under his eyes, it seemed. Panit judged me in a glance, his truth shredding my glib humor and ease of life that was my defense. I looked down.

"Wally, the horse?" I asked, softly. "Risa, the café? Will you explain? I'm tired, and sore."

Risa shifted in her seat and retold a story about smoke and fire, blood and glass. And calm in the midst of it all.

21

Risa

When you're eleven, days are a mélange of order and chaos. Order from your family, school, and home are punctuated by outbursts of youth. Laughter. Running. Shouting. All of it in a dizzying array that leaves you tired and happy each day if you have a good life. I had a very good life. My family was loving and boisterous. I was rarely alone. I spent entire days outside in the sun and had a room full of books that brought the world inside. I also got to travel with family. My uncle Zev was a tailor with three shops, one in Tel Aviv. To me, it was visiting a place of mysteries and colors. Rolls of fabric lay in orderly rows, stacked nearly to the ceiling in the long, narrow building. The smell of linen and wool and an acrid hint of dye hung in the desultory heat of the back storage. A single air conditioning unit chugged in protestation from a high window near the front. It was, and will always be, my home away from home. The spools of thread arced away from the gleam of beautifully maintained sewing machines. Their cowls shined under the lights, and the folding tables were crowded with orders in various states of completion. His staff always knew exactly what went where. In a scene of disorder, everything had a place.

I was playing with a lurid red ribbon, wrapping it around an empty spool and rolling the spool across the smooth tiles, when a flash of disturbance broke the normal chatter of the busy street outside. My uncle and one of his helpers, a stout woman named Sarah, briskly walked to the front of the store, opening the door wide enough for both of them to see the street. I followed, my interest piqued by the noise.

It was the last thing they would do on this earth. A young woman crashed through the crowd, her western style clothes soaked with sweat. Dark eyes looked across the tables of the café next door and found mine as I stood holding my uncle's leg. Her face was beautiful but hollow, the gaze bright with mania as she was tackled from behind by a female police officer, red ponytail lashing her neck as she rode the wiry, crazed girl into the heavy edge of a table, chairs rattling away across the concrete as she detonated her suicide vest and a small spot of the sun opened in front of my vision. A peony of fire and metal turned the area into an open air coffin, screams and sobs bursting forth from the victims even as the shattered furniture and bodies began to thump to the ground in a drumbeat of horror. The smell of cordite and flesh lay over the street like a layer of sin.

Zev and Sarah gurgled and whistled to their death in seconds, their lungs rent by flying nails and bolts from the bomb that carved them into a frothy red pantomime of humans. Their hands shook and went limp almost as one. I stood on the balls of my feet and exhaled the breath I had held, letting go of my uncle's pant leg. His body collapsed to the ground, devoid of motion. The sirens screamed into the air, and, after some period of time, I was led by the hand to a gurney, my body sticky with the blood of others. I was floating.

My pulse never quickened. I never flinched. Years later, I knew why. I respected and sensed danger, but never feared anything. I was born as such.

Now, with my partners, I know the truth. It's a dangerous world, but, even within the very darkest parts of it, I am not a victim. If I've learned anything with Ring and Wally, it is that I am something to be feared.

22

Florida

Suma drew a conclusion and gestured at me, then Risa, and then settled uncertainly on Wally, pointing an inquiry. "So, if I think I understand, you can kill these creatures because you cannot be afraid? Is that right?"

"There's a difference between being free of fear and being stupid," I began. "Mostly, if you're brave but dumb, you just end up dead. None of us are ready for the grave. Seriously, look at those women. Do you think I'd do anything to jeopardize their privilege of living with me, caring for me, seeing me in my underwear, drinking milk in front of the fridge at three in the morning?"

Risa snorted. Wally nodded in confirmation of my general disregard for manners and hygienic kitchen behavior. I remained dignified given my admission of being a serial nudist, despite our physical relationships. Just because we were sleeping together didn't mean they want to see my underwear, I've been informed on more than one occasion.

"We three are just capable of stepping outside of our fear. We don't deny that it exists, but we deny it the ability to gain a purchase on us or our actions. Especially during extreme duress. Traffic is another issue for *certain* team members," I looked pointedly at Wally, "but we were always free of that curse. Even as children. In fact, Wally knew even sooner than Risa or me that she was wired differently. Didn't you, Slim?" I asked.

Wally pursed her lips and then asked Boon "You know I was raised on a horse farm, yes? Well, I wasn't always the most *obedient* child..."

23

Waleska

Please work. Please work. Please Work. Waleska beseeched the humble chip of soap that she rubbed against the heavy wooden pin on the barn door. Her small hands shot the dowel bolt without a sound. *Hinges next.* She moved with the exaggerated care of a seven-year-old engaging in a serious breach of familial rules. One hinge, then two. The third, she greased with a flourish as the soap disintegrated, its heroic duty complete.

She held her breath and swung the enormous door open, exhaling as the bulky steel strapped wood arced silently past her, coming to a stop inches from the wall. Waleska crept forward, straw *skritching* lightly beneath her boots. After dressing in the dark, she had shimmied down the spreading branches of the espinillo tree that sagged lazily against the sash of her second floor window. Looking east, she spied the first fingers of dawn amongst the wispy cirrus clouds. The Criollo mare heard her and whickered questioningly at her presence. It was still dark, and rarely did anyone visit the barn at night, unless a foal was imminent. Waleska's father had bought the mare a week earlier, but the headstrong beast had rejected every hand on the farm. She *loved* roan horses more than anything in the world, and she had seen the mare sporting about in a paddock while visiting a nearby farm, carefree and headstrong. It was an equine version of her own heart, and love at first sight as the girl's eyes filled with joy, as her eyes drank in the rippling colors and sleek muscle of the shapely mare. Wally told her father with the gravity only a seven-year-old can know that she *must* ride that horse or she would cry. The owner, a rangy woman who, Wally had sniffed, was far too refined to be a true horseman, had seen the interchange between them and sold the horse on the spot for less money than it would cost to buy a saddle. As her father paid, the seller admonished Waleska, telling her that horses such as that one were meant for adults and seasoned riders. *The nerve.* The fact that her gift rolled over on every rider mattered not a bit to the grim-faced child, who would not be denied a ride on the mare she had claimed for her own.

Spirit was fine, thought the girl, but being thrown was *verboten.* Wally would have none of that, and she meant to prove it this night.

Climbing the heavy pine stall, she knew that saddling the horse was out of the question, so her legs and hands would have to do. Her bravado ran wild in the dark, where the horses were shadows and sounds. The stall door opened easily; it was the big door that had worried her, but, now, she squatted before the mare with her hand out. Slowly, she fed the sugar cubes secreted in her pocket to the skittish head looming in the darkness above her. Her plan was simple. Ride the mare on the turf track that circled the outbuildings and have her put up before her parents awakened. She could groom her later while uttering a steady stream of reassurance in low tones, just like she had seen her father do time and again. She breathed deeply, thinking about being calm with the focus of a much older rider. Fear was her enemy. Fear would expose her to the mare as a pretender to the throne rather than as someone who would rule the saddle with ease and grace. Wally had no fear. She felt nothing but the preternatural calm that cloaked her during times when most children would quiver with fright. After several nights of these rides, Wally knew, with the certainty that only a child can feel, that she would have a horse all her own.

I must neck rein only, like Father does when he is being the boss, Wally thought, slipping the rope over the mare in a fluid motion. She cooed and chatted amiably, quietly, never ending the commentary as she stepped up the slatted wall and onto the broad back of the still-penned horse. Looking outside, she saw that the sky had gone from ash to rose and hints of gold. She had to hurry, so she nudged the flank and led the resistant horse out into the feedlot. Wally knew the test would come soon, that this quiet was a false front. She had earned nothing from this mare, but, with a single tug at the rein, a neck turn to the left placed them on the turf that yawned away in the growing light.

Wally rubbed the muscled neck and was rewarded with a single snort as the mare turned back to look at her as perched with confidence on the horse's back.

"Time to go. Hup," Wally urged, but to no avail. With the sun beginning to heat the day and fingers of light spilling wildly from the horizon, Wally drew her heels back once and planted them with a meaty whump into the obstinate sides of the horse.

The mare whickered once in irritation, then flattened her ears to her skull and *jumped*, carrying Wally forward ten feet in a blast of muscle and noise that slammed her chest against her own hands. In seconds, they flew down the track, chipping free clods of earth shaped like black crescents that hurtled *left right left right*, Wally gripping the back firmly with her long legs and laughing, urging the horse on, and then crying with the abandon and joy of it all. Only when Wally felt a heavy sweat on the mare's neck did she turn her, now compliant, towards the barn, tears of joy still streaking her dusty face as she gasped at the sight of her father. And mother. Waiting, and watching, by the barn.

She approached them, her tall father glaring at her with murderous intent. He mother had tears in her eyes, of relief, anger, and a wry admission of pride.

"Horst, gently with her, now, she is safe. Please," Wally's mother pleaded. Her father stood, impotent with rage, and, for a moment, nobody spoke, until Wally commanded the mare in a voice that was no longer that of a child.

"Park, Boudicca. Park out, now," Wally issued the order to her newly named mare, who complied, spreading her legs wide for her rider to dismount. It was the first willing direction Horst had seen the mare take since her arrival. He was stunned, but then looked at his daughter and realized he should not be.

"Boudicca? An appropriate name for a spirit like hers. Or yours, Waleska," Horst granted, his anger fading, replaced with something more like respect. Her mother sobbed lightly and rushed to hug Wally, admonishing her to never bring fear like this to their home again.

Wally looked up at her parents, their faces colored with relief and grudging admiration. "But mother, I wasn't afraid. I'm never afraid. Not even when I saw you and father standing here. And Boudicca . . . she was going to like me. They all like me. I just picked her, that's all."

24

Florida

It was full dark, and Wally cleared her throat from the doorway where she had been leaning and speaking. "I know that there may be more questions, but they can wait. Ring is tired. Risa, you go home. I will stay with Ring. In the morning, we will talk again. For now, rest."

Her tone crackled with authority, and she slid past our friends who filed obediently from my room, saying their goodbyes in various degrees of thoughtful shock. Risa patted my arm and asked Wally if we needed anything. "No. Take my truck home, sleep with that beast on the couch, and, then, in the morning, think about what we will do next. I don't want you up all night scheming." Her gaze took us all in. "We will be fine."

With that, Risa left, the front door shutting with a thump. Muted voices followed her outside, as I expected. This evening had been too jarring for the psyche of our friends. It was only one discussion, but it would have to do for now.

Wally placed a bottle of water next to the bed, but it wasn't for me. Wordlessly, she disrobed, then put on a t-shirt and climbed into bed. She rested on an elbow, looking at me softly. "We will not allow this thing to happen again, you know. We will be too vigilant, and Risa is smoldering with her anger. You know this."

I nodded, drifting with the weakness borne of healing. "We take care of each other. Thank you for staying." It didn't seem adequate, even to me, knowing how close we were. The bond superseded normalcy and edged into a connection that was forged rather than grown. We had seen too much and disguised our fears with glibness and play. That time was gone.

Wally cocked one coltish leg on my stomach and began dragging her fingers across my brow. It was intimacy and caring in the purest state. Her hair lay on my shoulder, like a golden zephyr. I was safe. Tonight, I could heal. A deep sigh left me, and I slept.

25

"What am I looking at?" Morning was unkind to me at first as my mind and body began to limber up after an extended sleep. Wally had been a lithe companion, keeping me still and restful for ten hours. I knew that, soon, I would feel renewed, but, right now, I felt disjointed and muffled. Risa and Wally sat on the bed, coffees in hand. Mine was untouched as I struggled to a sitting position. I was tense and wanted to be in motion, but Risa put an envelope in my lap. I was immediately curious. It was airmail. International. And it was addressed to all three of us, an unheard of occurrence. There was no return address, but the stamp and postmark were Cyrillic.

"This is Russian?" I asked Risa.

"No. Polish. The postmark is from a highly unusual place, but, when you read the letter, you'll understand." I opened the heavy paper envelope and took out a meticulously folded set of pages. The heft was significant, hinting at a mannerly respect for the fading art of penmanship. There was wealth in weight, too, and a feel of vellum. I knew the words would be as carefully crafted. I was not wrong.

Dear Hring, Risa, and Waleska,

I apologize for the presumption that this letter represents, but I wish to begin a dialogue concerning matters of some delicacy with which your assistance will be invaluable. In the spirit of honesty, let me dispense with any possibility that the information I possess shall ever be shared with anyone outside my home. You may be assured, upon my honor, that all members of my household practice the utmost in discretion. The facts of this letter will not be known to the rabble that cannot—and will not—understand the sensitive nature of your chosen occupation. You have my word, and should you consider rendering me assistance, you shall have far more.

I am a steward of sorts. I reside in an area that you would consider both remote and primal, but one that is beautiful, nonetheless. My house is surrounded by a crescent of green forest that has been undisturbed since the glaciers left the continent we call Europe. I am from no country and call no nation my own, but, rather, belong to two places: the forest and the subterranean spaces below.

Some time ago, my family began an undertaking that was anathema to the time and social class from which we hailed. You must understand that feudal Europe was not bereft of good leadership but that history has a penchant for remembering the bad. I prefer to believe that our attempts to preserve and protect certain elements of this place reflect the very best of humanity. My detractors have branded me vainglorious and foolish. I leave your judgments of my actions and work to you, alone.

I like to think that I am more than a mere herdsman, and, over the years, I have nurtured my passion as a craftsman who works in stone. Or, to be more precise, an artisan of jewelry. I again defer to your taste and cultural leanings to render decision upon my skills. I sincerely hope that, in my work, you will see the passion and relationship I have labored to build with each bauble. I have amassed a considerable collection from my hobby, nearing a count of 300 pieces at this time. I work quickly, and, as I hope you will find, have a superior network of suppliers from which to choose my materials.

And, now, to the point. Please forgive my digression, but I cannot ask so grave a question without proper context in order to impart the scope of the task.

The 300 pieces of my life's work are, at this time, missing. They were stolen in a single act of criminal brazenness that riddles me with anger and doubt. I do not need remuneration for these objects—of that I have no pressing desire. My interest lies elsewhere. I am, however, emotionally bereft after this act of betrayal because the thief is, in fact, my daughter.

And I believe that Hring and Elizabeth have already met.

Should you deign to hear my proposal in full, I will be most thankful. It is, of course, centered on tracking these objects for the purpose of familial unity rather than a punitive action against Elizabeth. Please take your time to consider the matter, and contact me for a video conference at your soonest convenience. I have limited electrical power here but am available for brief periods, and I offer the full capabilities of my sporadic modern communications to you at any time.

I remain hopefully yours,
Baron Cazimir Byk

I dropped the pages wordlessly and looked into Risa and Wally's faces. Naked fury simmered under the surface of both, and more than a little fear. This was our first great unknown in our years together.

"This Elizabeth has been a busy girl." My tone was cool and dry. Inside me, a vertiginous glut of emotion caromed about. Here was a connection to our problem—my tormentor—but the questions the letter raised were potentially deadly. To respond to the Baron, if he was, indeed, such, was to reveal and confirm the contents of the letter as they pertained to us.

We would also be discarding a decade of carefully crafted anonymity. Risa took up the letter and reread it, her eyes plundering the paper for additional clues. Wally leaned in and sighed. "Before we contact him, let us agree on what we share and what we ask. And we must contact him. He has already shown part of his hand. He has sources. Very good ones. We must contact him today, yes?"

I knew she was right. Risa knew she was right. Our silence was our blessing. Wally took an envelope from her purse and flattened it on her thigh, ready to write.

"So, what do we ask him first?"

26

At some nameless juncture in the afternoon, the lack of protestation from my body slyly announced my healing was nearly complete. I could inhale without constriction or pain. After two solid meals and some time on the dock, I realized that I was merely delaying our conversation with the good Baron. I woke Wally, who was dozing in the chaise lounge, and we walked inside to gather Risa, who had thoughtfully set the table with her laptop, a speaker link, and chairs crowded in unity. Risa was pouring wine. I motioned for two more, and we settled at the table in a breathless crush. Risa was in front of the screen; Wally and I flanked her. The camera on the top of the screen was a small, gleaming eye, devoid of color. I couldn't look away. My hand reached for Risa's leg even as I my fingers twined with Wally's long hand on the chair back. We were ready, and I knew that we were also overwhelmingly curious. Risa tapped the touch screen and placed a request for a video chat. The picture-in-picture was a blue square, and, then, with a blink, the Baron was there.

    He was dressed simply in a white linen shirt, his hands flat on a fine-grained wooden table shaded with a patina of time and use. His eyes were dark but friendly, his short graying hair modestly combed in the manner of a businessman. His nose was long, and he had a mobile mouth with a hint of smile. An overall patrician air, but approachable, nonetheless. The table was neatly populated with the tools of an artist. His workspace was lit by a single lamp, a bronze post capped by a narrow burgundy shade. A small vise rested to his left, with a silver ring perched birdlike in the fine jaws. Beyond the lamp's casting, the room stretched into darkness. Hints of a large space bulged from the recesses behind him. A grandfather clock uttered a single soft *bong* and fell silent. After seconds of mutual observation, he spoke.

"Most importantly, thank you for accepting my invitation to speak. I am Cazimir, and I would offer you, first, the opportunity to ask me what questions you will. I shall freely answer anything you might wish, but let me first assure you of one simple fact: I am most certainly not immortal. If anything, I am painfully aware that my time is limited. How I express this awareness is something I hope you will allow me to share." The introduction was delivered in a way that revealed the Baron as highly mannered but aware of the discomfiture present. He folded his hands in a gesture of patience and supplication and then stilled.

Our collective wariness was denuded slightly by his appearance and speech. Nodding slightly, Risa sensed our decision and began.

"If it is not too rude, may we ask a series of questions in order to maximize our time together?" It seemed reasonable that we wanted to learn as much as possible in the most direct method. Risa thought of logistics in her sleep. I usually just snored. Then again, so did Wally, albeit in a much more beautiful manner. When the Baron smiled and said, "That is quite agreeable," we were off to the races.

"How did you find us, and what is the potential reward for assisting you? And, just where are you? Right now, that is?" These seemed like broad enough issues to give us a platform to decide if we would move forward with this . . . partnership or just excuse ourselves with as little exposure as possible, although I suspected we could forget anonymity of any kind in the future.

The Baron twitched at his cuff and got comfortable in his chair, the wood creaking in mellow protest as he leaned back. "At the risk of seeming patronizing, may I share some history first, and then expand upon it as you see fit?" We gave our assent, and he paused, thinking.

The Baron, a man of whom we knew nothing, then began to tell a story that spanned millennia. History, as he told it, began in a place that was remote and ancient. The Baron spoke of giants.

27

Cazimir

I built my house among looming oaks. Not any ordinary trees, these were behemoths of stately grandeur, their canopies spreading out in vigorous disarray. Even the location of my lodge defies description, being a borderland between modern nations that remains untouched even today. For the sake of brevity, I will spare you the many names and call this place the Bialowicza or, simply, the forest. Between Belarus and Poland, the vestige of the great European wood thrives, protected and nurtured after brief periods of threat.

This home of mine is much more than a preserve. It is a place of invasion, retreat, and resurgence over time. Only the forest remains continual, timeless, and unknowable. Humanity is a recent addition to this sacred ground, following on the heels of mega fauna that rumbled about in a shaggy diaspora, their horns and feet marking the landscape as they lived, bred, and died over millennia.

With beasts came hunters. From the depths of human time, the forest was visited by men, alternately frightened and bold in their desperate war for survival. When the great ice departed, travelers from the Danube began to arrive, and, upon settling, they began to dig. Copper was beaded, hammered, and shaped into tools of cultures known now only by their relics. The Lengyel, the Polgar, the Malice cultures, gone. Yet, we would learn about them as a result of their apparatus used in daily life, crafted from clay and stone. Flint was worried from ground, tools were shaped, and the first-named peoples, now long forgotten, embarked on the enormous task of shaping the upper European Plain into a locus for their descendants. They hunted game for fur, tendons, meat, blood, and bone in numbers that established humanity as the dominant, sometimes ruthless, master of the Bialowicza. Among their prey was the Wisent, a medium-sized bison that is in the forest to this day. But it was the pursuit of an enormous bull, the aurochs, a heavily muscled, horned steer that ranged through the European plain, which would change my family history.

Romans were, originally, a martial society that prized the science of warfare and self-discipline among soldiers. But, the arrival of viticulture became a sort of undoing for these warriors, as the state they fought to protect began to corrupt with each successive Bacchanalia. Gone were the rigors of a society devoted to the morality and structure of Rome. And, so, the *Circus Maximus* became the light from Rome's long, meteoric arc of dissolution.

Left to her own devices, the decaying Empire was forced to distract her people from the increasing difficulty of their lives. Human gladiators battled each other and beasts from every Roman province—and beyond. Wolves were pitted against bulls, bears against lions, and combinations of predators churned the bloody sand of the arenas to the howls of drunken mobs screaming for blood.

They were rarely disappointed.

The aurochs became a favorite. Huge, aggressive, and incredibly agile for such a large beast, the slashing horns and hooves spun death for man and animal, alike, when they pitted against the bull. Their performance in the ring would be their undoing, as arena procurators combed every acre of the aurochs home range, eventually driving the once prominent herds into rarity, rumor, and legend.

But the aurochs was crafty, and, deep in the confines of the Bialowicza, the remaining members of the species found a place to hide. For a thousand years after Rome was sacked by waves of Vandals and Goths, the bulls of the forest hid and thrived, their small herd picking delicately through the oaks and birch. They were relatively safe, but meat is a commodity, and the feudal system of Europe led hunger to the doorstep of many rustic families. It is at this point, in the sixteenth century, that my family intervened as a bulwark between the hungry poor and the fatted elites.

My progenitor built a lodge, but there was no hunting, only nurturing a small group of regal beasts whose breath layered the early morning sun in a verdant swath of meadow. This Baron, my namesake, was the first ranger, a man who knew the value of the aurochs and the oaks and the river surrounding his secret lands. Our family's existence was simple but rewarding, and education about our property was a premium concern. So, we turned our curiosity to the land under, not just around, our holdings, and began to dig where others had never gone, in natural fissures, bluffs, and caves.

The fruits of this secondary occupation are what you will soon hold in your hands.

28

We were rapt. He was a brilliant speaker, his tone that of a natural teacher. Our fascination was shattered with a harsh knock at the door, jarring us from our receptive mood.

"I'll get it." Wally uncoiled from her chair and went to the front door, disappearing outside for a brief moment. The Baron watched from the screen, smiling.

"Delivery. From the Baron? How did you do that—magic?" Wally's tone was suspicious.

"Not magic. Federal Express," The Baron, a man we would now call Cazimir, laughed across the miles as we fell to the package, our curiosity burning. Wally prized a small rosewood box from the fat envelope.

"The box slides out, right to left," Cazimir offered helpfully, as the wood was polished to be seamless. Inside was a wonder.

A necklace dangled from Wally's hand, eliciting a collective noise of appreciation from the three of us. This was art. A single square of silver was chased with copper in the form of a stallion in profile, one bead of carnelian marking the eye of the proud animal. A chain of small silver links attached cleverly to a fore and rear hoof that touched the border of the two inch shape. The horse seemed to pulse with life in the metal. If ever there was a debate about what Cazimir's primary pursuit should be, the piece ended it with finality.

"You are gifted beyond words. I cannot fathom what it feels like to have things like this stolen from you." Risa's voice was reverent.

"You are too kind. Yes, the collection is valuable, but there is another, larger concern at hand regarding my baubles. It is the primary reason for contacting you after careful research among persons who possess your *particular* abilities." The Baron's emphasis was light but definite. He was revealing a great deal for someone who stood to lose so much.

"How did you find us, if we may ask?" Risa asked, the picture of decorum.

"To put your minds at rest, it was not an easy task. I began with a simple question: Who finds things that do not want to be found? The answer lay in the nature of the lost objects. Since Elizabeth is immortal, I needed a very specific type of finder. Someone, or some people, as it turned out, who could operate comfortably in a world where the threats were outside the scope of normal humanity. To that end, I employed some of the same tactics that you use and was led by the trail of disregard for humanity. Crime brought me, through my proxy agent, to you, although, in truth, the search took more than a year. The woman you dispatched, Senya?" His eyes shifted directly to me. "My agent saw you leave with her but did not see . . . the unpleasantness of her demise, let us say, but did report motes of light drifting away on the salt air. You were followed, discreetly, and then further observations and inquiries were made, leading me to the three of you. And here we are."

"Cazimir, forgive me, but you don't exist. We searched online, books, newspapers, every repository of information we have access to. Your name is a dead end. The lodge you live in is built of air. Your family name is a ghost. Can you explain how this is possible?" I was as respectful as I could be, but the answer we got to this question would determine a great deal of how our interaction would proceed from that point on.

"That is a testament to the value my family puts on discretion. Did you, perhaps, find mention of another protector of the aurochs, ambitious Germans who sought to reverse their plight?" We had, and he knew it.

He continued, "That scheme took place in the 1920s, but, under Catherine of Poland three centuries earlier, a very minor relative of hers built an extravagant hunting lodge in the Bialowicza. King Wladislawa IV seized that lodge and began to actively manage the forest beyond simple hunting laws, imagining himself as the true guardian of the natural world. What he did not know is that opposite his plush abode, in a sheltered valley, my family, with funds Catherine had granted a century earlier, built what would become my home and the home of the aurochs, which miraculously survived until the time that they came under the care of my people."

"Your agent?" Risa seized on that thread first, Wally nodding in accord. We had all picked up on the fact that he had a contact here that was skilled enough to observe us, unseen.

"Yes. My apology for the intrusion, but, as you will see, quite necessary. I have revealed nothing of your existence whatsoever, and my observer has reported to my complete satisfaction." Cazimir remained unperturbed that we asked about this, of all details, first.

"Well . . ." and Wally drew the word out, voicing so many of our concerns. "May I ask that, if your family has no need of money, why do you need the collection returned? Is there a value that we are unaware of, perhaps?"

Cazimir's face was shadowed, his smile waning. The lamp at his desk flickered, and he glanced over with a sigh of resignation. "We will lose our connection in a moment. I shall be brief. I do not, as you say, need the items for monetary reasons. In fact, I care not at all for them other than in a superficial manner. I want Elizabeth back, or at least something of her. My family is nearly gone. There is Elizabeth, and there is me. She is immortal. My time is limited. I have staff here, a modest number, but my promise to this land has, with her departure, rendered me a prisoner here. While I am bound to this place, Elizabeth is not. She is gone, and I remain. I know that you are more than human now, and that is requisite for this task. Were you not augmented by your lifestyle, you would be dead. Find the baubles, and you will find Elizabeth. That which you recover is yours to keep. Remember, she does not wish to be known, so you must pursue her with great care. My instincts reveal that you will both choose to assist me and succeed. I will speak to you two days hence. Good night."

The screen blinked once, and the connection was cut. The Baron, a man trapped in a castle of wood, had asked us not to retrieve jewelry, but something, someone, more important to him than a king's fortune—his daughter.

And I wanted her dead.

29

Petra

Viktor leaned back in anticipation, the buffed leather of the custom chaise squeaking under his muscular frame. Unlike many billionaires, his vanity demanded that he keep his body in enviable condition. To be slovenly was, in his opinion, a sin of the commoner, and one that he would not allow himself to commit. Defiling young women was another issue entirely. His 200-foot yacht was ripe with the most beautiful women culled from the shoreline during an orgiastic day of purchasing cars in Miami. The men and women who worked for him knew to bring only the best to the deck of *Inquisitor*. From that pool of beauty, he had selected the flawless girl before him. Viktor glibly commented on the beauty of her unusual blood-colored earrings, the dark jewels held in antique silver. It was a typical opening foray intended to begin his brutish seduction of the girl.

Her earrings swayed as she laughed, shining with stately worth. He had seen her comically-elongated pinky nail as she sipped white wine on the deck and made his determination. *Coke whore*. Although he never touched drugs, he kept a small quantity in his suite as an enticement for certain women. If a line of high grade cocaine did not remove their doubts about the immediacy of his lust, then other, more physical means could be used. He had a reputation to protect, and momentary prudish behavior could not interfere with his image. Simply stepping onto the deck of *Inquisitor* was, in Viktor's mind, tacit approval for him to take what he wished. A woman's refusal was unacceptable, no matter what reason she gave.

They retired to his suite after he made his wishes known with a possessive hand in the small of Petra's graceful back. The other social climbers saw their chances for notoriety or money die in a gesture.

Petra paused and sinuously dropped her silk dress to the floor in a rippling circle. She stood before him in nude blonde magnificence, clad only in heels that accentuated her legs. Her Czech lineage gifted her with beauty of a rare nature. She picked up her dress and bound her hands with a languorous motion, kneeling before him in complete supplication. It was exactly as he wished. Busy fingers unzipped his trousers and freed him in one motion. Even constricted by the silk, her movement was serpentine and free of awkwardness. His anticipation grew acute.

She hesitated. Viktor *hated* teasing. He reached out to guide her but his hand was rebuffed as exquisite heat washed over him, a paralytic of unmatched pleasure. She drew him out of her mouth and encircled his entire manhood in her hands, her touch maddeningly light. Viktor looked out from heavily lidded eyes at the golden angel kneeling before him.

"Keep going. Now. And do not stop." His voice was thick with lust.

"As you say." Petra leaned forward to her work, her fingers teasing, probing and dancing around his base in a flutter. Her grip tightened. She bore down with her mouth, the conflicting pleasures stoking Viktor to near climax as her fingernail punctured his skin and neatly severed a gossamer strand, the only nerve that mattered to a cocksman like Viktor. He burst into her even as his organ began to detumesce, the last erection of his life fleeing him just as his pleasure ebbed.

Now he felt the wound. "What . . . what have you . . . ," he sputtered, his eyes rolling in fear as the woman who had stolen his claim to manhood rose up, smirking. "What have you *done* to me?" he whimpered, but he knew. He knew even as Petra's heel snapped forward, shattering his nose and pitching him, unconscious, over the chair, back into the deep woolen rug. He lay on his back, arms spread as if crucified, his limp member lolling as it would for the remainder of his life. Petra spat in his open mouth. Smiling, she pulled her dress over her head before smoothing it to go back to the party. With a final look mixed of triumph and pity, she pulled the door to the suite closed, thinking, *Mother would be proud.*

30

Florida

The mood in our house was frosty the next morning. I was simmering with what I imagined to be well-deserved anger. Wally was strangely dispassionate, and Risa avoided me altogether after a brief discussion over breakfast during which she called me a self-serving prick. Lest anyone think we are an unwaveringly united collective voice, we had occasional arguments that ranged from tame to paint-blistering brawls that raged just short of physical violence. Without even asking Risa, who was like a human lie detector, I could smell bullshit in the Baron's story. My doubt did not mean that every statement was a lie. But there were too many red flags in his narrative to escape notice. If Elizabeth was immortal, why wasn't he? How did she turn? Was she really his daughter or something else? These questions seemed natural to me, and I know Wally and Risa were thinking within the same framework. I was being forced into the unsavory position of playacting with the Baron until we could determine the truth or whatever nuanced history passed for fact when dealing with a family as unique as that of Cazimir.

I have money. I have a home. These are tools for me, and, as long as I am physically able to strip wealth away from immortals, I can continue to rid my world of evil. That salient point is where Risa and Wally and I disagree. I want Elizabeth to answer for what I know is a long life of spreading death and sadness. I have been unflagging in my desire to eliminate immortals quickly and without hesitation. There is, in my mind, no nuance to evil. And yet, the respect I have for my partners demanded that I at least listen to their case for why the Baron's needs should circumvent my desire for vengeance.

I needed information about Elizabeth, about the Baron, and about why my wrath directed at my near executioner should be held in check.

I was asked to lunch by Suma and seized the opportunity for a change of scenery. We met at an Italian deli on Sheridan Street and took to a booth, sliding across the plastic seats in the midst of utter chaos. It was incredibly busy, and the background was a nice distraction from the intense chill at home. Suma ordered a sandwich with so many varieties of garlicky meat that I was glad we had arrived separately. I kept true to my first love on the menu, a chipped ham sandwich with homemade dressing and fries. Suma wasted no time in expressing her reasoning for our newfound status as lunch pals.

"You talked a great deal during your recuperation, and, until our group discussion, I thought you were delirious. I am a person of science. I am a trained skeptic, but I know evidence must override my inhibitions to expand what I think can be possible. I am also," she slowed her speech, clearly attempting to reconcile divergent ideas, "a Thai. I am the product of a culture that is steeped in spiritualism. It is a second skin for me, and no amount of university can make me deny what I feel at a cellular level. I also respect my family, not because I am an automaton who is expected to do so. No, I respect results. My parents were excellent people of great character. They worked, they saved, and they took duty to family so seriously it was like law. They lived in a world where the veil between reality and the supernatural was a curtain to be passed through each day."

She paused, appraising the mountainous sandwiches that had arrived. "Occam's razor notwithstanding, I want to hear from you how you came to be . . . what you are. How did you and Wally and Risa become a unit? Are you an enhanced *ménage a trois*, or just what the hell is your connection? Is it convenience borne of an unusual gift? Hatred due to your respective losses? Is it love? Or is it something I cannot imagine because I am from a more ordinary place?" Her frustration bubbled forth now as she tried to understand how her family had come to danger from what might be sexual dilettantes with a penchant for killing. I understood. The curtain had been pulled back, and her own flesh and blood were now at risk from something that she did not fully grasp. Nursing me to health had given her evidence, though, that the threat was real. She feared that powerlessness, but her cool exterior demanded that she approach the situation with logic in order to understand what she could do. In truth, I was surprised at her relative calm. I suspected that she was intensely passionate but measured in her actions. As a physician, it was expected. As a woman of discipline, it was what she had chosen.

After a deep breath and a gulp of tea, she asked, softly, "Can you really defend my family?" That, I knew, was the most important question she would ever pose to me, and she deserved a thoughtful, honest answer. Around contemplative bites of ham, I parsed the truth and expounded where necessary, clarifying terms unfamiliar to her.

"I have very little family left," I began, "so you can imagine how I feel about yours. I admire them, and I'm even a little bit jealous of them at times. They are at an intersection right now. I care for them but feel real hate for immortals, but I don't imagine you can understand that type of incandescent fury. Risa and Wally, we keep each other from combusting with it. We see the effects, you know."

Suma sat, rapt. "We were party kids, amateur students who were drifting, careless; we met in college, but, after a drunken weekend of *in vino veritas*, we realized that we shared a collective ghost story, but this one was real. Can you imagine two other people who felt the same bizarre thing, how rare that would be? The same brush with evil? Who believed you? In one second, I found my purpose. I'm not saying we were a well-oiled machine at first; we didn't even really know what the hell we were doing. But we sensed the rightness of it all, and we made peace with the violence, especially Wally. She was such a gentle soul then. One of my first kills was some sort of vampire who looked about ten years old. He bit through my watch band and broke my collarbone before I pounded my knife up into his chest. I pinned him to the door of my car, and, even as he was dying, he tried to rip my throat out with his thumbs. I almost died because I hesitated to murder what *looked* like a child. Risa found out he had been killing people, good people, since the dustbowl years in Oklahoma. I swore I wouldn't make that mistake again, but I knew I needed help. I puked into the tub for hours and slept for a solid day. This was when we all lived separately. After that, we decided to move in here, where we could watch each other, and help, and hold each other when no amount of hot water could wash the sin from us after a kill. So when you ask me, do I love them, I can tell you that love isn't a big enough word for what we feel for each other. The danger makes it something more. "

I ducked my head into the last of my sandwich. After a quiet moment I asked Suma, "Do you want me to talk less or more?"

"More. And you can start with some basics. How long have you been paired off, partners? How long have you known Risa and Wally?" She paused, pensive and looking at me anew. I could tell our conversation was shifting her view of me, but, in what manner, I was uncertain. In an existence as bizarre as mine, the truth always won out because it trumped any fantasy I could concoct.

"Fourteen years. Each. I'm thirty-eight years old, and we've been ferreting out immortals full-time for almost thirteen years."

"Stop. You're thirty-eight?" Suma was incredulous. "Is this another challenge to my scientific bedrock?" Her eyes narrowed as she leaned back in the booth. She was skeptical, even after seeing me vomit acorns, presumably put in my stomach by an evil being that defied the facts she held dear. The evidence was contrary, since I knew I looked to be in my mid-twenties.

"I noticed something was different about me after our third kill. It was a small thing. I was swimming the canal when I heard Risa yelling. I had been just under the surface, kicking and watching the sun break through the water. She was panicked and getting ready to jump in, for some reason. I yelled at her and swam to the dock. She was *pissed*. She asked me, with a poke to the chest, if I thought I was funny. We all know I'm hilarious, but this was something else, which she made clear with more jabs. Finally, she told me that I'd been under water for six minutes. Now, I can hold my breath well because of diving, but that was new to me. Then, I realized that I felt some sort of tension in my muscles that I couldn't explain. Wally joined us later, and I felt like a prize hog at a fair. They poked and prodded, but there was nothing wrong. It was a few days later that I sussed out what was happening. Turned out it was happening to them, as well, but they hadn't realized it because they were dealing with something missing from their bodies rather than something being added to it, after a fashion."

"What was different?" Suma asked.

"They had stopped menstruating. Completely, in unison, for three months." I thought back to the hysteria of pregnancy tests in the bathroom at Walgreen's and the dawning realization that our bodies were not entirely our own to control.

"No immaculate twins, then, but what brought on the amenorrhea? Was it stress or shared illness?" The doctor in Suma was calculating possible causes, I could see.

"I don't think so. We think it is acquired. Like me swimming underwater or being a bit faster, or Risa reading faces and intuiting people's thoughts, word for word. You see, this was the first proof we had that change was coming for us with each contact. I was thrilled. Risa was dour, and Wally cried in gales for an afternoon before she went out to the solace of the yard. They knew what it meant, what was happening. Fourteen years later, hindsight is cheap. We've never seen an immortal infant. Do you know why?" I asked, my eyes downcast. I knew Suma would understand the reason.

"The immortals are sterile, right? Whatever it is that infects them must happen outside the womb. They cannot breed, so they must create. Yet, with each 'birth,' they expose themselves to the possibility of a new form that may lay them bare to us. To the world. Still, they bite and seduce, or whatever their vector is and they do it because their organs are barren. And you found this out in a moment of understanding and decided to stay the path." Now her expression matched the kindness in her voice. She saw it all.

Suma clasped my hand lightly. "I'm so sorry. What a cost."

"I think you see why we are so intractable. I'm not vicious. I put them down like rabid dogs, not born of hate for the animal, but because the dog is no longer in charge of its own body. The distinction is that these animals look like us, but they are very different. They kill wantonly. They're good at it. But, even if there is a small core of their former humanity, it has to be sacrificed. That makes me the blade man almost every time. The girls have different skills from mine. You might not know it, but Wally is incredibly lethal, although her violence is wild and unfocused. She is less clinical than Risa, but so angry; she's been intermittently angry for years. It flares with her, almost uncontrollable. We are three sides of a coin, and we work well together, which is fortunate, because it seems like we'll be doing it for a long time. You might think it's a hellish way to live, but I suspect that hell is *far* beyond my imagination. "

I knew this to be true because I saw the handiwork of these creatures much too often.

"To answer something you haven't asked, Suma, the answer is yes. Yes, I can protect your family because, if something gets close enough to hurt them, it won't matter. Wally and Risa and I will be dead. And the knives we wield against these lost beasts will be gone, along with more innocents, falling to the darkness, and nothing to stop it."

From Risa's Files

July 19: Patient is outwardly healthy 28-year-old male complaining of insomnia, lethargy, and shortness of breath. Exam reveals mild anemia. Lungs clear. Dismissed with vitamin samples and prescription for sleep aid.

July 26: Patient has moderate weight loss and persistent insomnia, despite sleep aid. Mild rash presents on chest and thighs, with some confusion and dementia, insisting that all night visitors be kept from room. Patient admitted under care of Dr. Pratbahd. Intravenous fluids given. Topical steroid for rash.

July 30: Patient weight loss is noticeable, and lesions are present on thighs, ribcage, and chest. Aggressive treatment with steroids has not affected skin condition. Fever, delusion, night terrors. Extremely low urine output. Patient incapable of speech. Hypertrophy of skin near ribs, thorax, and neck. Tongue is swollen. Patient communicated through writing before losing consciousness. Patient requests euthanasia due to being "eaten at night." Dr. Pratbahd has restrained the patient for safety reasons.

July 31: Death.

31

Florida

I hold Saturdays in a special regard. It's the day to put the boat in the water, go fishing, make umbrella drinks, and feel my muscles atrophy in front of sports on television. I tend to get up early and swim or run. I then return to a state of near coma after eating waffles until I am psychologically prepared for the rigors of fishing and drinking. Wally and Risa share this passion for the finest day of the week, so it was no great surprise when I woke from my post-breakfast nap and found the girls out on the dock, sunning like oily iguanas. In between their respective lounges, ice settled in a rolling cooler, completely devoid of bottles. Several empties were rolled casually across the wooden planks. The girls had either started early, or I had napped late. Wally stared mournfully into the barren ice from beneath her lowered sunglasses while Risa purposely ignored her.

"Ring, tell that brunette slut to get up and grab more beer. She's ahead four to three, and I am not going for more because she drinks like a dolphin." Wally was too comfortable to do more than complain, incorrect analogy and all, and was probably well on her way to a healthy buzz. I wondered whose bladder would yield first.

Risa responded to Wally with a yeasty belch and stuck out her tongue. The atmosphere was one of prim adulthood and silken manners. I made a noise of agreement and turned back to the house in order to keep the peace by delivering beer.

"Blue texted me," Wally continued at my shoulder. "She wants to talk to you and . . . ," her pause made me look to see her mime driving our boat, "maybe tomorrow . . . ," thus indicating that our friend wanted to borrow the boat for a day on the water with her son. "And, while inside, be good and make us peanut butter sandwiches. With cinnamon. And much more beer." She settled back on the chaise in dismissal.

Risa spoke up, "Make mine toasted." I gave an obedient sigh and went in to fulfill my stint as a short order cook, and to call Blue.

Keeping a minimal profile is in our collective best interest, but Blue is a friend. She has a direct line of information we need through her business. At thirty-nine, she is one of the youngest strip club owners in the area. Blue had gone to school for textiles, only to find the job market a wilderness of nepotism and unpaid internships. She seized a retail position at the first chance, working her way into the management staff of a high-end men's store. It was there that she was romantically pursued by a customer named Walid, whose hot pursuit of her resulted in a marriage that was cut short by his untimely death. Walid, an unrepentant Arabic chain smoker, suffered a fatal heart attack that left Blue a young widow with a controlling interest in a strip club and a one-year-old son. Her adaptation to the role as a club owner was a testament to her boundless character and intellect. As a woman, and an unrelentingly honest human, she is a rarity among the seedier establishments. In addition to her many qualities, Blue doesn't ask excessive questions. We love her style, and her club. Since the adult industry is awash with European women, men, and their castoffs, we mine that group for immortals and their crimes. Rarely is investigative work quite as engaging as being surrounded by gyrating naked women. It's a sacrifice I make for the good of our team and for the children. Or something like that.

We are never unsuccessful. The anonymity, cash business, and late nights make strip clubs and all that they entail one of our primary places of business. The cast of characters is fluid. Blue sits squarely in the middle, and she asks nothing of us, other than personal favors that benefit her son. Since Evan likes the water, our boat is hers. In return, we enjoy tips and other perks without undue interrogation from Blue. Her sense of fair play dictated that she only asked for the boat when she heard or saw something of interest to us.

After the girls dozed in the sun all day, I would ask if they felt like enjoying a little neon and nudity for dinner at Blue's club. It would, of course, be rude to ignore her implied invitation to chat, and I am nothing if not courteous.

Our achievements for the day as a group were, to be kind, minimal. While the girls acquired deep tans and an all-day state of inebriation, I cleaned and spooled my fishing reels, breaking only to doze with Gyro after he tired of the nonstop laughter on the dock and joined me in the living room. I checked my email to find that the Baron was awake and eager to chat. While my partners slept away the early evening in a gently sodden dreamstate, I connected with Cazimir, uncertain of what I would say. As it turned out, I said very little, since he judged our rapport sufficient to offer additional history to the lost collection.

Again at his desk, he began our chat by holding up a ring of smooth wood. Not all permanent things were stone, it seemed. Some, he explained, could be as timeless as stone. Like a simple ring.

Or a cross.

"Are you familiar with the larch tree, Ring?" he asked, rolling the object between his fingers in a gentle, reverent motion. I was not and said as much.

"The wood is hard but not remarkably so. This ring is larch. I did not carve it, but I wish I had. Simplicity is elegance in this case. By oiling and buffing the simple circle, a common piece of wood becomes something notable, valued. The grain becomes visible and demands the attention of an admirer; it is whorled and free but still orderly. It is history in a small circle. The minutiae of the band indicate dry years when they are tightly bound. Wet years, too, years with fire or clouds. In a sense, the ring is a story to whoever is willing to read it. It has passed from hand to hand for centuries. Isn't that hopeful? That something this small can survive the rigors of time while only becoming more polished?" He stared, shortsighted, at the ring, admiration coloring his expression.

"What is the purpose of the ring? Was it a wedding band?" I felt obtuse, but curious.

"I do not know. Larch has been a favorite wood of the animists and pagans for millennia. Perhaps it is the shape of the tree, or the color, that lends itself to being a fulcrum between some people and the supernatural. Look at the effects of a simple cross, two millennia later after a woodworker was hung to die in the sun. Do you think that the Romans could have possibly foreseen the boulder they were carelessly tossing into the pond of history? I doubt it. I show you this ring because it represents a bookend to my collection. I began as a keeper of these antiquities before I ever set my hammer to a gem or any metal. Value is rarely universal, but, to me, something as simple as this," he brandished the ring, tersely, "is worth keeping and protecting, if only for respect of its history."

He set the ring down, regaining his composure, as a woman came into the picture, carrying a glass of wine. Tall and blonde, she moved with soundless efficiency. "Thank you, Ilsa." He returned his gaze as she wordlessly departed the screen. "My staff is efficient but rarely verbose. It makes for quiet evenings." His face betrayed a hint of boredom at this admission.

"I understand the scope of your labors a bit better now. Do you have any family left, other than Elizabeth? Is the collection your legacy?" I asked this man, who was nearly alone in a glorified log fortress, hidden from the world.

"It would seem so. I can feel my time here becoming thin. I am, or I should say, *was* prideful, a terrible sin, to be so, but now, I feel myself losing depth, like an echo or a reflection of a man. The beasts here are unaware of my presence, anymore. My time for challenging and changing is past. I only hope, rudely, for my own benefit, to recover some of what once was. In my wistfulness, I am becoming that which I would mock, looking back into the sunset. That same pride demands that I bring Elizabeth to heel and not leave a legacy of sinful jetsam spurred by my own hands. I cannot allow it, so I implore you to find her. And, when you do, to keep my legacy for yourself, or sell it to create lives for the helpless. Please leave me with that knowledge, that my sins will be expiated through the good of strangers. And, if you succeed, I leave here fulfilled, completely."

I nodded to his fading image. I knew he was right, and assuaging my own pride could wait.

32

Sandrine

P<i>osers. I should be in surgery; not standing here smiling like a simpleton among these people,</i> thought Arnaud, although he was far too meek to say so out loud. His dumpy shape and thinning hair made him stand out in the midst of the beautiful, wealthy crowd around him. At the nexus of the room stood an auctioneer, his hair as slick as his delivery, droning in a playful British intonation under the enormous white tent. Thin, tanned arms glittering with gold, rose to bid on more jewels, all in the name of charity. It was a farce, and Arnaud would not have attended were it not for the fact that these people funded his work at the hospital in West Palm Beach. His penance for offering his surgical skills to fix the broken bodies of women and children marred by abuse was to stand here, pretending as if he could afford the jewelry being offered. It was a display that was anathema to his personal morality, but he endured it in quiet misery.

He took a polite sip from his champagne flute and tried to focus on the object being held up by an auctioneer. The screen behind the podium displayed a ring of unusual beauty, setting the tent abuzz.

"*Magnifique,*" said a soft voice at his ear. He turned, smiling to hear his mother tongue. He smiled wider when he saw the speaker.

She was young, perhaps in her late teens, willowy and Gallic in every way. Her close-cut hair and eyes were black, her skin pale, and her countenance silky, a touch disdainful. Her eyes were even with his, but he felt small next to her grace. Arnaud was instantly enchanted.

She pointed with her chin at the auctioneer. "Bid for me, please? I will pay as high as twenty thousand American dollars. I am a bit shy for this room," she concluded, with a glance from under her lashes. His arm rose, unbidden, to enter the fray of the auction. When her breath caught at his clear tone as he shouted above the others, he made his decision.

The girl will have the ring no matter what price, he thought, *and, maybe this time, I will get the girl.*

"Look at the light in it. Like falling stars. So perfect." Sandrine rested her hand on Arnaud's thigh, his pulse racing higher with each miniscule motion. They sat, shoulder-to-shoulder, in the sand, the sun long since set. The crowd had dispersed in their fleet of cars, their collective social duty complete, and their egos sufficiently caressed by the charity staff that had grown tired of pandering. It was quiet, save the waves. She laid her arm over his shoulder and leaned to him, her lips curled in a smile. Arnaud sighed in pure submission. *This is real. Not like emailing the prostitute from the advertisement and answering her questions, exposing my loneliness to a whore who would not even send me her picture until she could investigate me. I will never feel that shame again.*

"How many surgeries will your hands do this year," she asked, close enough to kiss. "They are so beautiful. Like an artist's."

"I hope to . . . well, I shall, as many as I can afford, we can afford, rather, so, a hundred, but more if I can. There are always so many, from so far away. There is so much violence and I only have so much time," his voice fluttered away into her mouth, which met his softly.

She pulled back, the kiss still hot on his face. Her arm wrapped around his neck, hugging him with a possession he had yearned for. Her grip began to tighten. *How can she be so strong,* he mused, as spots flooded his vision, floating red starbursts of pain. Sparks. Shadows. A red curtain, descending.

"You are quite right. Our time here is rarely as long as we wish." Laying his inert form on the soft sand, she began to drag him, his body leaving a furrow in the shells.

Arnaud awoke to the first steely gray hints of dawn. *I am nude. And I am buried? In sand?* He was still at the beach, but under a copse of trees. Above him waved palmetto fronds, a sea grape, and an oak. He felt air on his stomach, and his face was clear, but he was held tight by the sand. Wriggling, he strained and groaned at the pain in his neck, a deep bruise from being choked. It was a miracle his hyoid bone had not broken. He sensed she was near, and then she spoke.

He felt his first genuine whisper of terror, like a spigot being turned on slowly.

"I did not intend to kill you, of course. That would be wasteful, not to mention rude. I do love the ring so, and my mother taught me that I should reward the men who are kind to me," Sandrine said as she appeared above him, unbuttoning her blouse. She was very thin. Her skirt and shoes were gone. She straddled him, nude, her hands braced on either side of his head. Her pelvic bones pressed into his abdomen like spikes. Naked, he realized how angular her frame truly was. Sweat beaded her brow and lip. She was straining, but at what Arnaud could not guess. She gave him a cursory smile as she leaned to kiss him.

"I would like to give you a gift in return. It is only proper, since you would be most generous to my children. In fact, they could thank you for every meal," she murmured, raising her torso high above his exposed midsection. A clicking noise emanated from where her sex should have been, as a bone white appendage extended from her dark junction. It glistened malevolently in the growing light. She pressed in to kiss him, a fleshy dart under her tongue flicking forth and piercing his soft palate. Bitter venom flooded his mouth as he began to numb instantly. Arnaud felt himself deaden as the lassitude from her poison worked through his body.

I cannot move. Dear God, I can feel, but I cannot move. She is like a parasitic wasp. I am her children's food. The scientist in him was dispassionate, even removed, from her real nature, but observant of how she would bring death. The man in him screamed wordlessly in a helpless, piteous roar.

He felt the shock of her ovipositor puncturing his navel, but no pain. It pulsed once, and again, and then a last time, the sterile eggs spearing into his thoracic cavern to be enclosed in warmth, safety, and blood. They would yield no live births, but would result in certain death for Arnaud. She withdrew from him, spent, her skin flushed with the effort of insertion. Arnaud could not even scream as she stood, brushing sand from her legs and hands as she reached for her clothes, hanging on a low oak limb. The sun began to warm his face, and he became aware of an itching from within as his body went to war against the hostile invaders who would survive only long enough to kill, the egg cases rotting within him as he decayed under the sands of a picturesque beach.

Her heels now on, Sandrine kicked sand over Arnaud's stomach and face, thinking to keep him hidden until he had been consumed.

As I was taught. A good mother leaves nothing to chance.

33

I opted to drive to Blue's club, as the girls were still rowdily drunk, although showered and dressed. Both wore cowboy hats in honor of our destination's unique theme. The Corral was appropriately rife with western imagery, neon, saloon doors, and pleather couches, where girls could grind their marks into submission, one three-minute song at a time. I parked discreetly in the gravel lot next door; the Corral was across the street from the Intracoastal, and the smell of saltwater and mud spiked the breeze with each draft. Even though Risa was quietly arguing with Wally about what type of champagne they would order, we were all casually investigating our area as we approached the growing rowdy locus of noise and light under the canopy at the front door.

A bouncer I didn't know politely asked us for our identification, looming over us in a white dress shirt that fit him as if it was sprayed on. He moved with the heavy rigor of many power lifters, but he was friendly and invited us in with a flourish as we pushed the second set of swinging doors open and stepped inside.

Atmosphere cannot be underestimated in setting a tone, and Blue was hardly subtle in her shrewd approach. In essence, a well-run strip club is a flawless business model. All efforts are made to peel as much money away from patrons over an extended period of time, with the least resistance possible. Liquor is king. Bar profits are astronomical when management is honest and present. Blue was both. Add to the mix loud music, beautiful nude women in numbers, and a charged atmosphere of lust and gender warfare, and you have a concoction that simultaneously creates and destroys.

We loved it. It was like setting an ambush in a narrow pass. There was little chance of failure, given the realities of the business. Foreign women flooded the clubs, some working as dancers, others as escorts. They gyrated alongside American girls who were locals, or worked a circuit, or short-timers who stepped onstage with the sole intent of landing a man—or woman—that would see to their needs permanently. It was desperate, outrageous, and exhilarating, even genuinely fun at times, but I never forgot that peering from underneath the feast before me was danger. Petty crime, drugs, assault, and more sinister events percolated in a permanent cycle of chaos. The money held many of the dancers and other employees hostage. So did the late nights, late mornings, sexual freedom, and anonymity even under the glare of the club's lights. I knew to be outwardly carefree but observant. We were here to learn something, hopefully.

At least I knew I was, as the girls ordered a magnum of Cristal. Some nights, they were too clubby for their own good. I let the room wash over me. A miasma of noises and smells came to me uninvited, assertive and raucously lewd. Body spray, beer, whiskey, cigarette smoke, and lust were raw on my soft palate from my first inhalation as I leaned back in my chair. I assessed the patrons, and then, the dancers. None of the talent could compare to the natural beauty of Wally, but they were still tanned, prancing about for customers in a lazy circle. Like sharks, but with long, smooth legs and glittering makeup.

The waitress, clad only in a thong, hat, and boots, brought the bottle to the table, and I gave her my credit card. On the tray was a folded note that simply read *"Office."* As the girls poured and settled in, I stood and headed to the back corner, where the money room door was hidden behind a partition. Even inebriated, I knew that nothing would evade the constant, darting eyes of my partners, so I left, wondering only what we were here for, other than the scenery.

The door clicked solidly behind me as I blinked in the glare of a modern, fully lit office devoid of nudity and western décor. Blue slid from her desk to embrace me and kiss my cheek with a, "Hullo, kid." I smiled back and slid into a cloth chair, frankly admiring her in the process. She was naturally beautiful but tiny, with a competitive edge to her smile that made it known she was the pack leader on her premises. Her vibe was pure alpha out of necessity. She exuded stable, genuine confidence. In her business, the unending drama would consume a lesser human. There was no risk of that, I thought, looking at her intelligent green eyes in a face that was heart-shaped and capped with brown curls. A pair of sunglasses still rested, forgotten, on her head from her arrival at work earlier that day. She was driven.

"I gassed up the boat and spooled the rods. I thought you guys might anchor at that rock pile where the coast guard cutters go to dry dock." I knew Blue was not as interested in catching fish as her son was, but a productive spot would assure them of a single spot to anchor, eat, sun, and talk, without having to move due to inactivity among sea life. While Blue appreciated the Zen of angling, her son was more of a results-oriented sportsman.

"Oooh, thanks. He loves that spot. Did they move that one ship so we can sit there without having our guts pounded by wakes all day?" Their last trip there had been more like punishment than rest, due to unceasing waves from boat traffic.

"It's gone. All clear. You'll have no trouble. So, what day? It's ready even for tomorrow, if you want," I told her. Her excitement was plainly visible. It must have been some time since she had savored a day of motherhood that didn't involve a sobbing stripper with a litany of problems. I felt a twinge of pity, which I knew she would hate. I schooled my face and smiled as she began to rifle through her desk.

"So, business first. Two women were here, for, like, a week. Even the slow times. They smoked ciggies from somewhere I didn't recognize and laughed at our best liquor like we were bumpkins. But they left killer tips, so the girls let them camp out without hassling them for dances. I watched them, sort of casual at first, but, the third night, I wondered if they were vice or something. Although the one woman, she was a bit older, maybe thirty-five, she was dressed *way* above pay grade for a cop. I never really saw them that well but the older one was, according to our bouncer Brian, "shit your pants" beautiful, which is saying something, given his record with the girls here. She was white, had dark hair, and came from money, I think, just a hunch. It wasn't flash. It was real. She drank a lot less than the other woman, but they both sort of sized up the girls. And some of the patrons, too, I think. The younger one was well dressed, too, but more like a vacation wardrobe than someone who took their life with them, you know?"

I did. It was the difference between a tourist and a traveler. A traveler hired cars, had things done for them, and never lifted a finger unless it was to hail a sommelier.

"Brandi waited on their table the last two nights. She said that the younger one kept flashing a ring that looked like big money, a diamond with other stones around it. And here's the fun part: she left it as a tip when they finished their last drink on Thursday night. Brandi showed me, I'd say it was worth enough to buy a house. Maybe a small one, but a house. And I haven't seen Brandi since. She was sleeping with our new liquor rep, they met out one night away from here, and he said she's gone. Like, totally gone. Her apartment is empty, and her car is sitting right where it has since that night. It just feels a bit more like, I don't know . . . they were recruiting for something? Brandi had a degree, you know. Chemistry. She was going to finish her master's in Industrial Chem. But she got knocked up by some asshole from the Navy who headed for Guam on the next boat. She was book smart, not street cagey like the other girls here. And I know she was dead set against hooking, so my question is, what did they want her for?" she finished and folded her arms. I could tell she was pissed that something—although she didn't know exactly what—had transpired here, in her place.

I thought for a moment. "Brandi, was she pretty, not makeup pretty, but smart or elegant, a sort of cerebral beauty?"

"Exactly." Blue edged closer.

I had to tell her something, so I offered her what I could. "Nothing is happening in here now, I know that. Let me talk to the girls, and we'll discuss it before you fish. Everyone is safe, this was a sort of search. That's all I can tell you now. More soon, I promise."

That was good enough for her. She was a pragmatist at heart. She opened the door and kissed me again, reaching up on her toes to do so. I felt like a liar and was ready for a drink.

"Come get the boat. Then we'll talk," I said as I walked back into the barrage of the club.

From Risa's Files

Dear Pat,

Since you won't return my calls and you're too frigging dumb to get online, I have to write you a letter even with my arthritis. Thanks a lot.

You need to get your ass out of Virginia and come down here and talk sense to your idiot brother before I kill him. He's got himself a whore that is gonna spend every single dollar he made with my sister in twenty years of busting ass at the shop. I met her and let me tell you, it ain't going the way you want it if you think the kids will have a penny left to their name come Christmas. Her name is Silky (some kinda stripper name or some other kinda slut) and for starters she's thirty years younger than he is. She's got him buying her high priced sushi every night up on Las Olas like he's some Prince and she dresses him like a retard on vacation. She won't eat a damn thing except for expensive fish! They got a apartment up on the water and she's got him swimming like a frigging dolphin every day and now she gets him to swim at night cause she likes the quiet, she says. I think she's full of shit and believe me one day he ain't coming back from that swim. You get down here right now and send this whore packing so I don't have to bury him because he likes the young stuff, you hear?

I mean it!
Marion

34

Karolina

Sixty feet to feed a world. The greenhouse was twenty yards long but was filled with miles of potential. His creation, a wholly new strain of beans, grew riotous, hemmed only by their artificial borders of matrix made to perfectly aerate and distribute water for their hardy roots. Adam surveyed the agricultural project with the satisfaction of a man whose life's work had come to fruition. Eleven years, three million dollars, and a flash of brilliance as a newly minted Ph.D. had brought him to this point of triumph. Long monofilaments run as trellises groaned under the weight of the latest trial. With more than a dozen replications of the initial wild success, Adam was ready to publish. More importantly, he was ready to feed people. The accolades and money would come, he knew it, but his gift would be to everyone who went to bed hungry. No more meaningless starvation, and they would have him to thank.

Drought resistant, impervious to blight, and hated by insects, the beans were loaded with the nutrients for a starved world that was too poor in money and water to turn fields from dust to life. The first ripples from Adam's success were being felt. No less than ten genetics firms had made initial forays into acquiring his variant. Some had been less than noble in their attempts to apply pressure to him for a sale, and he suddenly had numerous volunteers and applicants for farmhand positions, all of whom he turned down ,knowing full well they were spies and thieves. He trusted himself. He trusted his miniscule staff, all of whom had been with him for years.

But he loved Karolina. Coltish, shy, brilliant Karolina. She had a mind more beautiful than any he had encountered in his thirty years of life. Studious and hardworking, he had first met her when the university had ended his funding after four contentious years of no progress. When a private charity asked for a grant proposal, he was met by Karolina alone at a suite in a bland business hotel in Miami. Across three yards of faux mahogany table, he exhausted what few oratorical tricks he knew within moments, finally reduced to staring helplessly at a woman who held the key to his future. As an idealist, he saw it as the world's future, too. Karolina had asked him, simply, if he was right. Could he grow a plant to feed the masses?

In a meteoric moment of bravado, he had slapped the table and said yes. And she had opened her briefcase without a word, arched a brow on her mobile face, and asked, "How much?"

Karolina was as plain as she was intelligent, tall and thin with long brown hair that she wore in a hat more often than not. Hardly shy of work, she was more proxy venture capitalist than charitable liaison, joining Adam in the greenhouse and lab daily. He came to know her wry wit and inquisitive nature. In time, they came to know each other. He was penniless and smelled of soil at all times, his hands chapped with labor, but, on the rare occasions he showered and dressed for the world outside, Karolina would tell him, "I like you in your own element, love."

The confirmation of his work meant that he could have things a bookish dreamer once thought impossible, even a woman like Karolina and her unending passion as she climbed him like ivy. Many times, they lay twined on the soft earth of the greenhouse, the ventilation fans wafting humid air over the rise and fall of their bodies, perfect in their syncopation. Today would be the day for rewarding himself. They could marry. A family, and the money to support them and let Karolina live a life free of work. She would wear the ring her mother gave her until he could afford something more modern. For now, the antique gold and opal would have to do.

This plant is from Eden. I will have everything now. Years of rooting in dirt, squinting into a lens, and now . . . all of it. Money, books, Karolina. Any woman at all, actually. It's all here for the taking. And I am going to take every bit of what I can, and people will love me for it. Adam and his magic beans. It's no fairy tale.

A car door thumping closed broke his reverie. Karolina was here, now, and they would celebrate this final step before his glory. He warmed in anticipation as the inner door to the greenhouse opened and she stepped in.

"You're certain about it?" she asked, moving to him. She shrugged out of her wet coat; it was raining lightly. His concentration had blocked the sound of the rain pattering on the transparent roof, rivulets running hurriedly to the ground. He heard it now over the rush of the ventilators. Karolina sniffed at him and toyed with the buttons on his denim shirt that were ringed with sweat and grime. Her nose was very sensitive.

"Take that off. I want you, not that rag." Her green eyes were shining, her brown hair hanging limp in the moist air. She kissed him hard twice in succession and pulled the shirt from his back as she slid back onto the potting table they leaned against. In a violent sweep, Adam cleared the surface and lifted her cotton skirt. She wore nothing underneath, and he was in her smoothly, his gallantry outmatched only by his need.

"My turn" she croaked, turning him to lay him flat and never breaking their intimate contact. She rode him in a wave, biting his chest in tiny nips and pushing his arms over his head. He relaxed, letting her work. Her tongue flickered across his chest, his neck, coming to rest at the tender pulse of his axillary artery. She inhaled, her eyes rolling in delight at the unmasked scent of his flesh. *So pure.*

Hidden beneath her upper lip, a single, needle-like tooth slid from hiding, luminously hollow. Her bite was serpentine, the pleasure exquisite, and his flavor much richer for having cultivated him for so long. The fang sank to the root without resistance, filling the artery in a perfect diversion. Patience made him delicious in her mouth. He continued thrusting into her, unaware his lifeblood pumped down her greedy throat ounce by heated ounce in a coppery flood that left him pale, and then softly wheezing, only to buck slightly under her iron grip. At last, he slipped from inside her, limp, bloodless, desiccated, his heart silent and still. His booted foot kicked once and swung to a stop.

She wiped her mouth on the hair of his chest, pausing once to take a questing lick at his sightless eye. *You were never meant to feed the world, Adam. Only me.*

35

Florida

Among my vices are fishing, beer, my boat, sunshine, and trading vehicles. I planned on indulging in all of them within the next twenty-four hours. Purchasing an unending array of used cars wasn't just a hobby, it was a tool. At times, an unobtrusive ride was a much-needed accessory for surveillance, travel, or transporting the former personal property of immortals that had departed the premises. My current ride, a solid but forgettable tan sedan, had served its purpose, but, after six months, it was time to move on. I called the least reputable used car lot in Broward County, owned and operated by one Jim Broward, whose true name was an incomprehensible Armenian monstrosity I knew he kept wisely hidden as part of his *nom de guerre*.

Jim answered on the second ring, a voice that was nicotine-scorched, deep, and Southern, all the more impressive considering he was from Chicago.

"Broward cars, here," he managed to drawl, making the last word a polysyllabic cough.

"Jim, it's Ring. I think it's time I took a look at your lot. You around later?" I enjoyed the familiarity of a frequent customer.

"Sure am, Ring, I was wondering when you'd get the itch. How 'bout an SUV this time? I've got something special sitting in the wash bay, pretty as a peach." He wasted no time in appealing to my habit.

"I'm interested. It might be nice to sit up high. I'll see you after lunch with my checkbook." I couldn't negotiate on an empty stomach.

"Music to my ears. See y'all later." And we were done, as I wondered what color my new vehicle would be. Jim was a heluva salesman. I was sold before I left my house.

Suma texted, and we agreed to dinner on the boat with a side of fishing. That meant that I had several minor but enjoyable errands, not the least of which was a trip to Publix, which I treat as a sort of pilgrimage each and every time. I entered, turned right, and headed to the deli. I sampled. I wandered, perused, picked up vegetables, and engaged in flights of fancy in which I envisioned myself a white-coated chef with minions of followers, all as I selected a masterful array of ingredients for two immense sandwiches. I then added tubs of salads and chips and made an inevitable trip through the beer aisle. When I arrived at the checkout lane, a relentlessly perky employee briskly moved me through the line. I was then disgorged into the sunlight, my wallet lighter, boat meal in hand, belching happily from Sample Row.

I keep a cooler in my car. It's the habit of an inveterate fisherman, beer aficionado, and resident of Florida who respects the heat. In went the boat lunch, to be covered with beer, ice, then beer and ice. I pack in layers. Since salmonella was being held at bay by my prescience, I turned west and headed to University drive, where Jim had my new vehicle waiting for me.

It was time to get acquainted with my new ride.

36

The lot was crowded with cars roasting in the sun. I parked near the office, which was a converted hamburger franchise from the 1950s, covered in white stucco, with a single steel sign announcing that Broward's cars did, indeed, refuse to be undersold. To the left of the building, a three-bay steel hut housed the get-ready area, where Jim's staff buffed and scrubbed years of use off of cars. The glass door swung open, and Jim ambled out, his cabana shirt straining over his stomach. His grey hair was slicked back, and his intense brown eyes sized me up as I stuck out my hand. He was having none of it. I was pulled into an Armenian bear hug as he said, "Good tuh see you, Ring!" and then deposited back on the ground, a bit flustered.

"Same here. How's Deb?" I inquired after his wife, who was indispensable to both his business interests.

"She's dandy. Says you have to come in after you see what I got for you out here." He turned towards the last bay. "I think this is exactly what you and the girls want. Style! None of that economical horseshit, an honest to God two tons of style." He waved his arm with a flourish as I saw what he had, shined up and ready.

He was right. A steel grey Jeep Grand Wagoneer sat majestically awaiting my arrival, the red leather interior gleaming with polish. A seeming acre of wood paneling ran down the sides underneath immense windows. Chrome was everywhere. It was a Yankee fantasy made real, twenty-five years old but kept perfectly by someone who had appreciated the vehicle as much as I did at that moment. I didn't need to drive it. I knew. So did Jim.

"Let's write it up," I told him, shaking his meaty hand.

He laughed a spastic rumble. "Already did."

We settled in his office, the paperwork complete. He called for Deb, who was in the other room. I heard her feet tapping on the tile, and then she entered.

"Hi Ring. It's nice, isn't it?" Her eyes flicked toward the Wagoneer. "Jim didn't even bother putting it on the lot because he knew you were ready for something a bit more masculine." Her tone was borderline flirtatious, which was at odds with her appearance. Deb was funny and smart, and regarding her looks, she was funny and smart. Tall, skinny, with a long nose, she had a distinctly bony presence. But her smile was warm, and she was unfailingly polite, qualities that go a long way in the world.

Jim brought me back to the present. "And how will you be paying today, Ring? Cash? Check? Or perhaps something more interesting?"

"Cash is so dull. How about these instead?" I placed Senya's hair combs on the desk. Neither he nor Deb moved.

She asked, "May I?" Seeing my assent, she picked them up and held them to the light. Jim's other business interest was the acquisition and disposition of unusual items that were not benefitted by being on the open market. Jewelry, weapons, and the odd wayward artwork—all was within his, and Deb's, field of expertise, along with the profitable and wholly legitimate car lot.

I sat quietly while they conferred in the other room, ascertaining a value for the combs. After a few moments, they returned. The combs were nowhere to be seen. That boded well for me, I thought.

"They're special, that's for sure," Deb began. "Probably fourth century, Byzantine or Roman. Would you take," she shrugged at Jim, "six?"

Jim seemed a bit tense. The combs must be *really* unusual to get a reaction from a pair of old pros.

"And the vehicle? Tax included, of course?" I smiled. I had leverage. It was deeply satisfying, even knowing that they probably had a buyer lined up already who would pay a ghastly number for the trinkets.

"Taxes. Of course. Always a pleasure, Ring." Jim shook my hand, and Deb began to count out money.

The combs must have been much nicer than we could have imagined because she counted out six thousand dollars and set the Wagoneer keys on top of the stack. I was pleasantly surprised.

"Do me a favor, Jim." I had another matter in mind, for later. "I need something for protection for the girls. No guns. Anything light, maybe a blade. Something very personal. Keep me in mind. Functional but well designed. I'll go a thousand each for whatever you run across. It should be small enough for a woman's hand, but lethal. Not decorative."

Deb and Jim both closed their eyes for a second in thought. Jim spoke first. "You betcha. I'll send you anything appropriate that I might find."

We said our goodbyes, and I strolled through the sun to my new pride and joy. I shut the door with a satisfying *thump*. The engine turned over immediately and settled into the rich purr of an eight cylinder powertrain. With a tweak to the mirror, I pulled out into traffic and headed for home, a yuppie to the core.

And an elementary school art class was six grand richer.

37

When Suma pulled up to our place, the boat was ready. Gyro greeted her at the door with a single reverberating *WOOF*, and then fell to the floor, his security requirements fulfilled. Wally was cycling, and Risa had been at the heavy bag in our carport gymnasium. Her grunts of satisfaction with each strike had punctuated the last hour. She was working hard, and I didn't wish to interrupt her, so I had Suma follow me to the dock, where we stepped aboard and cast off. The canal shone brilliant in the afternoon sun. The tide was running out, so I took a leisurely pace, opened two beers, and asked her what she felt like fishing for.

"I don't know. Can we sit still, drink beer, and technically still be fishing?" Her look was mischievous. I appreciated that type of angler.

"Absolutely. In fact, the less we move, the better. It gains us tremendous fishing cred to remain in one location. I know just the place; it's in Port Everglades. We'll still be inshore, but there's a deep hole where we might accidentally catch fish while we get sun." I pushed the throttle forward, and we turned east, our destination minutes away.

We coasted to a stop at the corner of two seawalls, where a lazy eddy circled underneath us. I dropped the blade anchor and let the line pay out until I felt the subtle underwater clink that meant we were relatively stuck.

"Okay, so, we have a hook, a small weight, and a shrimp. We drop this over," I demonstrated with my spinning reel, "until the line goes slack. Then, you reel up until there is a hint of tension and pray that nothing tugs at the bait, which would interrupt your sandwich and beer time." I finished by sitting on a cushion with my legs overboard so that they could be slapped by wavelets.

"Like this?" Suma was very careful with the rod and had one finger lightly poised on the line.

"Just right. That way, you feel the line, not the tip. If you get a bite, don't reel—pull up quickly and *then* reel as you lower the rod, like a seesaw, up and down." I mimicked my flawless strategy as she watched.

"Can we have a snack? I'm starving," she asked, smiling winningly at me from under her hat. I leaned toward the cooler and began to rummage.

"Sandwich time?" I asked, and she reached with her free hand across the space between us. I noticed for the first time that her eyes were hazel. I handed her a one-pound section of sub, dripping lettuce and dressing onto the deck. It was an inelegant but rewarding way to eat.

"Are you from Thailand or the States?" I asked, squinting out at the water. It was that particular fragmented green of late afternoon.

"I'm American. And a little bit French. Our grandfather was from Marseilles. He met our grandmother in Thailand, though, so some of my family had dual citizenship. We—hey! A bite!" She cut off her speech and began to reel furiously, the rod tip dancing merrily. After a few seconds, a wriggling fish swayed in the air, gill plates pumping in frustration.

"Swing it over here. I'll take it off for you, Fish Master." I bowed solemnly as she led the fish through the air to my waiting hands.

"What is it? It's beautiful, like a blue and yellow mirror." Her gaze was admiring. It was a gorgeous little fish.

"It's a grunt. They carpet the bottom, but they're delicious. Since we have sandwiches, we'll let him go." I held the foot-long fish out for Suma to inspect.

"A grunt? What a name."

The fish obliged me, barking several times like an old man clearing his throat. I tossed him back in as Suma laughed.

"That's truth in advertising. I never knew fish could talk," she said, looking into the water where the grunt had submerged with a miffed flip of the tail.

"They certainly can. Translated, it said we should have another beer, and I, for one, always listen to nature." I reached for the cooler as she laughingly accepted the bottle, and we both decided to work on becoming better friends before the sun went down.

38

I know the rhythm of our house, from the creaks and pops of roof joints cooling after a day in the sun to the low whirr of the refrigerator. I walked silently to the back door. It was three in the morning, and Gyro rose quietly to join me on the dock. I replayed my afternoon on the boat with Suma and realized that I liked hearing her laugh more than I should. I noticed things about her. She had flecks of green in her eyes when the sun hit them under the brim of her hat. She hated the texture of fish but loved their colors. Enormous ships throwing wakes made her a bit sick, but she thought the shape of the waves was graceful, and she tanned without burning. There was no Nightingale syndrome between us, but I intrigued her for unknown reasons, even with the danger that surrounded me. In turn, I found her immensely likeable. Absently scratching Gyro, I knew that our day together was our last. She was family of family, and I refused to be the vector that brought death to her door. I hoped I would be determined enough to avoid an emotional attachment that could only lead to danger.

The canal was quiet, and the streets were still. I let the illusion of solitude swirl around me. Even amidst the lights of the unending coastal city, stars burned sparsely in the sky. I knew the Milky Way stretched above, invisible to me, but still present, unending from horizon to horizon. So much of the world was beyond our perceptions. We were obtuse for so many reasons, our poor senses laughable in the animal kingdom. We could be blind by choice, or by design. That type of ignorance was no longer an option for me and the girls. We had lifted the curtain, and we could not lower it again, the stain of knowledge permanent in our minds.

I had Risa and Wally. I had a dog. Still, looking out over the dark water, it seemed that there were many things I would never have, and anger stirred within me at the loss of a future I could not know.

I went inside, resolving to call the Baron and ask him if someday there might be room in the forest for three more people. Our lives suddenly felt more dangerous.

Cazimir connected immediately and seemed genuinely glad to be in contact. After a description of fishing and my general leisure, he grew quiet.

"Ring, I do not wish to sound paternal or brash, but may I ask you if you are serious about finding Elizabeth?" He waited for my answer, hands folded on his desk. His expression was one of mild curiosity, not anger.

I was brought up short. I didn't have a legitimate reason for my inactivity. In fact, his question caused more introspection than I was prepared for, and I hesitated to answer. I didn't want to lie. Was it fear? Perhaps I was unable to be fully engaged in a task that was outside my original skillset, and my discomfort made me unfocused. I didn't know, but it was a fair question, not an interrogation, so I waited a long moment before I began speaking.

"I don't know. I feel like I may need a point of origin, or something, I can't exactly articulate what is missing here." I was nonplussed by my own vagueness. I knew to Cazimir I must appear to be a braggart at best and a coward at worst. He had unwittingly, or by design, struck at the very root of my entire life with the girls. I had morphed from a laconic teen into a sporadic soldier who found casual death inoffensive and forgettable, only to find that, as an adult, I was repeating the exact same behaviors to our detriment. I had even found a nontraditional but intense relationship with two women who, for some reason, returned my feelings and respect tenfold. I'd been dipped in luck and yet here I was being mildly rebuked because I couldn't maintain an intensity that we needed if we were to succeed.

"Allow me to give you some direction, if I may, Ring. You recall that I was able to identify you by looking for oddities within the news. Let me pass along something you may find useful. One of your local news sources reported a murder, quite gruesome, involving a highly respected surgeon who was found buried near the beach. After reading what is present and lacking in the crime description, I think you may be interested. I'll email it directly, and please give me your opinion when you have read it."

I felt a bit like a recalcitrant child, but I agreed and we signed off, my resolve a bit more firm than it had been an hour before.

We had a lead.

We all read the article describing the death of one Arnaud LeConte, a surgeon who had donated countless hours to corrective surgery free of charge. He was, on the surface, a highly unlikely target for an immortal of Elizabeth's standing. Internet searches revealed him to be of relatively modest means and an all-around good citizen. Risa keyed on the body. Rather, she keyed on who found the unfortunate Arnaud, and where. A caterer returning to clean up after the charity event stumbled, quite literally, on the good doctor and called the police. Photographs from the affair were everywhere online. For the people in attendance, being seen doing good works was more important than the act itself. Social sites were laden with smiling faces of perfectly coiffed socialites sacrificing for the greater good. In one photo, a caterer's truck was parked in the background, the distinct blue and gold logo clearly visible. *Le Renard Gris* Catering.

Arnaud's body was discovered by a male, we knew that much. In all likelihood he was young, self-assured, and attractive, if the hiring model held true for Palm Beach caterers as a whole. Our next move was simple. We needed information, and it had to be extracted with the least possible resistance. I smiled grandly at Wally who was already rolling her eyes at me in disgust. After a quick search, I located the company and found that they also staffed a yacht club in North Lauderdale. In all likelihood, our target could be found there, pouring stiff drinks for boating enthusiasts who dressed more casually than their bank accounts would allow.

"Get your miniskirt, gorgeous. You're going to shake down a bartender for some gossip." I was already laughing. I knew her evening would consist of, at the very least, an interminable flirting session with a side order of personal space violation. I planned on cleaning the boat and then taking Risa for pizza. That seemed like a solid occupation of our valuable time while Wally played inspector.

Wally hung her head in dejection and made tracks for her room to prepare for her interrogation by flirtation, one of her specialties.

Risa put down the remote and softly called from the couch, "Be home by eleven, you tramp." In answer, a flip-flop hurtled her way, followed by a slew of cursing as we heard the shower being turned on. Risa stood and grabbed her keys.

"Pizza and beer? I'm buying," she said. The boat would remain grimy. My response was the only one a sane man could offer. I opened the door with a flourish and wondered if Wally would have any luck.

39

Stacia

His shoulders shook with hidden sobs. This was a man coming apart at the seams, and it was no surprise to his family and friends. Privately, they were amazed that Don had been able to hold it together for this long after losing Janice. A long, ugly pitched battle against ovarian cancer had ended in a Miami hospital where his wife of three decades had slipped into a coma and exhaled one last time, her pallor instantly shifting to that of the deceased. Even a year later, the smell of disinfectant left Don shaking and uneasy, like the specter of her sickness had come to visit again, and brought little details to remind him of the pain with a sadistic hint. He was a big man, with long limbs and the rough hands of a hard worker. His black hair was still cut short, and he dressed crisply every day after drinking a single cup of coffee while looking over the rock garden he had built for Janice. The water still bubbled merrily from the fountain they had placed in the middle of it all, oblivious to the crashing sorrow in the man standing a few feet away.

But Don had found hope.

At the brink of a breakdown, he had sought help. His pride eroded, his resolve weakened, he had turned outward and found a grief counselor who met his demands for discretion and budgetary constraints. Janice's illness had left him far less secure than he liked, and he needed to clear his head in order to regain the desire to live. To breathe. To survive.

Stacia had been the only counselor willing to come to him. It was a huge step to even admit he needed assistance, but to publicly reach out was too much for Don. He had been, at turns in his life, reticent, quiet, and even taciturn. But sitting in his own chair, with the familiar trappings of his life around him, Don learned with each session to let go, just the smallest bit. It was an internal war of control. Stacia, a well-groomed woman in her forties, would sit across from him and introduce small questions. Did he dream? Did he remember them? Did he cry, and how often? She paid close attention to whether or not he could express himself around her, an outsider.

He could not. She was fine with that, and pressed no further, leading Don to trust her with more imagery of his sorrow. His deep, penetrating sadness. How he still picked up the phone to call Janice at work and then, crying, hung the phone up, wondering if he was losing his mind. After an hour or more of talking each day, Don realized he was shedding his burden. He slept a bit more and ate quietly at his solitary table, aware that the food had no flavor, but at least he was eating.

He came out of his shell in small ways. Progress was being made. He complimented Stacia's necklace, a single green stone. Green was Janice's favorite color, and she had loved to feel feminine. She would have loved the piece. *I know*, said Stacia. After three weeks, Stacia solemnly informed him that, for their next meeting, he would learn. She needed him to understand concepts that were alien to his Western mind, but she felt it critical that he grasped them in order to heal fully and move on.

So for a day, he listened. Over coffee gone cold, the dark-eyed woman sat primly at his table and told him of how the world defined the soul. She spoke of Prana, and Ch'i and of the spirit in terms that were simple and clear. When the sun set through Janice's gingham kitchen curtains, she asked Don one simple question.

"In that large body, you have a small but pure soul. Knowing this, are you ready to tell me, in full, how Janice loved, lived, and left you? The pain? And now, perhaps, hope? The after, so to speak? Can you do that?" she asked, her gaze maternal and warm.

He folded and unfolded his large, bony hands. He looked at the lines and scars bespeaking a life lived in service to his love. He nodded once and looked blearily into the lights of the kitchen.

"Don, you should speak. It is time to let go," she urged, but softly, warily.

He was aware of her becoming very still, like a hunter fearful of spooking game. Her head was poised, listening, her hand inches from his, the fingers curled lightly inward. He began from his first memory of Janice, with her cursing at a cyclist who tore her dress on a crowded street in Rochester, New York, when they were both young. His eyes grew soft, far too soft to match his hands, and the lights began to lose their focus as the memories took command of his body. He felt Stacia take his hand, her warmth and caring urging him on. Through dates, and their first child, to the war and two years of wondering *do I die today* while choking on rain a world away... he told her all of it. And, eventually, the tears rolling freely now while he had to cut off a yawn, he dove into the blackness of the day that the doctor said simply, "The cancer is back." He recalled the hum of the fluorescents. The light scent of urine and cleanser on tile, rustling lab coats, and the faces carefully ignoring him as he led Janice, staggering, to the car to weep together, crying without end for the entire world to hear. Stacia stood behind him now, rubbing his wide, bony shoulders and leaning on him, his yawns growing wider and longer, his focus fading.

"What about the last day, Don? Did she move at all? Tell me... tell me about her eyes. Did she know it was close?" And now her voice was low, guttural, fat with pleasure. He felt a delicate probing of his body and then the lightest touch as her messenger tendril, an ethereal dark blue, twisted from within her and twined around his ribs and heart. It pulsed like a gorging snake with his sadness and lost love. Inside his body, synapses fired and went black, their charge stripped away by her questing presence, the filaments of her hungry light spreading in him like the canopy of an evil tree. Her eyes flickered under her lids in concentration. He had a vivid mind and a hardy soul. She laid her cheek against his head and asked him, while his heart hammered, "Do you want to join her? Do you love her that much, Don?"

Oh God how he did and he would tell her if he could just keep his eyes open. He became aware of a slight erection and moved his hand to cover it, but his arm only rolled weakly. He was so tired. So very tired. His lips kept moving as Stacia whispered again and again, "Tell me about her. About the sadness, Don," and then, finally, the tendril made of more shadow than light uncoiled one final time from his chest, and retreated into her body, now flushed and glowing. She was drunk with his memories and more than a little high on the depths of his pain. A patina of sweat covered her cheeks and forehead. His rugged frame had been very strong, and she had expended an intense effort to feed freely of it. His brain pan filled with blood, and he had bitten his tongue. A massive stroke, they would determine. Brought on by a broken heart, the neighbors would say.

She kissed Don's head, which now rested on his long forearms that were folded inert on the table, and stretched once. All of his fear and love and the remains of his broken soul now surged through her in flashes, his body a husk, hers fully engorged and already in motion to her next charitable act. She left the house and Don, but she took his life with her.

Mother was right. One cannot overstate the importance of being a good listener.

40

Florida

Fat raindrops woke me in the morning. The noise it made on our aluminum awnings had a jarring effect, regardless of how many times I had heard it. Smelling coffee and eggs, I moseyed to the kitchen. Risa was up and had been productive, but was now on the couch, lolling a bit next to Gyro, who occupied three cushions to her one. Wally was missing, so I filled a mug and took it to her door, tapping lightly and entering.

Wally was partially nude, in a tangle of covers and limbs that needed to be bordered by crime scene tape. She slept as if dead, and, like any good corpse, she cared little for her position. There was a slight stirring as I sat on the bed and a thin glint from her right eye betraying a state of awareness, so I wordlessly held the cup to her. Grumbling, she accepted.

"Give me ten minutes before I report, you goose-stepping martinet," she protested, struggling to a sitting position. I caught a ghastly whiff of morning breath as she exhaled, belched, and coughed in a series of actions that were befitting an aged cat.

"Agreed. See you at the table, gorgeous. And scrape your tongue before you come out of the bathroom. Do it for the children, if not me," I commanded in my most authoritative tone. Closing the door, a shoe hit the frame and fell to the floor. I had been answered and counted myself lucky to have emerged from her lair unscathed.

Wally shoved an irritated Gyro off a cushion and wedged underneath the beast, pulling her legs up as he re-settled his head on her lap, looking at her in adoration. She smoothed his ear and sipped her coffee, grimacing. Risa and I waited until she pulled the cup away. We were impatient, despite her under-caffeinated state.

"Clashes with toothpaste," Wally grunted, but she kept drinking. "So, I found our unlucky caterer. He was rather smart, actually. He's pre-med. He was also sober the morning he found the body. I think he looked it over a bit before he called the police. Quite talkative, that one."

Wally was a master at the hair-twisting, eye-batting flirtation method of peeling details and facts from sometimes reluctant targets. Yazin, as it turned out, was neither reticent nor immune to her charms. He told Wally more than he realized he knew.

"Yazin not only found the body, but he gave me a general description of the killer without realizing it. I'm not even certain the police are aware of the connection, but he worked the charity event and the cleanup crew that came in the next morning to break down tables and load the truck. Yazin is Moroccan, and he swears he heard a Moroccan woman speaking French at the party. Her accent was very faint, but he described it as a woman of the upper classes who spoke French as her second language, probably after Berber. He was very specific. Physically she was thin, dark hair, striking. Yazin caught an impression of money; it was something he couldn't quite articulate, but he felt certain."

She swigged her cooling coffee and continued.

"Yazin didn't remember seeing the victim at the party, but that's hardly surprising given the high wattage of the attendees. From the pictures I've seen, the trophy wives were stacked in layers. With all that silicone and Chanel No. 5, it's miraculous that he didn't sprain his neck staring. He's practically a kid, but, thankfully for us, an observant one with a great memory. He was able to give me even more details about the condition of the body. And here's where his medical training really comes into play. The body was buried in the sand, intentionally. When he checked for a pulse, he noticed two visible wounds. One was in Arnaud's navel. Clear fluid ringed the hole, and there was irregular swelling. There was a bit of blood running down his chin, and, when Yazin looked in, he saw a round puncture right through roof of his mouth. He had been buried like he was being... saved. Or protected."

As she finished and expounded on the boy's experience with the departed, Risa, who had been briskly taking notes, paused for a moment.

"I can't read Berber, but I can read French. Let's see if the Moroccan news has any footprints left by this killer. And then, let's bury her and see how she likes it."

From Risa's Files

Broward Sherriff's Office Records 911 Transcript
911: *What is your emergency?*
Kenneth Myall: *I've been robbed, I think. And I'm hurt.*
911: *What's the address? Who hurt you?*
Kenneth Myall: *I'm at the Lauderdale Beach Club . . . *unintelligible* move my, my hands*
911: *What apartment, sir? Who hurt you? Can you tell me the number?*
Kenneth Myall: *She's gone, she left the door open, the water is running*
911: *Are you in the water? Are you inside? I have police on the way. Are you inside?*
Kenneth Myall: *She made me sleepy, and now I'm, the water is coming up, please*
911: *Police are in front of the building. What floor, sir? What number?*
Kenneth Myall: **unintelligible* bit me and put me in, in the water, I, I,*unintelligible**
911: *Sir? Sir? Please talk to me, stay with me, sir . . . sir?*
Kenneth Myall: *(sound of water running and footsteps)*
911: *Sir?*
Kenneth Myall: *911? This is officer Callister. We are administering CPR to the victim; he drowned in the tub, or he bled out, trying to get a pulse. Send ambulance. He has a . . . bite wound.*
911: *Bite wound? Ambulance on the way, Officer.*

41

"Look at this." Risa stood in front of me, quivering with urgency. She had a small stack of printed sheets. I glanced at them. They were written in French.

"I assume you'll translate?" She nodded and waved me over to the table. The sun was at zenith and she looked like she hadn't slept all night. Wally was nowhere to be seen, but Gyro's leash was missing, so I knew I slept through her taking the beast out for a walk. I poured orange juice and sat down, as instructed. Risa frowned slightly at the top page, continuing her translation internally. I waited.

"These are three different news items from French language papers in Morocco. Two of them are nearly identical, with one exception." She paused and pulled a one-page map of Morocco from under the newspaper articles.

"We start in Rabat, north of Casablanca. I know you're disappointed, but that's where I found something unusual." Risa knew my love of the classic film bordered on insanity. I appreciated her nod to my excellent taste and remained silent.

"Rabat is the capitol. So, like the unfortunate Arnaud, a doctor was found murdered, partially buried near the beach. The reason this crime was deemed newsworthy was that he was a visiting Frenchman who had been very well received. He was free with his care and took a special interest in sick children. He was successful, too, so, when he was found with puncture wounds, it was assumed that he had been stabbed. A relatively swift manhunt was conducted by a local Imam who thought highly of the doctor, and a suspect was caught and beheaded. Then *another* suspect was caught and beheaded a week later."

"I take it there was no trial?" I asked, imagining that justice of that speed would be a bit more streamlined than I was used to seeing.

"Correct. This brings us to our next lucky contestant, in the city of Tangiers. This time it was a French shipping magnate who was known to be one of the most skilled smugglers in the area. He had half the city on his payroll, and the other half trying to buy their way on. You guessed it—he was supposedly stabbed and buried, face up, in the sand in between two pilings where fishing boats anchored. This time, there were no suspects, although that may have been due to the frenzy of crime that followed his death as local criminals rushed in to fill his highly profitable shoes."

She was handing me the pages as she finished her translations. She slid the last sheet across the table to me. I noticed she had her own copy of the same newspaper. This page was in Spanish, something we could both read.

"Read this and tell me what you make of it. I've read it, and I want to see if you see what I see." Risa was excited. I knew that look. It boded well for our efforts.

I took several minutes to read the item, carefully making mental notes at salient points that practically screamed *look here* to my investigative nature. Our killer had gone across the strait to Spain. She had seduced and attacked a wealthy, elderly glass importer and led him to the beach. She was, according to the hysterical language of the victim's son, a demon of some sort.

But the old man had lived. He was Moroccan, a widower, and had a single child. His son, a vain, jealous man, followed them to protect his father, not from altruism, but greed. He saw women as a threat to his inheritance. That is how, in the dying light on a Spanish beach, the son watched his father be mounted by a woman with a dagger extended from her stomach, poised to drive it into his gut. The son stalked up behind her and brained her with a wine jug, splitting her head and then freeing his father. The old man was unable to walk and remained so for three days. He had been injected with something. In his mouth. When the police went back to find her body, it was gone, presumably with the tide. The son said the dagger was attached to her, somehow, and looked like the stinger on a bee. With this tale, the details of Arnaud's horrific death were becoming clear. Done with my read, I asked Risa, "What does this last line describe? I can't translate it."

"The old man recovered and named the woman who attacked him. He said she held a needle in her mouth and poisoned him. And he saw the 'arrow' protruding from her body. He was never taken seriously, but, when he was able to speak well enough, he called the woman *al-Ribat*. The Archer."

"That's an apt name for her. Have you found evidence of this *al-Ribat* anywhere else, other than here?" I wondered why the immortal was moving.

"Oh, yes. And that's what makes me think there is much more to the story than one immortal killing lonely men on beaches. The last sheet has mention of her being named as a person of interest in the disappearance of an antiques dealer in Marseilles. It isn't by name, but it's her. I know it. But you need to see one more thing."

Risa rearranged the papers. She tapped the top corners of each. "One other thing. Look at the dates of these reports."

I whistled softly. If there was ever any doubt of who we were dealing with, it was gone in that second. The first murder, 1947. The second, 1948. The third attempt in Spain was in 1948, too. But the story in France was from less than a year ago.

I closed my eyes, thinking. I could sense Risa watching me.

"There are only two reasons for such a drastic move. She was either on the run from something—" I started.

"Or she was being called home" Risa finished. "But by whom?"

42

While I was online, reading, the Baron called. He was wearing glasses perched on the end of his nose and a yellowed newspaper article lay on the desk, folded crisply.

"Ring, good evening. I hope I'm not interrupting," He trailed off, mannerly to a fault. I was glad he had called, and told him.

"We've made progress in the past day. It seems that there is movement among certain immortals that we believe are tied to murders here in Florida. I'm not the analytical type, but I am curious. A killer from Morocco has crossed the Pond, so to speak, and is operating here. She's different. She isn't anything we've seen before."

"How so, may I ask?" The Baron raised a brow.

"She works near the coastlines. She's a predator, no doubt, but she doesn't feed on women. She has been altered, physically, in a way that is new to us. Her nickname '*al-Ribat*,' along with her description, is unsettling. I can't decide what she wants other than death."

"The Archer? A very specific nickname." It did not surprise me that the Baron understood the term. He seemed to be a polyglot of the first order, despite his secluded home.

"This woman, she preys on men. Yet I have information that refutes your belief that she wants to kill," he said as he unfolded the old, ragged news cutout. "This is from a French newspaper. Printed in 1948–such a busy year for the world, don't you think?" he asked, smiling.

It *had* been a chaotic year. The world had not taken a sober breath after the orgy of violence from the Second World War. Indochina was becoming a cauldron of hate. Greece, Eastern Europe, and the emergence of Israel had stoked the hot embers of war into another act of mass bloodshed. Mankind had not tired of the horrors of butchery, even after the most destructive event humanity had ever created.

"A woman was charged with assaulting a gem trader over a disputed purchase. The victim was a known cheat, so it isn't surprising that he would receive some form of comeuppance. "

"Was she prosecuted?" I was curious to see how an immortal would react to the banality of human law.

"No, sadly. She escaped after the victim died. He survived the initial assault but was unable to speak or move. He lingered in a Lisbon hospital, dying in silence after three days of agony." Cazimir glanced at the clipping, refreshing his narrative.

"Does it mention a cause of death?" I had to know.

"It does, but obliquely. You see, there was only one visible wound on the victim, Senhor Lorea. His navel had been violated. And, when he died, as a man of questionable breeding and character, he had no family to claim him. So, an inquisitive physician named in the article cut him open." Cazimir paused, his mouth a grim line.

"What was inside him?" I wasn't certain I wanted to know. To be victimized so intrusively was disturbing to me, even though it happened before my birth. This entire event felt personal.

"Three stones. Unremarkable, gray in color. Of no value at all. They were coated by his body in a furious attempt to expel the alien objects, like an oyster crafting a pearl. They crumbled upon examination by the investigating doctor, a Senhor Coelho. He said that they were soft, more like dried leather mixed with dust."

There was something about the doctor's discovery that disturbed me at a visceral level. I created and discarded lines of inquiry quickly, trying to glean a purpose for the attack. It was the idea that something had been intentionally *inserted* into the man and the victim further degraded by having objects left behind. Like he had been colonized. The disregard for his humanity was total.

While I had been ruminating on the crime, the Baron sat patiently. "Cazimir, is there anything else of note in the article?" I asked, hopeful.

"Most certainly, Ring. I am confident you will find one fact fascinating. You see, she was charged, but she escaped after charming a youthful jailer into an unplanned release." A mirthless smile curled his lips. "But bureaucracies can be useful at times, and the record of the allegations remains, despite her absence. I'll email the newspaper, as well as the court documents, but you may begin with the most important fact of all–Sandrine DeStot. Her name."

And with that, the search for Elizabeth narrowed in our favor.

43

Saturday night arrived, and the girls began their usual preparations for a special kind of evening out. Dressed in demure attire, they wore little makeup and jewelry. Their hairstyles were modest, and their heels were low.

They were going to evening Mass at St. Maurice's on Stirling Road, as they did on occasion. The reasons for attending were varied, but, in Wally's estimation, legitimate. An inveterate sinner, Wally's Germanic and Latin heritage demanded that she atone for her foul language while driving. Risa, a caring friend, chose to support this decision by attending a Catholic Mass, despite not having a gentile bone in her body. This tradition served a multitude of purposes. Wally was able to experience a religious catharsis fewer than three miles from home, which was both convenient and beneficial to her soul. It was also an opportunity for her, and, by default, Risa, to gain the high ground on me and my unrepentant Protestant spirit. Wally appreciated the fact that Saint Maurice led a Roman legion to honor. Risa found the protection of Saint Maurice given to swordsmiths a fascinating and noble attribute. The fact that the priest was a dashing forty-year-old ex-professional volleyball player from California had little to do with their interest in hearing Father Kevin call the catechism in his robust baritone. Of course, I chose to ignore their base reasoning for such a shameful dalliance with the Holy Spirit, but only to promote harmony in our home.

I also got the house to myself for two hours each week, which I used to the fullest by sleeping on the couch, eating pizza, and other constructive activities. On this night, though, my restlessness got the better of me, and I decided that research was in order. An idea had been percolating in my mind, so nascent that I had not shared it at all, but the quiet house gave me an opportunity to do some internet searching. I knew that vanity was a hallmark of many immortals. Pride and vanity were two sides of the same coin, an Achilles heel to be exploited when dealing with immortals. Surely, I reasoned, Sandrine had left her mark elsewhere. Given her earliest mention, it would most likely be in print. Her career had been decades long when I was born. That type of trail was difficult to mask in full, especially as the digital age brought dim history to the fingertips of the curious.

And my curiosity was intense.

I scrolled through newspaper databases until my eyes were bleary and the screen pulsed with haze. Microfiche news items had been transferred into a grainy torrent of forgotten scandal and crime. The process was cumbersome, as I translated passages from French, Portuguese and Spanish newspapers into small vignettes. The resulting syntax was broken English that I followed to a gradual conclusion.

Sandrine was a French citizen of unknown origin. She presented herself in court as a demure woman of the middle class who was surprised to have been charged with a crime but was too mannerly to ridicule the notion of her guilt, preferring to let the court see the absurdity of her presence in the hall populated by the brutal side of mankind. Marseilles. Lisbon. Earlier, Morocco. All sites of her curious bloodlust and places where she had slipped the leash of justice through murder, wile, and bribery. It seemed that Sandrine was a humanist, free of conscience. I couldn't wait to meet her. I felt like I needed Risa's logic or Wally's intuition, paging through newspaper columns that breathlessly urged public awareness and vigilance in the hunt for a killer. All, of course, in the name of safety. And, incidentally, advertising sales. I thought of Wally and how she would be mooning at the handsome priest, elbowing Risa as he moved through the Mass. It took a joyful soul to treat a religious ceremony as a source of sexual playfulness. It was congruent with Wally's sunny disposition to find romance in the austere grasp of a celibate priesthood. Finding such pearls was her gift.

And in flash, I knew where to find Sandrine. Why would a woman who harbored a century of arrogant disregard for men go among the chattel to be judged worthy? Nightclubs, bars, the stale air of bookstores and cloistered pretentious shops, these were beneath her. I began to warm to Sandrine's thoughts, her need to prequalify men as lonely. Free of families. Devoid of serious relationships. Out of their normal element, or uncomfortable in their stations. Perhaps, a bit desperate and willing to be put in a vulnerable position to get something that they needed in order to feel like a man. There was only one type of woman who granted a man the satisfaction of a virile identity far beyond his charms.

I sat back down at the keyboard and typed *Escorts. South Florida. French.* A single ad came up. With a picture. Her eyes were stone flat above a perfunctory smile. "Hello, Sandrine" I said to the air.

Gotcha.

44

I pinged the Baron with the news and found myself inordinately pleased with his reaction when he signed on and we began speaking.

"Impressive, Ring. You've made a logic leap that I would not have contrived in any amount of time. How will you proceed? She is quite dangerous, despite your abilities." He was understating the case. She was terrifying. There was something deeply offensive about her method of killing. I knew that murder in and of itself should be the supreme violation of a person, but Sandrine brought new elements of fear and disgust with her crimes.

"I'll have to approach her as a customer. A public meeting is too uncertain. I don't know how cagey she is, but I'm betting that, after a century or so of predation, she's hard to corner. So it has to be me, alone, and I have to take her alive, at first." I needed interrogation rather than instant elimination. It was new territory for me.

"She won't be held. She cannot be domesticated for the purposes of turning on her own kind. That means you must act quickly, decisively, and with a maximum violence in order to subdue her." Cazimir's tone was instructive but urgent. He knew that paralysis of any kind would mean my death, and it could happen at her leisure.

"My last name, Byk? You know the meaning?" he continued. "It is the word for a bull, an animal never known for subtlety." He smiled at me and put his hands up in an imitation of horns. "Bulls are always charging, they do not submit lightly. They are capable of enormous destruction in a short amount of time, crushing and using bunched muscles to drive them ever forward until they win. Or die. There is little middle ground in the mind of the bull. But, in spite of our name, my family has chosen to live through avoidance, some would even say deception. We had to, in order to survive a vicious political landscape through these centuries. Europe has been at war, Ring. War of unending variety and violence. There have been countless local skirmishes due to petty feudal grievances about succession, lands, money, religion, divorce. The reasons are as varied as the dates that blood was shed in the name of some forgotten lord, born of a cause lost to the depths of time. Only the bones remain, Ring, and they pave the continent with the residue of sorrow, each death piling on the last in a tower of loss that would scratch at the heavens if it were made real. Do you know who pays the price of royal vanity? The rustics. Stoop-backed laborers enslaved to their land, their pittances worried away by men they never see who give them nothing. My family took only from the forest; we would not bear the shame of a parasitic existence on the shoulders of the poor. So we have hidden our herd, and our family, and our wealth in this life, by folding ourselves fully into the green depths around us. Do you know of the KGB?" he asked.

I said, yes, of course. Who didn't?

"The KGB is timeless. If one goes far enough back in Soviet history, their name changes, but their sinister purpose and brutality remains unchanged. Before the KGB, there was the NKVD, the OGPU, oh, so many names, Ring, but always called by their original name: the Cheka. How they were feared. We took in ragged refugees often; their flight from the organization in power at the time was that of a terrified animal. The Slavic fetish for paranoia did not begin with the Bolsheviks, though. Even as far in the past as the reign of Tsar Nicholas, there were secret police that walked amidst the populace, ever vigilant for enemies of the state. Real or imagined, Ring, there were always bodies for the hangman. The Cheka used to drive cars know as Black Crows. To see one park in front of a neighbor's house was a death sentence for the unfortunate subject of their gaze. There are several Black Crows rusting into the moss near my home, along with many other cars, long rows of decrepit boxes rusting through the somber colored paint from the Soviet years. "

"Who owned the other cars, Cazimir? Surely not all of them were serious threats to your home. Your family. Or your secrets, for that matter." I was dubious about the guilt of so many; doubtless, their bones were forgotten under the leaves of decades, a secret garden of missing souls under the towering canopy.

"Not all were secret police, true. Many were commonplace thieves masquerading as local officials, their greed too powerful for their fading common sense. Hunters visited our land, too, to be turned away peacefully whenever possible. Unintentional interlopers trod the Bialowicza for all manner of reasons, many coming due to richness of the land in a starved time. Oh, the Soviets and their execrable Five Year Plans. So many victims of the State during those years, just as the Tsars had done to the serfs. A different flag, but the same hunger and pain."

"We were not unknown, you may surmise. Myths surrounded our private enclave, and we fed them whenever possible. Is it not better to avoid confrontation altogether, even if that means embracing a false, supernatural identity? I think so, although I wish our attempts had been more fruitful. The automobiles dissolving into the earth are a testament to my own personal failures to be less visible. So many, like dying poplars along a rutted track." His gaze was distant, loaded with the burden of time.

"Do you see why I must stay here, in this lonely, verdant prison? Why I wish Elizabeth to come home? I am no coward, Ring, but I am chilled to the bone by the thought of losing her. That is why it is so bitter for me to have you do vile murder on my behalf, regardless of the greater service you are giving to mankind."

I knew a great deal more about the man after his call. I wondered if children ever really knew how much their parents loved them. Was that even possible? My resolve hardened after hearing a history that made the forest seem ever more desirable. When the girls got home, I would tell them that time was now of the essence, and I would be making plans with Sandrine as soon as possible.

Tomorrow, if all went well, it would be a brief but memorable date and the last of Sandrine's poisonous career.

A lover is coming, Sandrine. And I will be most attentive.

From Risa's Files

This Weekend: Elite French companion available for incall only. Ft. Lauderdale Beach. Donations 550 per hour, 900 for two hours. Room visits only, no travel or dinner possible, although moonlit walks on the beach are possible for select gentlemen. Email for appointment. References required. No locals. Picture unimportant. Mature men preferred. This is not an offer of prostitution but merely for time spent together. All other contact is between two adults at their discretion. Please be properly groomed and respectful of my wishes. Kisses, Sandrine.

45

Gyro could sense my tension even if I chose not to display the turmoil I felt. Planning, waiting. He stayed close to me in the yard as I wandered, apart from everyone else. A fat moon began to rise over the canal, adding a buttery line of light to the flickering panels of cobalt water. Suma and Wally were putting a medical kit together in case Sandrine got the better of me; they would ride together, while Risa drove me to the hotel. Wally's frenetic energy in traffic was too distracting, so I would sit quietly next to Risa and her projection of quiet calm. I was to meet Sandrine at ten, well after dark. Through email, I had baited the hook with a false persona of a lonely, childless technocrat on business. No wife. No family. A faceless, salaried employee on foreign ground without any discernible defenses against his own carnal needs. I was perfect for Sandrine's dark purpose, and she scheduled a visit without hesitation.

Under a loose-fitting shirt, I tucked my knife, the cool metal resting with a comfortable heft against the small of my back. I didn't know if she had the same tendencies as Elizabeth, but I could not allow her hands near my face. Her curious biology precluded any kissing. *What a shame.* Even if I could metabolize her poison, any slowdown would expose me to her other weapon, and I had no intent of being used as a pincushion. That meant I had to disable her quickly and with maximum force. Sandrine was a nail, and I was the hammer. A gentle touch on my shoulder from Risa alerted me that it was time to go. With a final stretch and pat of Gyro, we paired off, Suma and Wally in the other vehicle, and left for the beach.

Risa drove. I sat loosely, as she quizzed me gently about our plan. Her voice was soothing to my nerves; at least until I would feel my fighting instincts take control with a chill at my neck and a leaden calm in my mind.

"When you walk in the lobby, what's first?" Risa began.

"It's too nice a hotel for escorts to work without bribing a staff member. I'll look for a concierge to recognize me. She might even have a Helper, but I doubt it. It's too obvious, and they tend to be a bit awkward in upscale settings, especially this close to their mistress when she is killing." We had discussed the possibility of human collaborators earlier. It seemed thin, especially since three was a crowd when the blood started flowing. Helpers and Friends were like drug dealers. They never died old.

"Elevator up to fourth floor. Her room is a suite on the end, like we expected. It will be quiet there. You have the envelope?" Risa asked.

I patted my pants leg. "In my pocket. I'll put the money on the bathroom counter. She'll pretend to check it and come out. I can't let her undress me or get undressed. I don't know exactly how she kills, but it's attached to her. No contact with her hands or mouth. I need to hit her quickly and without hesitation. That won't be a problem. I'll go for a knockout and text you immediately. She's at least a century old, I think, so we won't be able to hold her for long. I'll start questioning her right away, but I'll have to get up to open the door unless you break in. That's a bit loud, I think, so I'll have to be fast."

Risa nodded periodically as I spoke. "Wally's worried; call her on your way up. Suma, too."

"What about you? Have I got this?" I asked her as we pulled in the parking lot of the hotel. She turned to me and put her hand on my face.

"You're too fast for her. But if she wounds you, run. Run fast, and come to us. Come to me. And then we'll take care of it, or her, whatever. And she'll regret being born." Her eyes were bright. I knew she meant it, and I knew she was worried. As I opened the door, she squeezed my hand once and turned away, her pride keeping any hint of tears from my view.

My heels were muffled in the sumptuous carpet of the doorway, only to *clop* lightly as I crossed into a tiled foyer with Mediterranean décor. I peeled right to the waiting bank of elevators after a discreet glance around the room. It was staffed lightly, and I saw no obvious candidates in league with Sandrine until I met the eyes of an unblinking bellman. He averted his gaze as I punched the four on the controls and waited for the soundless elevator doors to slide open. As the doors closed, I noted his brisk walk to the bar area. *Maybe two working with Sandrine, one human, one Helper.* I filed that thought and turned to the matter at hand, my heart rate rising slightly as the elevator stopped with a minor twitch.

Odd numbers left, even on right, to the end of the left hall. With a final check of my blade and one other surprise I had, I knocked twice, softly, and stepped back. It was date night.

She opened the door and stepped back as I came in. Thin and waiflike, she had an elfin quality to her bordering on androgyny. A black skirt covered her thighs, and a white silk top clung to her frame. A gold chain hung between her small breasts. She was beautiful, with doe-like eyes and a pixie cut that accentuated her apparent fragility.

I knew better.

"Thomas?" She asked, her voice cultured, French, quiet. I had to remain focused as she sat on the edge of the bed and crossed her legs, displaying them for maximum effect. With a start, I remembered my role and cast my eyes down, playing the awkward john. It was exceedingly easy. She had an aura of refinement that was palpable.

"Yes, hi, hi. Sandrine, hi. May I excuse myself to the restroom for a moment?" She smiled and waved me towards the inner door as I made a show of fumbling with the envelope. I went into the separate bathroom, laying the fee on the vanity and quietly checking my knife. So far, so good. I walked back out to find her in the same position on the bed. Her hand patted the mattress soundlessly, once.

"Do come over, please. Would you care for some wine? Or something stronger? The bar is excellent."

Her manners were impeccable. I sat. There was a mild tension, but she reached out and grasped my hand, softly, and smiled. "Tell me a bit about yourself. And about what you like. You shouldn't be nervous. I'm here for you, and I'm very experienced. Would you like to kiss me, perhaps? A massage?" Her flirtation was seamlessly woven with her hand steadily moving about my leg, my stomach, a brief caress of my upper arm. I'd been frisked for weapons in the most erotic, disarming way imaginable. I was impressed, even if she did miss my blade. She was a pro. I could respect that.

"I am not with women very often. At all, really. So, I was on business, here, you see . . . ," I stumbled, offering her an opening. She accepted. Out of position, I could not refuse her kiss. She was gentle, very coy. I felt nothing odd, even though I knew she was built to kill, and I had let her in far too close. Memories of Elizabeth percolated in my thoughts. I shut them down. I had to be present for this.

Her perfume was Chanel, but, under it, there were hints of vinegar and almond. Not the smells of a woman. Nor the scents of humans, for that matter. I forced a blush and stammered, "Could you, you know, kneel in front of me? Just to start? And then maybe, we can walk on the beach, like we are lovers? I miss that sort of thing. And the other thing, too. If I ever really even had it. I don't know . . . ," I trailed off as she stood, removing her heels and delicately placing them on the bed. They looked expensive. I wondered what size they were and how many she had. I knew Wally would like to know.

She knelt, smiling, crossing her feet behind her, and began to slide her hands up my legs. It was electric. I could see how she had been so lethal for so long. Her smile was secretive, and she raised a single brow of inquiry. I placed my hands behind me, flat on the bed, my legs and torso tense with her charged eroticism. She leaned forward, reaching for my zipper as I exhaled in anticipation. A light chuckle escaped her throat. It was the laugh of a woman who knows she is in total control.

Without warning, I drove the pommel of my knife into her temple hard enough to make her teeth *crack* against each other as she sagged to the carpet, stunned. From my pocket I withdrew a pair of titanium zip ties. In seconds, she was trussed on the bed and very, very disoriented. It was time for questions, and she had, after all, advertised that she was an excellent conversationalist. I intended to get my full hours' worth of her company, whether she felt chatty or not. Climbing on the bed, I straddled her, careful to remain on her chest. I wasn't concerned with her comfort. I was concerned about my life.

She wheezed to consciousness, her eyes rolling like an animal in distress. A circular dent in her skull remained from my knife handle, a killing blow for a human. It gave her left eye the curious tilt of an impressionist sketch gone wrong.

"What do you want?" Her voice was chilly, and free of inflection. I had to admire that type of recovery. She was resilient. "You paid for my body. I don't think you want anything more, Thomas. You will find that I am a prickly blossom."

"Prickly. What a descriptive," I said and reached back under her skirt. I found her secret, its chitinous length tucked up against her abdomen. How many men had felt that violation? How many women? It was cool and glassy under my grip. I squeezed once, hard. She gasped and bucked under my weight, her head rolling side to side in a symphony of nerves shrieking at once. I had her Achilles heel in hand, and I intended to use it. Even the genitalia of an insect were highly sensitive to pain, it would seem.

"Call me Ring. The ruse was necessary, and I feel compelled to apologize after bearing witness to your stellar manners. Quite continental of you. Since you know I am aware of your enhancements, if you will, let me tell you what I want, and we'll attempt to remain cordial, shall we?" I was feeling gallant, and a bit confident. My plan seemed to be working. So far.

When she remained silent, I continued. "First, don't scream. Any excessive noise results in this blade," I tapped the point against her breastbone, "being driven through to the mattress. Blue stars, ashes, poof, no Sandrine. Okay?" She nodded once, grimacing. "Second issue. Do you know what you are going to tell me tonight?" I cocked my head, listening.

"No, I do not. I hope you will explain what you wish to hear." She seemed unsettled, even a bit fearful. That was a new and unusual sensation for her, I was certain.

"I want to find Elizabeth. I want her with no misdirection. No warnings. No tripwires, verbal or otherwise, that will alert her in any way. You will tell me, beginning this instant, or you will live much longer than you ever thought possible. While dissolving. You see, my friends and I are compulsive researchers. We love facts. Information is power, as I am sure you know. And the fact that I find most relevant now is that you will find this," I waved a small plastic bag, filled with white powder, "is going to prove very persuasive, should you choose to be less than forthcoming."

Even restrained and with a fractured skull, she managed a derisive laugh. "Heroin? Or something else? Do you seriously think that flooding my body with narcotics will do anything other than anger me further, let alone debilitate me? My metabolism will shrug that off without hesitation. Please, allow me to assist you."

She opened her mouth wide. Her tongue was very pink and narrow. I halted my hand from moving too close, unsure about the range of her stinger hidden underneath that curving palate.

"I wouldn't do that if I were you. Boric acid is quite fatal to your kind. A common insect killer, easy to find, and easy to administer. The death is rather slow, and doubtless, painful. So, your vaunted metabolism will heal you, only to be overwhelmed by the next round I administer to you, which you will, of course recover from. Somewhat. And the beat goes on. You see? Unending pain. Continual living death and renewal until I tire of your presence or run out of poison. Neither of which will happen quickly, Sandrine."

As I spoke, she closed her mouth, her face paling from my gravid tone.

"So, first things first. Tell me about yourself. From the beginning. And leave nothing hidden. Begin." I tapped the knife handle in her skull fracture. She hissed and stiffened. But then, she began to speak.

"I was born the bastard of a defrocked bishop who backed the wrong Papal court. After Avignon surrendered the seat of Catholicism in 1377, my father was another castoff who had lived a life without concern, suckling at the teat of the Mother Church in repugnant glory."

She ignored my expression of shock at her age. She was far, far older than I had known. It presented an unusual opportunity for me to gain insight into the immortals and their culture if she kept talking. I chose silence, inviting her to fill the void.

"Rome inexorably wrested control of the Papal throne from France, and I was young, born without title, and had precious little chance of marrying anyone substantive. At best, my father hoped for me to wed another by-blow and remove myself from his demesnes, which edged closer to penury with each passing year."

"Is Sandrine your real name?" I asked out of pure curiosity.

"No. I cannot even recall my birth name. Memory is imperfect after so much time. Even glass becomes warped with age, and so it is with my mind's eye. Sandrine was a hatchet-faced nun who slept with my father for political favors. Her, I still remember clearly, a horrid woman. Stick thin, with nose hair and a braying laugh, but enormous breasts and no scruples whatsoever. I killed her when I was sixteen. Not that I regret it. Not one bit." Her tone was dreamy as she peered through a river of memory. "My last name is a shabby joke. Humor is so thin among the everlasting."

"Destot? What is the joke, then?" I asked with interest.

"I would show you, but I do not think you will remove these bonds, so I shall explain. When Jesus or any other victim of crucifixion was impaled, they were not hung by their hands. That myth is a creation of artists who sought visual symmetry in their work or who were lazy and ignorant of anatomy. No, the nexus of three major tendons in the wrist is the perfect weight-bearing locale for a sadistic excursion on the cross. Oh, to be sure, one might expire from shock, or other wounds, but the intent was for the victim to endure an unending war against asphyxiation and thirst. A most creative punishment, in my eyes. And I have seen many. That point on the wrist is called Destots place, after the French anatomist. My little nod to a countryman who named something quite useful in cowing the populace." She smiled and her eye leaked a stream of aqueous fluid, which she ignored. She was a tough one, to the bone.

"When did you become an immortal?" I assumed at a young age, but I wanted a definite answer. Thus far, I had not been forced to urge her to speak. I remained alert, nonetheless.

"Truly? Two years earlier. On Michaelmas, we had a visiting party from the Church who brought countless servants, scribes, whores. An ostentatious waste to remind us that Rome was the true muscle behind the Fisherman's ring. Among them was a woman who was so regal that every country priest found a reason, no matter how thin, to seek her company. It was as if Aphrodite had appeared in our midst. Even the most desiccated clergy found their loins afire for the woman." Her expression was one of proud remembrance. I could see she spoke of her maker.

"Elizabeth?" I asked to confirm. "What was her position at that time?"

"No one ever truly knew. She was a confidant of the Papal secretary, that much was certain. He listened to her as if his life hung in the balance, which later would make a great deal of sense, since it did. All of our lives existed by her whim. My seduction at her hand was so complete, so overwhelming. She summoned me to her room after vespers. I was to deliver candles and a trencher with hard cheese and pears, as she had missed dinner due to illness. I was expected, as a child of the house, to extend the utmost in courtesy for our guests despite the tension between the parties. I knocked at her door, a heavy, iron-bound affair of bleached wood, and I heard her call to me. I was bid to open the door and enter, which I did hesitantly. She sat in a sagging cane chair; the fire hinted at, by moving light, a physical perfection that was rare. Her face, her hands, every part of her. Even her voice was charged with unknown treasures. A pervasive aura of sexuality clung to Elizabeth, even sitting in a shapeless, woolen gown. I stood transfixed, captive in her gravity. She never blinked as she took my measure. I wilted under her intensity.

'Put them down,' she told me. I could not disobey. With a thump, I dropped the food and stood at attention. I quivered like a tuning fork until she spoke again.

'Do you find your life here austere, despite your devotions? Has your work for the Lord given you succor?' she then asked me. My ascetic appearance was amusing to her. I felt small.

'No, my lady. I mean to say, yes. I have many blessings. I can ride horses when I wish, and there are books here. My master allows me to read on Sundays if there is time. And I am never hungry, really,' I revealed, shrinking further as the words hung in the room, mocking the insignificance of my existence.

'Your master must be kind indeed. Bind not the mouths of the oxen that tread out your grain,'" she quoted to me. "'I do not see hooves on you, I see hands. Are you a beast of burden?' the lady teased me." She paused, gulped air and winced. Then she continued.

"She mocked me, but I welcomed it because it meant I had her attention. I felt the pressure of her gaze, do you understand?" She asked, adjusting her arms behind her. I knew she was in discomfort, and it bothered me. "I was being recognized. It was a generosity I had not experienced, and I found it to my liking. Even my youthful senses detected a kinetic threat from Elizabeth, although I was too naïve to quantify exactly what I felt. In moments, I was sitting next to her, on her bed, and the blood roared in my ears as she whispered secrets and promises in a single kiss. When she touched my face, I knew, somehow, that I was in danger. I became a marionette to her fingertips, and she pushed me flat, sliding over me in a serpentine glide. I saw the ridged timbers in the firelight, and then her face, and then she laughingly drew me into her and I was mounted. Raped, you might say, but I would not because I gave her my entire will and spirit in my childish thrusting, calling to my God to stop the pleasure and absolve me of my guilt at wanting her mouth, her hands, body, all of her covering me in a smothering wave of sin."

"Raped? What? Is that how you were turned? Did she . . . ?" And I really looked at Sandrine, beyond my suppositions and everything I allowed myself to believe.

"Paul. I remember it now. My name was Paul, and I was a young man. But no more. Elizabeth saw to that. Over the years, I grew smooth, fine-boned, and feminine in every way. Except one. I felt my innards rearranging. I became sensitive to sounds and scents. That abomination between my legs grew, and I became a slave of my desire to breed. Elizabeth told me I would feel like a youth forever. I would command lust with a glance. What could be truer than wishing to live to see what was around every curve of the road? Bend in the river? I had never ranged beyond sight of my birthplace. As for the lust, she created a burning want for something I had been unaware of before her ministrations. I found I had a taste for it. My thirst for capitulation has been unending, thanks to her." She stopped speaking, as a trickle of blood rolled thickly on the pillow, spilling from her delicate ear. Pain shadowed her face, now growing taut and pale. She was fading from my wound, which had been more savage than I realized.

I had suffered through the penance of awkward teen years, as did nearly everyone I knew, save Wally, who transitioned from childhood to godhood without breaking stride. Sandrine, though, she had endured a theft of her youth. Her identity. Even the boy Paul's death was now part of a purloined future he would never know. Elizabeth possessed a sophistication that elevated her crimes into layered iniquities, stretching beyond the vanishing point of time. Paul, the subtle, seductive killer, was a prisoner of his childish greed. It was humanizing and nearly gave me pause, until I thought of the bodies she had buried over the centuries, stretching into time. They had been given no choice. Nor would she be granted one, either.

"Elizabeth is nearby, I think. It feels like she brought you here? Or was it of your own volition?" I asked. She was breathing hard from my weight.

She considered this for a second. "Sent. Called. Both are the same act, only the timing is different. I was called. I know others have been sent, personally. I made my way here, now, on my own time and by my own means, but I have been moving about freely for longer than your nation has existed. As to my sisters, I cannot say where they are, exactly. We seem to squabble quite often, which is rather dangerous for us. And you. I know that when you dispatch me, they will become *very* interested in meeting you. And your partners." Her threat was open, palpable. I believed her. "I think it safe to say that you will not wait long at all before unwanted visitors come to call."

She shuddered once as I let the knife tip draw another jeweled drop of blood from her chest.

My blood boiled at her threat. "Do you know how easy this was? I can take your sisters at will if you're any indication of their abilities. And when I bury this knife in you, do you know what happens? I get a little bit faster. A little bit stronger. Less likely to make a mistake. And let me assure, you, *Paul*, no one will weep for your ashes when I close this door. A maid will vacuum your memory up, along with any threat you might have posed."

I slid the blade along her chest again, lingering on the nape of her slender neck. "So, then. Where is she?" The blade slipped under her milky skin, a chilly violation. She shivered.

"I do not think you want the answer to that question, boy," she sneered, even in her agony. "We built a castle on foundations of sin. Money. Power. Souls. All are delicacies on the palate of the true predators among you. You bray and jostle like cattle on the ramp to their deaths and know nothing of the true seat of power. It hides in plain sight, an iceberg of manipulation that seems a small threat until you plumb the depths and see, with dull, captive eyes, what the Horned One is building. A labyrinthine empire hidden beneath the cool shade of a forgotten forest. But I have said enough for this body, and I think it is time for my last kiss." She curved her lips, playful to the end. Fully evil. Completely inhuman.

I looked at the blade's path and began to part her ribs with the tip when she sat up, impossibly strong, her body arcing in a whiplike action fueled by hate. My knife struck true through her flesh, reaching a grating stop in her spine as it angled towards her heart. Her face was at my ear, a searing sting as her dart pierced my lobe and withdrew with the speed of a mongoose. Before I could react, her breath was light in my ear, whispering to me.

"*Did you think the Horned One would remain in the forest forever? You don't know shit about pain, yet. But you will.*"

My bulk settled on the mattress as her corpse sublimed, ashes and faerie lights, and then silence. And in my bones, instantly, the first salvo of a night-long war as I became imbued with the residuals of a seasoned killer.

I was still sitting in the circle of Sandrine's dust when the light tap at the door announced my back-up had arrived. I stood carefully, not knowing what to expect. It was a good policy, this going slow, because the room seemed to tilt as I lurched to the door and opened it, only to have Wally catch me. Suma and Risa were nowhere to be seen, which meant that a hotel staff member was having a *very* uncomfortable conversation right then.

"Are you hurt?" Wally searched me, her face lined with worry. I stood against the doorway, feeling steadied by her presence.

"I'm good. I got to her first and put everything I had into the first shot. Nothing but ashes, now, Blondie." Wally kissed my cheek in relief.

"But, she was very different, totally new to us, and very old. I think I need to go home, and we can talk on the way before I crash."

We left without a backwards glance and turned down the carpeted hallway, just two more anonymous faces in a building made for them.

46

Muscles have memory, and, by the time Wally pulled in our driveway, mine had acquired another lifetime from Sandrine. I noticed high spots of color on her cheeks as she walked with me, arm in arm.

"Contact buzz, or out of shape?" I asked her.

"Buzz! I am sailing just from being near you. Crazy! I've *never* felt this way, like our best sex ever, but we're upright and walking. This is . . . ,"and she shivered, pulling me closer as we opened the door to find Suma and Risa in the living room, pouring wine.

"Our little friend here is quite high from the kill." I said to them, tugging at Wally. "Sandrine packs quite a punch. I'm already feeling her all over me, in me, and Wally's got a bad case of the chats."

She disengaged from me and downed a whole glass of wine in two gulps, motioning to Risa to fill it again. The surge from Sandrine was pervasive. I felt like chewing a chain in two and then ravishing every woman in a three mile radius. Not bad for an aftereffect.

That's when I noticed the man sitting quietly at the kitchen table, admiring the necklace Wally had gotten from the Baron.

"Hello?" I cut my eyes askance. "Who's our new friend?"

He turned and waved, somewhat meekly. A beer sat in front of him, and his shoes were off. He was clearly comfortable, which was odd, because we usually just bludgeon intruders. He was early thirties, professional-looking, brown-eyed and sandy-haired. Innocuously covered with the air of middle management, he seemed a friendly sort and was doing well, given the circumstances.

"Ring, meet Marcus. Marcus, Ring. The knockout drinking like a twelve-stepper is Wally."

Wally waved carelessly, her nose buried in another glass of red wine. Risa indicated he should come over to the living room, which he did, albeit slowly. Wally caressed his face as he passed, winking lasciviously. "And please ignore her trashy behavior. She's got quite the glow from Sandrine, -the escort Ring popped in your hotel tonight, by the way, so she's even more randy than usual." She rolled her eyes to indicate this was not a unique situation.

To Marcus' credit, he didn't blink but merely sat on the cushion next to Suma and looked awkwardly at each of us in turn.

"Sandrine? The French girl? She's dead?" he asked, worry on his face. "You killed her? I knew something wasn't right about her. Knew it."

I nodded. "I wouldn't call her a girl, exactly. But yes, she's dead, I killed her, and I assume that you're not here for just a cold one?"

I raised an eyebrow at Risa, inviting her to elaborate where Marcus could not. Wally belched and stretched with an erotic groan. Quite the lady. Suma snickered and then caught herself, focusing on our guest.

"Marcus was in the hotel lounge, but he wasn't working. He's not a true Helper, either, not like we understand. He's sort of a . . . groupie? Or a really enthusiastic fan of a particular lady. Right, Marcus?" Risa inquired politely. "Why don't you start with how you got here? Then we can move on to other details, okay?"

She was being overly polite. I distrusted that voice; it reminded me of her interrogations about my use of her towels.

Marcus gathered his thoughts for a moment. You could see the wind filling the sails of a narrative in his mind, and then he spoke.

"I'm from Chicago. I'm a– well, it doesn't matter what I did. I was a nobody, but I made an okay living. My wife left me two years ago for some shithead from Colorado who wore a buckskin jacket, for Chrissakes, and to boot he had a–"

"*Marcus*" I snapped. "Let's focus on the other aspects of your story, m-kay?"

Suitably reprimanded, he continued, "Okay, so I'm single. No wife, no dog, living in some kind of country song. I'm on a cold streak with women, like I'm a penguin, I couldn't even get a look from the maid at my gym. So after about a year of that shit, I do something I've never done before." He paused, sipping his beer.

"You called a pro, right?" Wally spoke up from the floor where she lay supine, her feet in Risa's lap. She knew men.

"Err, right. But I wasn't about to bring some streetwalker into my house, so I looked around online a little, you know, just doing my homework. I'm an insurance actuary. Or I was. I know about risk." Marcus explained.

"That explains your shoes. Gah!" Wally piped up from the floor. Risa slapped her foot, hard. They glared at each other for a second and then fell back toward the conversation. Suma snickered again, clearly enjoying the fray. I remained dignified, as I always am. Ask anyone.

Marcus, unmoved by Wally's fashion criticism, pressed on. "I have a buddy at work. Derek. Or had, rather. He's dead." We all knew what was coming, but we let him continue. Only notes of the story would differ, but the tune would be familiar.

"He whored around on his wife all the time, so I asked him if he knew of a girl, you know, who was available. A sure thing. So he told me there was an escort he's been drooling over and that he would have her break me in the right way, in his words. She was *expensive* but when I saw her picture I thought it would be worth every penny. Only problem was, we had to travel to her, which was no worry for me, I didn't have anything to do, and Derek said he'd pay for my ticket. So we plan it out. Or Derek did, anyway. We arranged to meet her at a hotel bar for a drink. Derek set it up and he knows his shit, so he got a room upstairs."

"What did she look like?" Suma interjected. Wally stood up to grab the wine bottle, intrigued. We all were by now.

"Hot. Oh my God, was she hot. Blonde. Short. Tanned. Killer body, smelled like heaven and the angels all together. She looked kind of like you, Wally." he added. Wally curtsied, while Risa grimaced. "She was so far out of our league I almost couldn't look her in the eye. Her teeth were blinding. Even her hands were perfect. I felt like an idiot, sitting with her at the table, but she talked and flirted like we were old friends. Shit, I was hooked. I mean *really* hooked in, like, ten seconds. Her accent made me insane. I could've been happy listening to her reading an aspirin bottle."

"Describe her accent, Marcus. Again, if you would,." Risa asked.

"It was southern. But not like, redneck, you know, I mean . . ." he struggled to articulate the finer points of southern dialects. "She said she was from the Garden District, whatever that means."

"New Orleans. Louisiana. High class brood mares out of there." I said, earning a punch from Wally. "So how did this *date* proceed?"

"Right, New Orleans. That's where we ended up." Marcus took a long pull on his beer. "Like I was saying, I went up first. She already had a suite. Beautiful, way over my pay grade, just like she was. She kissed me and bent my mind; I mean I just about fainted. In about a minute, I was on the bed, nude—hey, is this part okay? You want details?" he hesitated, turning shy.

"It's okay; these are my lovers. Feel free to hit us with the good stuff," I stated flatly and then gave him a mock salute when his eyebrows went skyward. We get that reaction a lot.

Sliding his eyes from Wally's legs, Marcus continued. "Well there aren't many details. At least, not with me. She lay upside down on the bed with her head over the side and I . . . I had trouble with my lift-off, if you know what I mean. I tried to concentrate on her face and her perfect tits. I mean, they were world-beaters, but, when I thought it wasn't happening for me, I focused on this green necklace sitting in her cleavage. It shimmered constantly. I mean, what wouldn't if your camping spot was in the most beautiful valley of all time, right? Anyway, I was *pissed*. I think she was just too insanely hot for me, and I felt like a kid getting taught a lesson by some cougar. Anyway, she was so sweet, and she said that we would see each other again and that she would make it right. Blew my gaskets right there to think about being with her *again*. And, after I went downstairs, that's when Derek headed up. Looking back, that's the point where things really start to get weird." he paused in remembrance.

"A question: how long was it before Derek went up to her room?" Suma asked. I wasn't sure where she was going with that topic, but I listened, anyway.

"Right away. And he was up there for, like, an hour and a half. I knew he was a stud, but come on. That's world record stuff, right?" he gazed at me expectantly. I demurred and looked at my feet. He didn't know what Wally and Risa were capable of doing to a man. Or each other.

"Was Derek able to complete his 'lift-off, as you say?" Risa asked as seriously as possible, given the subject matter.

"And *how*," Marcus enthused. "Derek said she was not just the best ever, but better than he could have imagined, like legendary. And he said she was really into him, ever since their first phone call, and that we should come see her at her other place. You know, stay awhile."

Risa and Wally groaned. I laughed outright. Suma looked confused until I explained. "Let me get this straight. You and Derek left Chicago to fly a thousand miles to see a high class hooker because *she was really into both of you?* Is it amateur night? Aren't you professionally trained to assess risk? Am I wrong in finding this hilarious?" I finished with a derisive hoot, looking around at our collective stunned faces.

Marcus rubbed his face and shook his head. "I know, I know. And we did. But once we were there, she really took care of us. It was like we were visiting princes."

"Or cattle." Risa interjected.

"Right." Marcus admitted. "I used all my vacation time for her," he finished mournfully.

"Why didn't you leave? Other than being comatose from the attentions of Goldibox?" I asked, inwardly pleased with my phrasing. I laughed alone. No one understood my comedic touch.

"It was the details, man. She kept us in one of her places—she had four. I wasn't surprised; with that body, she could afford a castle if she wanted it. She would have a car bring us over one at a time—me during the day, Derek at night. Four, five hours of her and me. She knew my favorite foods, cooked like a chef. Or her staff would cook. Either way, best food I've eaten. Greeted me at the door with thirty year old whiskey that I couldn't afford, but have loved since I first tasted it on my honeymoon. Fed me sliced fruit, gave me massages, hot baths, shit you only dream about. And then on top of all that, the sex." He sighed heavily with memory. "I learned about things the human body can do but shouldn't. I felt my legs go numb and my face tingle at the same time, and, sometimes, she did it with one hand. See my eye?" he asked, pulling his eyelid back and turning to show us. Blood still filled the corner where vessels had burst.

"Conjunctive hemorrhage. Impressive. How'd that happen?" I asked. When I realized everyone was staring at me, I clarified my astute observation. "What? I read occasionally." My genius was met with skepticism.

"In the best carriage ride in the history of carriage rides, that's where. She had a horse drawn antique carriage pick us up. We're under these old oaks, the breeze smells like flowers, and she goes down on me.Right there! I'm looking up at this Spanish moss swaying, and I thought I was dying, that's how hard I got off. When I regained consciousness, she's sitting next to me, smiling, and I've got an eye that looks like a ruby made of jelly. I mean, seriously, I passed out from her mouth."

"That's not unheard of," Risa quipped. Marcus looked at her with amazement and me with newfound respect.

"Other than your eye, did you have any health problems from being with her? Dreams? Anything weird?" I wanted to ferret out the nature of this sexual dynamo from New Orleans.

"Me, no" Marcus said, finishing his beer and setting the bottle down. "But Derek was in trouble. He stopped sleeping. We were only there for a week, but I don't think he slept at all. He looked like shit, but I rarely saw him, she kept us so tied up with her, and, sometimes, she had a car take us into the city to do cool stuff, things that were really local and .personal. Like she was sharing her life history with us. It felt like she knew everything that had ever happened in the city. And she said she wanted us for herself, that she enjoyed our spirit and didn't want any of her sisters or family coming around. I got the feeling their family dinners must be like Armageddon."

That was closer to the truth than he knew. Marcus was immersed in the thought if this woman. It was uncomfortable to witness, knowing she had killed his friend. And many others, no doubt.

"Derek started to fade. He was really pale. She put us on a plane to go home, and neither of us wanted to. Who would? It was like leaving Eden and Aphrodite for the suburbs of Chicago. He didn't talk much on the plane, he was too tired. He said she just fucked him every night, nothing crazy, but that he couldn't tell when he was awake or asleep. It didn't matter, she was still there, naked, on him, and he couldn't stop." His eyes rimmed with tears. "He died in the car on the way home. I was thirty seconds from a hospital, but they couldn't save him. He was thirty-four."

The room was stilled by the memory of a man we had never met but a story we knew only too well. We stalled a moment to give Marcus time to regain his composure.

"And then you followed her here for the sex?" Wally asked, her voice soft with compassion.

"No, nothing like that" Marcus replied, his voice leaden. "I followed her here to kill her."

From Risa's Files

Savor the essence of New Orleans with a quiet evening hosted by the elegant Delphine. Worldly, gracious, and sensual, she and her southern hospitality are second to none. Let Delphine remind you exactly how gentlemen should be treated. A full evening of her care and company includes an introductory cocktail hour, followed by an in-home gourmet meal prepared by Delphine herself. Options include (but are not limited to): Carriage ride under the famous New Orleans oaks. Candlelit dessert hour overlooking a private lake. Champagne breakfast, massage, and dressing service. All of these memorable events are at the discretion of the gentleman in the event he chooses to leave the personal bedroom of Delphine during his visit. Few men do! Screening is, unfortunately, a must, as Delphine only sees select gentlemen. Her well trained staff awaits your call. Companionship is limited to established, refined men over the age of thirty five. Travelers welcome!

47

Florida

Marcus had clearly warmed to his narrative, but it was time for a reality check. Risa held up a hand to silence him, and to his credit, he obeyed. She's tough like that.

"Marcus, what makes you think Delphine should die?" she asked.

Bluntly, Wally added "What makes you think you are a killer? Of a woman like her?" They were legitimate questions. This was a medium-sized insurance employee with no presumptive experience as an assassin. It seemed like a reasonable point of contention.

He thought for a second and started speaking slowly, "Well, Derek was really healthy, you know? The whole thing was just so out of character for me, and Derek, even. I just know that she did something to him because, for him to die like that, with his face slumped against my car window . . . it's just so fucked up." He hesitated then added, "And, now, I still see her. At night, sometimes. Do you believe me?" He looked around for disbelief but found none, sinking appreciatively into his chair a bit. He had come to the right place for this type of problem.

Suma asked, "In your dreams?"

A violent shake of his head. Marcus was adamant. "No, I'm awake, I think. But I don't know how she gets in the house without me hearing. How does she not wake my dog up? We're five feet apart, for God's sake. She oozes onto me, and I'm in her, fucking for all I'm worth, and no one else knows. I feel like I'm coming unglued, but just the smell of her on my shirt makes me fucking insane. I mean, what do I do, announce to the world that every night I'm balls deep in a ghost orgy? So I keep the secret. And I know the only way to stop is to kill her, or make her go someplace else. I don't know."

"A succubus. Plain and simple." I spoke, Risa nodded, and Wally nearly growled. She *hated* sexual competition. "Marcus, she's not human, but you already knew that, right? And, now, this thing that defies every chart or data stream you've ever seen is taking your life from you, just like Derek. But you're holding out longer because you're probably a good guy with a clean slate who just wants to go to work, raise his family, and live your life, right?"

"I thought I was insane. I'm an evidence guy, no matter how contrary to my feelings. Occam's razor and all that, right? But then I think about Derek's headstone, and I just sort of *knew*." Marcus had lost his innocence to this creature. Now, he was losing even more in a slow drip that filled the succubus with his life and stolen memories with each nocturnal union. Sadly, he did so willingly in a haze of pleasure. Giving wanton gratification at the cost of life was an ace that immortals played too often. Few humans could resist the searing touch of a creature designed for seduction and Marcus, although resilient, was fortunate we could intervene. If he let us.

I thought for a moment. "Marcus, could you arrange an introduction with Delphine? Soon? I think that, in her line of work, money talks. Maybe a very generous offer can bring the lady south for a date with a tall, ravishing Midwesterner, skilled in the ways of love, a man whose very presence in the room makes women swoon.-"

"Okay, we get it, Your Highness. You want to play stud again and bring this succubus to us, rather than be in her lair." Risa could not roll her eyes any more dramatically in mockery. It's a good thing I'm not overly sensitive.

"It peels her away from the staff, which is probably complicit in her needs," Wally elaborated. "Getting her out of there gives us a chance to see if she makes contact with any other immortals while she's on our turf. I can convince the hotel staff to give us access. Or Risa can do it with a kick to the balls," she finished, earning a wintry smile from Risa, no matter how true. Risa simply cannot accept the fact that Wally is the consummate charmer, especially when it comes to bellhops and bartenders. I walked over to the table and picked up the necklace given to us by the Baron, watching the jeweled eye glint flirtatiously in the light.

"I don't know about all this, man. She's set up like a queen. Why the hell would she leave? Just to bang one single john a thousand miles away? What have you got that she needs?" Marcus openly doubted me.

"What she needs? A woman with money, staff, virtually eternal life? Dominion over men and a never ending river of lust and pleasure? You think I can lure her solely on the basis of my boyish good looks and some cash? No, Marcus. I don't think that , no matter how dashing I may be," Wally cooed mockingly, batting her eyes at me "- well; I could never have anything that she needs. But I have something far better."

"What's that?" Marcus asked me, puzzled. I brandished the necklace, turning lazily on its chain.

I tore my eyes away from the dancing horse to look at him. "I have something she *wants*."

48

Morning broke gently. Intermittent sunspots strutted across the canal in shards of whites and yellows, reluctantly giving way to the blue that shouldered upward towards the streaky clouds. I pulled on shorts and decided that I would watch our resident long-necked heron fishing by the dock until the house woke up, along with our guests. I walked softly past a deeply breathing Marcus, sleeping on the couch with Gyro, who had insinuated himself onto the couch in a tangle of knobby legs. Oddly, Marcus looked cradled in comfort, despite sharing his bunk with a beast. Crossing the yard, my feet welcomed the rough wood of the dock, and I perched, legs dangling, as the neighborhood came to life.

A click from the sliding glass doors announced I had a visitor, but I was so content, staring at the water, that only a waft of rose scent identified Risa, who dropped a familiar arm over my shoulders and leaned against me as she lowered herself to lean on my side.

"You smell like roses . . . and Wally. Sleepover last night for you girls?" I teased, nudging her as she yawned and slapped my thigh lightly in protest.

"Something like that." Her grin was wicked. "Suma took Wally's bed. We kicked Marcus to the couch after you went to sleep and we were done discussing our brilliant plans for the tramp from Louisiana."

"Hey now," I chided, "She's a courtesan, not a tramp. Big difference. Like three grand." I leered at her with what I hoped was my creepiest smile. I'm quite the charmer, especially before coffee. "Do you feel like things are changing beyond our control?" I asked her, giving voice to the inarticulate fear I was carrying.

"I think I do. I know Wally does. We talked about it. You know her impatience makes things seem much more immediate, but," her voice softened as she formed her thoughts, "I think she's right this time. I keep looking around corners, mentally, you know, wondering what it is that we're missing here in the larger scheme. I don't like being toyed with. Elizabeth is mocking us, somehow. All of these things are related. I just know it. I'm out of my element a bit here because you and Wally are so much better at using instinct. I just grind facts and then point you like a weapon. A very handsome weapon, especially when you don't shave or brush your teeth. One thing I don't understand about Elizabeth and her so-called daughters. Do they all get along? I've never seen a family that didn't squabble or compete in some way. If there's a way, maybe we can drive a wedge somewhere to make them come out and play." She kissed my shoulder, and I savored the familiarity of that small act, reminding myself to groom thoroughly in appreciation of the gesture.

"I'll call the Baron and throw a few things his way. Sibling rivalry . . . yes. Yes, every family fights. And these are killers. Good idea. Maybe he'll see a thread and run with it" I told her, but for the moment, we just sat quietly in contemplation of the water, the sun, and each other.

Wally drove Marcus back to his apartment after a late breakfast, but not before extracting a promise that he would return the same evening for dinner. There were many more questions to ask of him after a day of our minds percolating with the possibilities his information broached. Suma took my Wagoneer to the Hardigan Center in order to spend the day with Boon. Her leave of absence from work, taken at first as a simple vacation, looked to be more valuable each day, as her presence was welcome in our group. With quiet humor and an aura like a furtive smile, she complimented our rabble nicely.

49

As a chat with Cazimir was in order, I got comfortable on my bed, powered up the laptop, and briefly typed. I connected with the Baron and was greeted with a wan smile as he settled into his desk chair. He looked drawn and older. His vigor was somehow washed out by the lamps of his home, which threw light on more of the interior than we had previously seen. Stately arches of hewn wood were spanned by square beams, their lengths scored with axe marks that attested to the age of the structure. It was rugged but cultured, with meaningful-looking items placed on nearly every flat surface. On a table, a charger of burled wood and chased silver. Pears sat within the platter, huddled together in the middle of the smooth depression made from years of use. A museum-quality table spanned half the room, enhanced by turned wooden candelabras placed at every third chair. Tapers of beeswax sat unlit in their bases, and on each wall, tapestries hung with the stillness that only great weight and craftsmanship can bring to so large a weave. Lurid scenes of the hunt quivered with motion in the threads, still brilliant after years on the wall.

But these items paled in comparison with the crown jewels of the lodge, mounted on the beam closest to the Baron's desk. Five feet long, more than a foot in diameter, and tailing away to a lethal point, the aurochs horns shone like obsidian. I could not envision what type of beast might carry those upright, let alone wield them like swords. Periodic specks of gray broke through the unrelenting blackness of the horns, which were held in place by a bronze ring nearly a foot wide. The display was an otherworldly image out of time, driving home the point that the Baron's family- and residence- were far different than anything we had ever seen before. My house had the feel of a roadside motel; the Baron's was a portal to a life that disappeared centuries earlier. I sat mute in the face of this *otherness* and asked, somewhat cowed by the scene, "Sir, are you feeling well?"

"No, Ring. I will not draw out my answer, I am tired, and I have an inarticulate fear that something is happening with Elizabeth and the women she brings into her sphere of influence. I cannot say why, but I have an echo in my bones that she is moving inexorably to some sort of violent conclusion. I fear for her. I fear for those around her, and the good souls that she may take because of her moral corruption. And, for the first time, I fear not being here to help her." He bowed his head, looking more elderly than I thought possible. It shocked me to see him deteriorate this quickly, but stress can eat a person from within until he collapse in a rumbling heap. I tempered my sympathy by recalling the fact this man, essentially a stranger, still had someone watching us from a distance. That jolted me back to the middle regarding my opinion of the Baron, no matter how I felt about his current situation,. I decided to remain on his side, at least on the surface.

"I know we are getting closer to her, Cazimir. We'll find her, I promise you. One by one, her daughters make themselves known to us through their crimes or our diligence. So rest, sir. Rest, and I'll call you with each step as we narrow our search. I won't stop until I have my hands on her." I hoped my resolute tone would give him some solace.

"Thank you, Ring, I trust your efforts. Let me give you a bit of advice from an old man, if I may. When you get close, very close, be sure you are speaking to her directly. Because you do not want to grab a creature as spirited as Elizabeth by the tail," he finished. He bid me goodbye and cut the connection, leaving me to wonder about tigers, tails, and how I could convince Elizabeth that anything other than her surrender was suicide for her.

But first, I had to convince myself.

50

Delphine was no ordinary courtesan. While she certainly had a small presence on the internet, it quickly became apparent that seeing her involved a more traditional methodology. My email expressing interest in meeting her was returned promptly by a staff member named Joseph. He informed me that, after a brief description of myself, I might be permitted to speak directly with the lady herself. Given that I was going to tailor my personal history directly to her particular needs, I was confident that, no later than dinner, I would hear the voice of a succubus who had been operating in New Orleans for decades, if not centuries.

And, Delphine, who would certainly be the model of decorum, would hear the voice of her very last client: Me.

I called the given number, and Joseph answered on the second ring, neither anxious nor dismissive, but, nonetheless, making me aware that I wanted something to which he controlled access. His voice was silky, cultured, and capable of turning even the smallest words into insults. I hated him in seconds. He was the type of officious prick that graces desks in government agencies and salons, alike. But even roadblocks like Joseph can be surmounted, and, when I combined the words *inheritance* with *jewelry*, his voice quickly changed into a more subservient tone I instantly recognized as interest.

"Let me connect you to Miss Delphine, if you've a moment, Ring" he gushed. I had tickled the right ivories to hear the tune I wanted. A static click announced that Delphine was on the line, in more ways than one.

"Mister Hardigan, thank you for calling on me. I understand you're interested in the two of us getting acquainted?" she asked in the measured tones of a belle. She was good.

"I am, and thank you for taking my call without a prior, written appointment to chat. Manners are fading, I'm afraid, but I admit to being a bit anxious about meeting you. What with my new situation and all," I finished, leaving the unspoken dangling for her. She bit.

"Situation? Tell me, Ring-may I call you Ring, since we may be friends quite soon?" she asked, and I gave my permission, quickly. "How has your situation changed, that you find yourself wanting my company? You realize, of course, that I see only very select gentlemen, and, not to be rude, but may we start with me asking what it is you do?"

I knew that this was the delicate part of the conversation. A mixture of truth, lies, and something in between was what Wally and Risa suggested as a tactic to draw her into the discussion, that we might convince her to leave her gated walls.

"Well, to be honest, very little. I had hoped to enjoy your company, show you around my city," I was interrupted by her peal of laughter.

"Oh, Ring, that is *precious*. I think that Joseph- whom I'll deal with directly," her voice took an iron tone, "has sorely misread who you are. You most certainly do not meet the qualifications of the men I see." She finished and dragged on a cigarette, waiting for me to speak so she could end the conversation. Now was the time where I would demonstrate the fine line between carrot and stick. How she would react was uncertain, but appealing to vanity was a fine place to start.

"Miss Delphine, if you'll hear me out" I began in my most placating tone, "True, I have very little money and no job, currently. But I am a confident man. I'm also quite nice-looking, according to my neighbor. She says I remind her of her middle son, who lives in Illinois" I preened. I could not imagine Delphine's face. "I can show you a really nice time. We have a great pizzeria just around the corner that serves wine."

With that absurdity, she brought the hammer down. "Ring, I am holding a cigarette. Do you think I lit it? No. I cannot recall the last time I drew my own bath. I have a staff that respects and fears me because of my reputation and men who will gladly give their last cent to be with me. Now, I think this jest has gone on long enough, and I bid you a pleasant day."

Before she could hang up, I set the hook. "If you insist, Delphine. I only thought you would visit me because my uncle was a baron, and I wanted to use the jewelry he left me for something memorable. Like you *supposedly* are."

Her intake of breath told me all I needed to know about her curiosity, which was alive and well. It was time to close the negotiations.

"I can send you the same picture of the necklace I gave the other French lady. She told me she was very interested in visiting after she saw it, since she thought it might be a family heirloom." Now I brought the stick to bear. "I think that you might reconsider, given that the necklace was handcrafted by an artisan of incredible skill, one of the finest in Europe. What would it hurt for you to take a look? I mean, if it's good enough for someone as classy as—I think you pronounce her name Sandrine—is it good enough for you? I just want to have a really memorable time, you know?" I chided her and held my breath.

"Sandrine?" she asked, and I heard her breathing quicken. "I may be interested, after all. I do have some free time this week, as it turns out. Social seasons can be so *dull*." She was struggling to regain her velvety composure, and failing.

"Can you describe this jewelry, Ring?" she asked me, solidly on the line.

"Why don't I show you, instead? Remember, I'm just an unemployed nobody, so my description would be crude. Let the necklace speak for itself, right?" I asked her. She covered the receiver momentarily and then read off a phone number for me to send a picture.

"Send it right along, won't you?" she asked, letting her mask of control slip ever so slightly. "Who knows, Ring? It may be time for me to visit the tropics again."

51

Wally and Risa had gone for a run before dinner, so I had Gyro as my sous chef. We prepared, admittedly, with some sampling, an array of bread and olives, cheese, hummus, and basically every pickled item known to man. Peppers, artichokes, hearts of palm, and a sprinkling of capers lay on a large white platter that we could comfortably grab from in the center of the table. Our meals were often simple and informal, but that did not mean they were unsatisfying. I chilled wine and set the table family style, knowing that Marcus, and probably Suma, would be joining us, then opened a beer and took the beast into the yard for recreation. I sat at the dock while Gyro reinvestigated every single blade of Bermuda grass we had managed to keep alive in the backyard. His snorts were comical, and the sun was setting without fanfare as I fought the urge to doze in the light breeze. I rolled my shoulders to loosen them and stretched both legs and arms, getting ready for our dinner guests. I had a feeling that our meal would be memorable.

Suma joined us, along with Marcus, after picking him up at his hotel, and it made for a cheerful table as they traded war stories about the medical field, lawsuits, and the general decline of civilization. Now and then, it did us good to hear about less belligerent occupations and added an air of normalcy to our lives, at least for an hour or two. When the wine was gone and the plates were cleared, I asked Marcus if he had any training with weapons. His look confirmed my suspicions, so we all filed into the yard for an impromptu seminar on the finer points of knife fighting against ancient succubae that may or may not be wearing crinoline skirts. I really know very little about fashion among the moneyed immortals of New Orleans, but it seemed plausible.

"Stand light on your feet, okay?" I instructed Marcus, as Suma sat on the grass while Wally and Risa assisted me on posing his limbs properly. I hadn't given him a knife for the same reason I wouldn't strap a butcher knife to Gyro's paw; he simply wasn't ready for it and it was patently unsafe. We drank a lot of wine, too, which added to the general danger, although I had stopped at one glass, knowing that this lesson was going to occur.

"How does that feel?" I asked him, taking in his generally clumsy bearing.

"Okay. A bit stiff. Should I be moving around, or something, you know, lighter on my feet?" he asked, giving voice to a common mistake made by amateurs.

"No, stay still and breathing easy. Remember this: quiet mind, quiet feet. You want to be economical, not flying all over the place. All that does is make you unbalanced and at risk. Wally, reposition his legs and turn him a bit?" I asked her, as she moved to adjust his placing.

She placed her arms around his chest and turned him to face me in a side stance, narrowing his profile dramatically. I heard her inhale as she playfully nuzzled his neck. He reacted as expected, with wide eyes and a hint of a blush. Wally can do that to a man in an instant. It's her trademark. Well, that and a few other things, but this was the one she used at the moment.

"What is that cologne, Marcus? It's a panty-dropper." She asked him in her most lascivious tone. "Risa, come smell this guy. Amazing." She stepped aside as Risa leaned in and sniffed his neck appreciatively.

"Well? What is it, handsome? Risa flirted, outrageously. She was at her maximum wattage, gazing up at him with doe eyes and a soft smile. It was a killer look.

"It's, well, it's Armani. You like it that much, really? I'll wear it more often now," Marcus stammered, falling in love with his cologne choice just a bit more than he thought possible.

"Okay, dreamboat." I laughed, "Turn back, position again, like we showed you. Now, I'll extend my hand, blade backwards so you're not hurt. Show me what your instincts are when I come forward, and we'll see where your skills are at." Marcus settled again, trying to remain serious in the face of such flattery. It was challenging even for me, and I live with the girls.

I balanced on my back foot slightly in a sixty to forty ratio, arm out slightly and my knife turned towards me. "Ready?" I asked him, and he smiled. Over his shoulder, Risa gave an imperceptible nod, and I lunged forward in a blazing strike as my wrist turned to plunge the blade in his heart, stopping only when my knuckles thumped against his breastbone with a muffled noise signaling the end of Marcus' life as he knew it. Suma gasped. Risa and Wally stood, unmoving and imperturbable. Before his body could hit the patio, he began to sublimate like any immortal, old or new, and only Suma was surprised by the dainty motes of blue that scattered on the breeze as what had been Marcus, insurance actuary and toy of Delphine, vanished from the earth forever.

"How did you know?" Suma asked me, blanched and shaken.

"He smelled like Sandrine, but not a perfect match. Close enough for me. He must have begun to turn from fucking Delphine every night, not even knowing he was being recreated in her image. It was a matter of time until he began to kill on his own, probably starting with his ex-wife and moving on from there. I asked the girls to confirm it, and, once they did with their little bit of theater, it was time for him to go."

Suma shook her head sadly, her gaze lingering on the empty clothes that Marcus had worn. Risa snatched them up and began walking towards the trash cans on the side of the house, while Wally casually asked us all if we were ready for another bottle of wine. It was business as usual. But, I sensed that Suma was receiving an education in casual death that she could do without if it were her choice.

Being around us, it wasn't. With a steadying hand, I helped her to her feet and led her inside, where she could shake off the adrenaline in a more civilized setting than the scraggly Bermuda grass of our backyard.

"Why don't you stay over? No funny stuff, I promise." I beamed at her, conscious of her mental state. "But you can rest here, and, in the morning, you can head over to the Butterfly for a normal, death-free lunch."

"That sounds like just what I ordered." she replied gamely. Her good humor was returning, and we had wine to drink, so we joined Wally and Risa inside and gave Marcus no further thought. It was as if he had never been born, which was just one of the sad details that immortals brought to bear on innocents, day in and day out.

52

I stayed true to my word. Suma's virtue remained unsullied, at least by my hand. After coffee and some lounging in which we were miraculously alone, Suma asked me a question that caught me off guard as I was rummaging breakfast for us.

"When you were in the Army, did you think about what would happen afterwards? If you killed someone or did things that you thought you would have to answer for later? Like sins?" She was looking past me as she spoke.

It troubled me that she knew that detail of my life, as I couldn't remember telling her, but she had spoken to the girls at length. The topic may have come up. I certainly didn't hide my time overseas.

"I didn't think about it. I was hot and tired, hungry most of the time. Thirsty, miserable. I learned to despise the uncertainty of violence but relied on my team like they were family. The oldest in my squad was only twenty-six. Three of us were married, some had kids. We were all homesick. I would've strangled someone for a cheeseburger that didn't taste like dust. I was the loner among us, but that didn't mean I was an outsider. On the contrary, I was accepted. I always volunteered for shit duties because I knew that I could do the job. Don't get me wrong, I wasn't an exemplary soldier; I just sort of glided through things. Even combat. It was always a little easier for me. But, even though I was a bit different, my team always included me, accepted me. We were forged together. Some of us become men, a few of us died. I'm sure some went nuts. Or are going nuts, slowly. Every time I used my weapon, I did so in the interest of my team, never from raw anger. I was, like I said, floating." I paused to hand Suma a wedge of orange. She took it and inhaled the scent with appreciation.

"I'll never get tired of that smell. Like the sun." she said, nibbling. Around her bites, she asked "But you didn't think about sin?

About whether or not there would be some cost for doing what you were doing?" It was a fair question.

"Are you really asking me if I believe in God?" I countered. "Because the answer has to be yes."

I think that surprised her. She looked expectantly at me for details, finishing her orange.

"It just seems logical to me, that's all" I explained. "I don't know about heaven. I don't think that there is a hell, at least not like some of us portray it. There are no lakes of fire or beasts and ice and darkness. All of those things are here, now, with us every day, so it doesn't make sense to create a place to hold what is already a part of our daily lives. There is fire, endless fire from wars that we make. The cold of loneliness. Beasts that we hunt and kill, or the worst among humanity. Those people are beasts, at least to me. I see what they are capable of, up close and personal, and it's nauseating. And I believe in counterweights. After seeing what we have seen, here, in the dark and sometimes in the light, well, I just think that there has to be something, someone, holding onto the other side of the rope and stopping all of us here from sliding down some shithole to be lost forever. And I think that God doesn't really care what I'm doing, as long as I'm helping to hold the rope, instead of stepping on the heads of everyone who is circling the drain around a long, cold fall into the permanent darkness."

I sliced another wedge of the orange, perfect and simple. So different from all of the rest of what was becoming a very complicated life.

"Are you going to the Butterfly today?" I asked her, handing her the next section of her orange.

Reaching out, she nodded and said,. "I want to eat lunch with my sister and feel normal for ten seconds, not like—*merde!*"- She cursed abruptly in accented French when the orange slipped from her fingers and hit the floor. "Sorry. Clumsy!" she said, abashed at her minor outcry.

"You cuss like a sailor, but not in English?" I asked her, bending down to wipe the floor with a towel. I didn't want her to see my face at that moment. I had heard that same curse, once before. At the beach. With Senya.

"I do" she admitted, sheepish. "My grandfather taught me the best cursing was in French. It has more vibrancy when you're being dirty, don't you think?" she laughed, as she described the potency of lurid cussing in her second tongue.

"That it does" I agreed, with a forced smile. "I hope you enjoy lunch with Boon. It's important to have family. People you can rely on." I told her all this with a pasty grin, knowing that her simple little outburst had revealed who the Baron's informant was and how little I knew about Cazimir, Elizabeth, and everything.

When Suma left, I hurried to Risa's room to find her quietly reading on her laptop. Before I could say anything, she waved me over and pointedly turned the screen for me to see. On it hovered an email from Hayseed, with the simple message *Let's talk, all four of us, video, noon. Most important.* This was highly unusual for him or for any other members of our thin community, but, without any discussion, I told her "I'll go get Wally up and alert. I've got ninety minutes, which gives me one to spare."

With that, I went to wake the beast and Gyro, who was doubtless sharing her bed in all his furry glory.

We assembled in the kitchen, just as we had done the first time we spoke to Cazimir. Wally understood the gravity of the call, so she was ready, reasonably dressed, and had made some overture at grooming. It was a start. I decided that now was as good as any to drop the bombshell that Suma was a turncoat who was feeding information to the Baron.

"Before Hayseed comes on, since we're here, I found out who is working for the Baron." I started, grabbing the girls' undivided attention.

"Who?" they blurted in unison.

"How do you know?" Risa continued, while Wally's wheels began to turn, processing this information.

"Well, it's Suma." I said, expecting the worst. I was right.

"Bullshit. Seriously? How- wha-but she's *family*!" Wally spat, incensed. Risa glowered, already looking for angles.

"Explain," Risa said simply.

I gathered myself, looking quickly at the clock. We had three minutes. Not my best application of Army logistics, but what the hell.

"Senya. Remember her?" I asked, and, when the girls motioned that they did, continued. "The night I met her. At the beach, we were in the alcove of that turquoise hotel next to Vince's; that's where I offed her. Before we were in the clinches, I heard a woman's footsteps following us, then dropping her keys and swearing in French, but it wasn't some tourist who spoke the language naturally, it was accented. At the time, I didn't know how, but as of this morning, I do. It's a Thai accent, and the voice was Suma."

Before there were questions, I pressed on. "I handed her an orange, and she dropped it. She cursed in French. Her grandfather was from Marseilles, and he taught her the language. It was her that night. I know it. Same tone, same accent, same everything."

Risa asked, "Does she know you know?"

I shook my head. "No, I looked down, away, whatever I had to. I know I was shocked as shit, but I hid it. She suspects nothing. The questions are why? To what end? How the hell did the Baron find her?"

"Does she know Elizabeth? That's what I want to know. Because, if she leads that woman to her own family, then she is compromised beyond saving." Risa assessed Suma's level of depravity in sad tones.

Before we could continue, the laptop pinged, and it was time for our chat with Hayseed. I had no idea what to expect, but I knew I was sick of lies.

"I hope he isn't full of shit. I don't know if I can take any more lying and still be anything close to reasonable." I groused, voicing what we all felt.

The man who appeared on the screen looked like anything but a liar. He was in his late fifties and had the bearing of a steady Midwesterner. He had cheerful green eyes over a long nose with salt and pepper hair cut short, but not quite military regulation short. He smiled easily at us and dipped his head in acknowledgement of our image.

"I'll never feel like I've kept up with technology. Just when I think I'm current, something becomes commonplace from the science fiction I read as a kid. I'm Lyle Caldwell. Hayseed, by another name," he introduced himself to us with a nod and waited politely for a reply.

I made our introductions. "I'm Ring Hardigan. This is Risa Wexler." She smiled and said hello. "And Waleska Schmidt, or Wally, which will fit her once you see how she eats." Wally punched my arm and smiled brilliantly at the screen.

Lyle was captivated, even across the miles, which was not lost on Risa, who sighed under her breath.

"I handle most of our actual up-close-and-personal interaction with the immortals. Risa and Wally take care of anything that requires human persuasion, information, logistics, and things like that. And we live together, too, so feel free to say whatever you want. We have no secrets, although we will keep whatever information you discuss today completely private."

That seemed to please Lyle, who folded and unfolded his big, capable looking hands on the table in front of him once before he spoke.

"I have my target cornered. Twelve years of work. I'll finish it tonight." Lyle said in a neutral tone. I recognized it as someone who faces the end of their life's work and cannot see beyond that second. It's a form of mourning, and it was all over his broad, honest face.

Wally asked for details about the creature, giving voice to our collective morbid curiosity.

"There *were* two humans working in congress with the female" he began, "but, as of this morning, only one." He grimaced in memory of the kill. It must have been an entirely different kind of shock to kill a human, or someone who was nearly so. "She's holed up in the subcellar of an abandoned dairy barn, and her remaining partner is injured. I'm letting him bleed out. He's got some skill as a fighter, and the location is just close enough to a populated area that a gun is out of the question for dealing with him. For her, a knife- -just like you've learned, Ring–a knife is what is needed to do the job right." He stopped, drank from a bottle of water, and continued. "Tonight,

I'll take her. She'll be very hungry, a bit weak. I've harried her for a week straight, no meals, and no rest. She's ripe. That doesn't mean it's a sure thing, so we need to talk first, to make certain that what I'm doing is right," he concluded with a questioning look at all of us in turn.

"Right about killing her? What is she, anyway? A ghoul? Right?" I asked.

"Oh, you're right about what she is, Ring. She isn't human, not even close. Her story is, well, I don't know if it's unusual among their kind. She's living a long, slow burn towards complete depravity. In point of fact, she's there now, but her human partners—Helpers, as you named them so aptly—well, they point her like a weapon and follow her, east to west, west to east. With each mile and season, she descends a little further towards complete animalism, to a point where, eventually, even the Helpers cannot reach or communicate with her."

"Is she from that area?" Wally asked, trying to establish a relationship between origin and habit.

"Yes and no," Lyle said thoughtfully. "Yes, she is from here. But not from our time. Or rather, not from the time of European settlers."

I whistled inward. Risa and Wally both looked shocked. *Another old one*. They were popping up in our lives more regularly know. I can't say it was a trend I was comfortable with.

"How old, exactly?" I asked. The answer was worrisome.

"Pre-Columbus. Maybe Neolithic. I don't know. I took a sample, if you can call a finger a sample, of her DNA to the local college and had them test it, as a discreet favor to me. She's something other than what we would call modern American, maybe Clovis. That isn't the only evidence I've had examined as I've tried to pin down her identity. I got close, very close, about three years ago, caught a good look at her feeding, and saw a tattoo on her shoulder. It was grey, a hint of blue, very old. I think it was supposed to be antlers over a moon. It looked primitive and very personal, like something from a cave wall. It was simple but beautiful, quite different from the rest of her. She's a complete horror. Ropy, thin muscles and slate skin, streaked with someone's blood and viscera. Not big on hygiene" he joked. "She has teeth, if you can call them that. A mouthful. Sharp. Long nails, not pointed, but more like a mole. Or a badger. They're formidable. She's strong, can leap like a flea. Long, long black hair, a sodden, greasy mess—it hangs between her shoulder blades like a filthy rope. She's nude, always, although her Helpers have covered her in rough cured furs at times. I think it reminds her of her human life. Maybe they used it to pacify her when they were on the move."

"Why did she move at all? Prey?" Risa asked.

"Prey, sure. But there are undercurrents to her behavior. They bait the traps, she kills, and then they would . . . well, I wondered how they were both staying so young. I found out, and I wish I hadn't" he finished, his cheeks coloring with memory and shame.

"They were fucking her, right?" Wally blurted. Such language out of that mouth.

To his credit, Lyle didn't flinch. "Exactly. At the side of deserted roads. That's how they did it." Before I could interrupt, he explained. "For the last decade, at least, their bait has been a small roadside cross, a memorial. Like where people die in car crashes? You've seen them?"

I had. They were often garishly sad, fading plastic flowers and a crude memorial marking the end of what was usually a young life. I said as much, and he went on.

"They put out a cross with a name that can be anyone. It doesn't matter who, , it's just a detail. Small, wooden, hand-painted. Just another melancholy reminder of some forgotten sorrow. The cross is always at the edge of a larger field, preferably away from lights, not too close to town. Then the Helpers go to work. They used to infiltrate circles of young people, teenagers. They'd take a job at the drive-in, or McDonald's, wherever. And then, when they had access to these kids, they would tell a ghost story."

"About the cross? Or the ghoul?" I asked Lyle, sickened by the elegance of the plan. I could infer where he was going with this narrative.

"Both. I've heard variations going back as far as the earliest days of the frontier, but it's essentially unchanged. The gravesite is haunted, say the Helpers, but only on the night of the new moon. It's an atmospheric detail, but it serves a purpose. The curious come to a darkened, secluded place, unarmed, maybe drunk, giggling, the machismo of the boys in overdrive as they try to impress the girls who shriek at shadows, maybe the boys cop a quick squeeze of titty . . . sorry, I'm just tired of hearing the same story." He gathered his wits and went on, angering with the recollection of this movie that was playing out with every new moon.

"But, for every group of unbelievers who come and go, disappointed, there are the loners. The late arrivals. The genuinely curious. That's whom she hunts, kills. Rending, eating. That's whose blood hits the thirsty soil and draws crows the next day, a cacophony to commemorate someone who will be largely forgotten by the next hard rain. Well, goddamnit, *I won't*, not for secon, now I have this filthy bitch dead to rights in a hole and I'm going to gut her like a carp." He was incensed by his own speech, breathing in quick, shallow gulps. I would have been leery of sitting in the same room with him, his rage was that palpable.

We were taken aback momentarily, during which time Lyle regained his composure and said "I actually have a favor to ask of you. It's about money. Or, rather, spending some money."

"Okay. Umm, well, what about it?" I offered, cautiously.

"I'm not going to lie; I don't leave these immortals their worldly goods when I send them to the skies. I know that their wealth is ill-gotten, but I believe that it can be well spent. Do you understand?" Lyle inquired of all three of us.

We did, and we agreed. It was our policy, and we stated it, clearly. I went one step further and revealed the nature of our relationships with Boon and Pan and how they were extended family to us.

"In fact, I think we agree that, if anything happened to us, Liz Brenneman would be appointed executor of our collective estate. We trust her implicitly and know that our money would go to the right places— Boon, Pan, their kids, and anyone else who needed it." I elaborated. Lyle seemed impressed, and his body language changed, relaxing visibly when I gave him the framework of how we spent the money we collected from immortals. He nodded to himself as if reaching a decision.

"I think it's time for me to get ready for my visit. Thank you for taking the time to chat; it's a rarity to have real interactions anymore, after all these years alone." Lyle placed his hands flat on the table from which he spoke. They looked like weather-beaten wood.

Risa asked him in a rush, "Are you alone because of the ghoul, whatever she is called?" She was curious but respectful. Lyle had the aura of a gentleman, he deserved it.

He looked away and then at us, in turn, memory alive on his face and uncomfortably real.

"My daughter. Allison. She was the loner riding up last on a squeaky bicycle. The Helpers had placed a cross by the road three miles from my house. I was so busy, so involved in my own pursuit of money, I didn't retain that my own daughter told me she was riding her bike on a dark, moonless road to see a monster who was supposed to lurk in a shadowed ditch. And, because I was a selfish, thoughtless bastard, my own flesh and blood, the baby I held . . . she worshipped me from the minute her mother left, and I never paid her the respect and attention she deserved. What a brave and funny little child, so resilient, so loving. And I ignored her to the point that she rode a second-hand bike to the place where she was butchered and eaten like a prize hog, all alone. Even when she was with me, she was alone, and she died alone. And then those Helpers fucked that ghoul insensate, drawing life from her, just as she did from my daughter. That's how they're staying so young, you know? They rut like beasts after her kills, splattered with the blood of an innocent and howling their pleasure at the sky. And tonight, she dies. She dies baying at my hand, and then I can die, my life's work complete." And with that, he cut the connection, and we sat in horrified silence, edging closer to each other and thanking God that we did not know his pain.

Dinner was a muted affair where we tried to avoid talking about Lyle and whether he could survive his encounter with his daughter's killer. We ate listlessly and said as few words as possible, the pall of a child's passing lingering with us into the night.

The three of us fell asleep huddled together on the couch, all sharing the fear that, tonight, Lyle's life would end, but not his work.

From Risa's Files

Lyle Gaines Caldwell, 62, passed on to be with the Lord. A well-known and respected businessman, he built the area's most successful heavy farm implement dealership over three decades of work. He was preceded in death by his parents, his ex-wife, Marilyn, and his daughter, Allison. He leaves behind no family, and his will asks that, in lieu of flowers, donations be made to the Great Plains Missing Children's Fund. He will be interred at Sulfur Bluff Cemetery. There will be no services per his request.

53

Florida

If I've ever been a sleepwalker, I certainly don't remember it, but the next three days seemed to approximate my suspicions about what it might be like. The news of Suma was schismatic, a fundamental betrayal that left us in a position so unwelcome we weren't sure how to proceed. Risa and Wally would start a conversation on the topic, only to trail off in frustration. There was no solution that did not involve harming Boon and Pan. There was no direction that did not raise the specter that we were already in mortal danger due to Suma's lies. In short, we were fucked. And I hated every second of the powerlessness that accompanied knowing we had to find a resolution, regardless of the destruction it caused.

Over the next days, it was Risa who began asking questions first. We were watching Gyro bark at the ducks patrolling the seawall when she began to pepper Wally and me with a litany of queries.

"We know that the immortals don't necessarily like each other, right? It could be a bizarre form of sibling rivalry, or maybe elitism between the different age groups . . . I'm not sure. I think it's reasonable to start with some basics, like who benefits from knowing about our activities. Or is there even a benefit?" Risa asked us, beginning a dialogue encompassing all of the murder and weirdness that seemed to be accelerating around us.

"Follow the money" Wally replied. "Immortals can make or take wealth at will from the living, yes? What is their most important currency? Their equivalent to money?" It was a brilliant point. Until that second, I had been trapped in my thinking. Why would the everlasting care about money like we did? There was one thing that they all craved, every single one we met and killed.

"Power." I announced, and the girls quickly agreed. "They all love power. They lord it over us, exploit us, and toy with us. It's their drug of choice. So, if they love it so much, it must mean that it isn't an unlimited resource, right? They compete with each other for their positions?" I asked, uncertainly. I was thinking on the fly and unsure of my direction.

Risa asked, "If an immortal had the most power, it would reign. What is their kingdom? Is it here? Over all of us? Or is it actually something we cannot see?"

A thought pushed forth from my memory. "Sandrine. She told me about their power structure without meaning to, I think, but I didn't realize it until just now. She said that their master had built a labyrinth beneath the earth, under the forest. An empire we did not know about. I thought she was speaking in metaphors, but now I'm not sure. What if it's real, or at least something that is real to the immortals?"

"You men like Hell?" Wally asked thoughtfully.

"Exactly, but not like the Hell of our literature. More like a goal, a tangible thing that they control as a reward for their dominance. We know they crave power, right? Well, what if their rule isn't permanent? What if they can rise and fall in the hierarchy of the immortals based on . . . something? I don't know what, but they must be mobile within their structure. They would have to in order to chase power. Otherwise, wouldn't they just feed on us without end and let that be their reward?" I wondered. It was a Gordian knot of suppositions and assumptions. I wasn't sure that I would ever understand the motivations of immortals, but I thought that, since they had once been human, maybe we could grasp *that* remaining kernel of their drive.

Risa pulled at her lip and spoke. "How much would an immortal gain by bringing the three of us to heel?"

"Well, since we kill them, I would think quite a bit. Maybe enough to overthrow someone ahead of them in the pecking order, so to speak." I said, placing a modest value on our collectively lethal presence. I knew we were worth a king's ransom to the right creatures, but I have flashes of immodesty.

Wally spoke up. "We cannot be killed easily, right? It would require planning, much planning. These immortals have much more time than we do. So, they would plan for something like killing us, or whatever it is that would be done. They would plan for a long time, maybe longer than we think possible. We think like humans because we are humans, they think with a different clock ticking in the background. What if it was no accident that we met? That the three of us were pushed together, fall into this life, and we fit very well. And, then, we are pointed, like a gun, at someone specific—by someone else, who wants to move up this ladder in Hell. Past another immortal, to take more power, and eliminate some rivals along the way?"

It was brilliant. Find three kids who fear nothing. Give one a horse to prove it, the other a brush with death, and the third a knife to plunge in a leering face. Then, when the time is right, put them together, and let nature take its course, all of which meant that evil incarnate can plan on a scope I could not envision. Until now.

Our lives were changing. Gravity had found us, a heavy stone that was pulling us down, or forward, if I was being optimistic. Toward what, we were uncertain. Each encounter, each day carried inertia that sharpened my senses and kept my head on a swivel. My combat personality was at the surface every second. I did not have moments of lassitude, where the first decades of my life had been largely free of purpose or tension. I was getting tired, edgy. I felt an inarticulate need for a break, any break, something that we could hang our collective hopes on to bring the roiling waters of our current life to a glassy calm. I wanted the jewelry, or at least I thought I did. I wasn't sure that I really wanted to know the truth about the Baron, or Elizabeth and her daughters? Sisters? Whatever their relation might be, they were certainly in competition. My younger self would have relished the upcoming afternoon of carnal pleasure with Delphine, simply for the sake of the flesh. Now, I knew that there was genuine risk, perhaps even the cost of what I increasingly believed to be a very real soul that rested in my body, somewhere beyond the reach of reason but close enough for me to feel.

And lurking, at the edge of my vision and perception, was what was underneath the forest. Did we really want to know if Hell was real?

Did we really want to meet who reigned?

From Risa's Files

Dear Ring,

I am pleased to write you of Miss Delphine's upcoming visit. She is most excited about meeting you and has instructed me to extend a special invitation for your encounter. Rather than impose upon your hospitality, she has chosen to entertain you on her recently acquired yacht, a truly sumptuous vessel that has just undergone a tasteful redesign with her particular tastes in mind. I'm certain you will find it to be a singular experience, much like her company. The vessel will be ready for your visit on Friday, and Miss Delphine's driver will pick you up at your home at two o'clock in the afternoon. This will allow you time for pre-dinner conversation and champagne on the deck of the soon-to-be-renamed Inquisitor. *The setting really is quite spectacular, and she is most anxious for you to tour her newest acquisition. It seems the previous owner lost his passion for the sea, and many other things, much to the boon of Miss Delphine.*

I've readied a 46L dinner jacket, slacks, and wardrobe for your convenience, so please feel free to bring yourself, the gift, and a willingness to enjoy yourself for what should be a most stellar weekend.

Respectfully,
Joseph

54

Florida

"What takes this glorified hooker four days to get ready? What the hell does she have planned for you, anyway?" Risa sounded peevish, but I think it was the idea of me lounging on a yacht that made her jealous.

"She knows my taste in women and is undergoing a full wash, buffing, steaming her undercarriage, doubtless some sort of waxing thing or - whatever it is you women do when you want to reel in the big fish." I announced with modesty. It was good to be wanted, even if it was due to my ill-gotten jewelry rather than my dashing looks and magnetism. I'd take what I could get, especially if it involved silk sheets on a superyacht. And maybe a roll in the hay or three at the hands of an ageless sex goddess who was probably double-jointed. That thought I kept to myself out of a desire to remain free of bruises for my big day on the water. I'm smart like that.

Before Risa could deliver a punch with her tiny, hard fist, or some other stinging rebuke, Wally came into the house, mumbling over an envelope that looked suspiciously important. I was right because she handed it to me wordlessly and sat down at the kitchen table. She began running her foot absently over Gyro, who occupied the bulk of the cool tile floor. We were all present. Later, it would seem fitting, given the contents of the letter, but, just then, it was another moment in our lives, unremarkable. Familiar, comfortable. That was before I opened an envelope that was bitter but rewarding. That moment was a give and take in which we were given an opportunity to help at the cost of a good soul. Risa opened the letter, scanning it quickly and briefly referring to pages beyond the top sheet. I knew enough of her reading speed to sit patiently, as did Wally. Then, Risa delivered the bad news first with no filter.

"Lyle is dead," Risa said softly. "He fought and lost. Here, read it." She handed me the sheaf, disgusted and saddened by the loss of someone we had hardly known. But we knew *what* Lyle represented, even if we did not know much of the man. He had been a bulwark against evil, plying his trade out of vengeance and a greater sense of altruism than many people possessed. Now, he was gone. Looking at the letter and reading the high points, our conversation sprang into clarity because Lyle, a man who had built and sold an American success story, had just left every penny to us.

I slid the packet to Wally, who began to read, while her long finger tailed down the pages as she consumed each line of the lifechanging news.

We were now owners of two accounts that had several million dollars, none of which we needed. Lyle had known that, and his exploratory inquiry with us had advanced an idea that had languished for two years. We needed an attorney to help distribute the funds discreetly, a sort of windfall for the families left behind when their loved ones walked away from their lives into the predatory arms of an immortal. We needed someone trustworthy. We needed Liz Brenneman, so I asked aloud "Dinner tonight? Let's invite Liz and bring her up to speed. If she says yes, we're good. If not, I don't think we're hurt too badly, but I don't like making her unnecessarily aware of the real world, so to speak. What about it?" I asked the girls. They were attuned to the ragged history Liz had overcome to live again. I didn't want the sole responsibility of shaking that foundation, no matter how noble the intent.

Wally spoke first. "Yes. Full disclosure, tonight. She will agree because she loves her daughter, and, at heart, I think she is a crusader. Inside her is the will, we will give her the means."

I raised my hand. "I volunteer to cook. Flatbread pizza, salad, no wine. Fruit tea. I'll get dessert while I'm out—cake okay?" Two quick nods to my entirely rhetorical question, and I was out the door. We had plans to make, and we would be well fed.

Liz arrived at seven, and we ushered her with genuine warmth, as she has that effect on people. Gyro leaned appreciatively against her, jostling a woman half his weight with his enthusiastic brand of affection. Risa had suggested earlier that we let Liz ask whatever she needed to in order to get comfortable with the fact that world had an entire unknown layer, populated with a brand of viciousness she had not seen, despite her occupation. She was used to asking questions, as well as being told stories of variable truth. How she reacted was anyone's guess, although my instincts said that her intellect would allow her to assess and qualify the evidence fairly quickly. I began with a simple question that we had more or less scripted prior to the dinner.

"Liz, if we gave you a chance to really help people who have gone through a tragedy they cannot understand, and, we could pay you enough to care for your daughter and yourself, would you consider coming to work for the three of us as our legal and financial counsel?" I laid the proposition out as succinctly as I could, knowing that a soft sell of something so irregular would be impossible, and probably offensive.

Liz took our collective measure, and, seeing no incumbent laughter, set her tea down, smoothing her skirt with her hands out of habit.

She spoke slowly, and clearly. I could tell she was measuring her words. "We are friends, or at least friendly. So telling you my earnings are no revelation, you're my landlord, and you know my history. However, the opposite is true, as well. I know enough of your life to place some general values on what your holdings are. Until now, I never really asked how you earn your livings, but the fact that we are discussing this matter means, in all likelihood, that you've had a windfall. A fairly significant one, if I'm guessing. This leads me to believe that you have enough money to hire me. Also, since you know how I feel about, well, who I represent and what I do, I can presume that you aren't asking me to do anything illegal. Which leads me to the real question, I guess. What do you want me to do with the money that you have recently acquired, and why me?" She folded her hands in her lap and leaned back on the couch, her body language becoming that of a receiver rather than speaker.

"We're killers." It was Wally who broke the ice. Liz didn't blink. But we had even more of her attention than a moment earlier, if that was possible.

"And you do this legally?" Liz asked, dubious.

"We don't kill humans. Or animals, for that matter" I began, "but, rather than me tell you a decade of history, or try to do such a thing, we have a different idea. A format you might be more willing to trust. And you don't have to do anything except read."

With that, Risa flipped her laptop around, setting it on Liz' skirt. The screen was open to a document titled, simply, *Risa's Files*, which was as complete a database of sin and retribution as we could create. Immediately, Liz grasped what we were asking her, and, with a quiet settling into the cushions, she began to read.

From Risa's Files

Subject: Male, human, late thirties. Caucasian. Altered, drugs and alcohol. Assaulted Liz B., who was incoherently drunk and passed out in her car at Center. Subject was persuaded by Ring to leave the area after a brief physical altercation. Ring unhurt, subject no longer had the use of his left arm. Loose teeth were put in his pants pocket, admonished not to return to the area. Not immortal, merely a predator passing through. Do not expect to see him again, as he had a healthy desire to live when questioned by Ring.

The first rays of dawn arrived in an orange whisper as Liz finished her reading, closing the screen gently with a click. She began stretching her back in a grand, lush, groaning gesture, arms skyward, to shake off the effects of a long, immobile session of intense concentration. She had called the babysitter hours earlier when it became apparent that her task was going to involve more than a cursory glance at a few files. Her eyes were bright as I approached her with a glass of juice; I had risen earlier and let the girls and Gyro sleep in the massive heap they formed on my bed. I spent the night on the couch, listening to the tapping of Liz' fingers as she scrolled through the record of our personal vendetta against the undying.

"What do you think?" I asked, handing her the glass.

She drummed her fingers on her leg, looking around. "It's like finding out that my entire childhood has come back to life–every nightmare, every creature under the bed and in the dark water of my imagination . . . everything that I left behind in the light of reason, it's all back. And it's real. And you kill them? Apparently with ease?" She shook her head in amazement.

I gave a single slashing gesture to disabuse her of the notion that what we did was easy. "Not always. I have been injured, badly. I nearly died recently. The ones we are dealing with, they seem to be much older. Smarter, and more capable of planning in the long term. We think maybe that our entire living situation" I waved around at the quiet house, "might be a construct of one of them. A grand experiment—for what purpose, we don't know, but maybe you can help us understand. And I know you can help us clean up the wreckage, make those left behind a little more comfortable. Less frightened of how they will live, at least?"

"A crusade, like you said. I'll do it, but there is one issue that comes to mind before we agree to anything." Her mouth was set in a grim line.

"Oh? Tell me. Is it something I can fix? Offer? Just ask." We needed Liz, and I wanted to close the deal.

"The law? It will have to be stretched, on occasion. Nothing fraudulent or risky, since it's your money, but we'll have to create dummy insurance payouts, wills, probate. Trusts from long forgotten relatives. Fictitious awards or stock benefits. Anything to create a wall between the victims' families and the truth. And they cannot ever, ever meet you or the girls. The risk would be astronomical, both in terms of their finances and their lives. I don't think you want glory, but you must remain anonymous. Can you do that?" Her request was reasonable and made excellent sense.

I stuck out my hand. "Agreed, counselor. Your rent is waived. Your salary is one third more than whatever you make now, plus certain benefits that may come our way. We'll share. And, thank you. We need you to help, to make some of the wrongs less permanent, maybe pull some good from the ashes."

She gave my hand a firm pump and pulled me close for a hug. Whether that was because I was killing immortals or helping provide for her future, I couldn't be sure, but I enjoyed it, just the same.

55

The mood in our house had improved considerably. Risa and Wally took the boat for a victory lap to celebrate and soak up some sun. I suspect beer was a critical component to their plan, and, as I was not invited, I opted to visit the Butterfly for an early dinner. Since the Suma issue still hung over us like Damocles' lost cutlery, there was a chance that my meal would be awkward, at least in my mind. I resolved to keep my routine unchanged, or at least outwardly similar, until we could form a solution that didn't bring us collective heartbreak.

Boon's brilliant smile greeted me moments later as she took me, arm in arm, to a table near the east window. I exhaled fully, feeling tension leaving me as the warmth of the room permeated my mood. A blessing of calm enveloped me before my tea could arrive and Pan waved from the kitchen door as I mouthed *prawns* to Boon, a one-word order based on the heavenly smell drifting from a nearby table. This was home. There was so much more here than I had initially realized when they opened the restaurant. I was at ease from my first steps in the door, which made my actions toward Suma and her lies so magnified, so critical. So permanent.

Boon joined me with my meal, picking scandalously at my plate with merry eyes as I slapped at her hand. It was a dance we did often. She crunched the savory head of an enormous prawn and smiled around her pilfered treat as I did my best not to gulp my tea. Pan had been heavy with the chilies, and I had a thin sheen of sweat on my forehead early in the meal.

"Too hot for the tame American?" Boon teased, laughing and handing me another napkin to wipe my brow. Pan was being sadistic with the spices, and I would pay now. And later.

"Your hubby is cruel, but I can't stop eating." I confessed, dredging another prawn through the vivid red sauce pooling on my plate. "Where is Suma?" I looked for her, realizing she had not popped over yet.

"Hair. Nails. She has an appointment, and she's doing girly stuff. I told her my hair and nails were perfect, to which she snorted and informed me that, if I didn't get my nails done, she was going to refuse being seen with me in public." Boon appraised her fingers and wiggled them as if proving Suma's assessment was wrong. It was. Her hands were like a pianist's, long and thin. She sighed and stood, announcing her return to work.

"See you later. I'll tell Suma you stopped by." Her blissful lack of awareness gave me a pang of regret for something that had not happened, but could not be avoided. I finished my tea and left, my thoughts making the end of my meal far less pleasant than the beginning.

56

Wally stood brandishing a phone at me as I closed the door to my truck. Her face was a mix of anger and curiosity, never good on anyone but particularly worrisome on her. I took the proffered phone, wondering what disaster this particular call might bring.

"Ring, Deb Broward here. Jim would've called, but he's gotten himself worked up and had to use his inhaler, so I'll do the talking for the next few minutes." She was speaking hurriedly, with a hint of anger.

"I take it this isn't a quality control call about the truck?" I knew better.

"I wish, but we know we've got your business. Why waste the call? We just had a visitor asking some questions. He flounced in here, asking for you, said he was willing to triple whatever we paid for the jewelry you were selling us. Sound familiar?"

Did it ever. "What name did he use?" I was betting on Joseph. His arrogance was boundless.

"Joseph Lamarck. Said he worked for a buyer who knew you, and that they were *very* interested in buying any and every piece you've sold us over the past year. I'm not even going to ask how he found us; I imagine you'll tie up that loose end. But, as a friend, let me tell you something: whoever he represents has more money than God. I can smell it, and they don't give a shit about anything other than what they want. I've met his type before; he was so assured, oily, smug. He made my skin crawl, and that takes a heluva lot with me working in this business, you know?" She sounded worried.

Oh, Suma. "Deb, there is no loose end, I have it under control. I wanted my little side job to be- discovered, let's say." I lied, as smoothly as I could. "You're not at any risk. The hole will be closed this Friday, and you'll never hear from him again. They think I have a larger collection. I don't. But that misconception works for me, so we'll just let that ride, okay?"

Jim and Deb were no amateurs. I knew that they would be fine. Her next sentence proved it. "Oh, we caught on quickly. We told young Joseph that we didn't have any other jewelry from you but that we'd be happy to sell him the gold coins you'd liquidated, at a mere four hundred percent markup. He said he'd think about it and left. Very polite, that one."

I laughed heartily. They were slick. My concern about how those two horse traders could handle a fishing expedition was unwarranted, even if the pole was being cast by a seasoned dandy like Joseph. I said my goodbye and thought ahead to my upcoming time with Delphine. I didn't have multiple pieces of the Baron's jewelry, as Joseph had inferred, and probably still believed.

This made it the perfect time for me to begin bluffing, and I had a clear idea how I was going to do it.

57

"I'm telling you we should remain distant; let's keep this under wraps until we know which direction we're going to go with Suma, the Baron. *Everything.*" Risa was adamant. As usual, she was also right, which made arguing senseless. I could tell by the obstinate set of Wally's lip that she was in agreement, and that meant no contact with the Baron, even for chitchat. It was Friday morning, and the sun was pouring in the house to announce that today was a day for romance. My date with Delphine had arrived.

Joseph called, announcing that a driver would pick me up, and no, he didn't need our address, thank you, as a professional, it was his place to know his Mistress' clients and . . . the rest, I tuned out, liking him even less if that were possible. I packed a simple bag. I don't own a tuxedo, despite Wally's enthusiasm for the orchestra. First, I packed the only two things that I truly needed: my knife and the necklace. Both were keys to bringing us closer to Elizabeth, and, hopefully, some sort of peace.

Risa was in a foul mood. "That bitch has neatly cut us out of the picture. She's smart. A boat we can't get on, where we can't watch you, help you. We don't even know how many staff will be onboard or if they're all immortals. Or, even worse, Helpers who want to let blood merely to please their mistress." She stewed in her anger.

Wally was fidgety, a sure sign that she was unhappy about these developments. I grasped both their shoulders gently. "I know she's getting me alone. That's fine, we knew that would happen, so let's not obsess on possibilities. Let's plan for realities. I go in, drop the hint that there is more loot, maybe she gives me the royal treatment or maybe not. Either way, I'm on board a vessel owned by someone who knows and competes with Elizabeth. That's a win in my book."

I was right, but they didn't have to like it. A knock at the door broke the tension of the room, and Wally opened up to a driver in black livery, wearing an expression of competence and professionalism. I had expected nothing less.

"Mr. Hardigan? I'm Crow Hop, your driver for the afternoon. May I take your bag?" He smiled at me with even, white teeth that stood out from his ebony skin. He was in his late twenties, six feet tall, athletically built, and had an intelligent, friendly face. I was expecting a cadaverous relic in moth-eaten tails. Crow Hop, along with his name, was a complete surprise.

"Thank you, Crow Hop. Goodbye for now, roomies. I'll be back tomorrow." I let the charade speak for itself, handing my bag to Crow Hop and stepping outside. A Rolls Royce Silver Ghost sat idling silently, magnificent and shining with the care properly accorded a classic. Approving, I went through the open door into an interior that made clouds seem like flypaper by comparison. I slid smoothly across the leather as Crow Hop pulled away from my home, pointing the nose of the Ghost towards the water and Delphine. The necklace rested cool against my chest and my knife was cinched perfectly in the small of my back. I was ready.

"How did you acquire such an unusual name?" I asked across the distance to the front.

"It's actually a fairly mundane reason. I was a running back in college, and I tended to hop side to side when I was in traffic. My high school team mascot was a crow, so there you have it. No mystical family history, no heroic deeds. Just me, hopping side to side and trying not to get crushed by guys who looked like elephants wearing helmets." He smiled as he delivered the story of his name. It was a good one, and I told him so as we pulled into the parking area adjutant to the *Inquisitor's* slip. He opened the door in a smooth motion and gathered my bag from the trunk while I stood, sizing up the ostentatious yacht. It was a bit much for my tastes, but I would do my best to make do. I'm a trooper when it comes to roughing it.

The gangway was polished aluminum, bright and scuffed from countless feet ringing the grooves with heels and luggage. At the top of the stairs stood my nemesis, Joseph, resplendent with his unique arrogance. It could be no one else, and, when he spoke, I knew I was right.

"Mister Hardigan, we are delighted to have you aboard for holiday," he began, in a vaguely southern accent with European syntax that was as off putting as his cologne. I gritted my teeth and shook his hand. I hate it when Americans drop words in an attempt to be continental. It's phony, but, for all I knew, he *was* a continental. Perhaps I was just spoiling for a fight with him. I walked aboard without further offense, and Crow Hop said goodbye, unobtrusively vanishing in an instant. Good help, there.

"Would you care for a cocktail before your shower?" Joseph asked, poised like a raptor as his eyes furtively searched me for evidence of the necklace. *Bad form, Joseph. Far too obvious.*

I decided to go all in, right away. "Here, Joseph." I handed the necklace over after making a show of removing it from my neck. "This one is for the lady as payment for this weekend."

He didn't miss a trick. "This one?" His eyes glittered with greed. Or something even more repugnant. "You mean that there may be other opportunities for you to spend time with Miss Delphine?" I loved his vernacular. It implied I was being canonized by fucking his mistress. I can appreciate that type of adroit language, especially on the fly.

"Yep. I just figured we would see how it went and all, you know, this being my first time in a long time with a lady, if you know what I mean." He both did and did not know, but he presented a knowing, conspiratorial face to me, just two guys enjoying a joke about potentially mind-bending sex with an immortal hooker. You know, everyday stuff. I glanced down, gathering myself for a question, the picture of an awed plebe.

"Joseph, what does she look like? I never even thought to ask." Oh, how shy I could be. It made prying information free and setting a mood much easier, especially when dealing with my supposed betters. Joseph did not disappoint me.

"Miss Delphine is hard to describe. Her beauty is timely, and timeless. She is actually smaller than one would think, given her considerable presence. She is womanly, flawless, but nothing of her body harkens to the days when steatopygia was all the rage. A phase that has thankfully passed." Joseph delivered this opinion assuming

I would be ignorant or cowed by the topic. As a veteran of multiple art history classes in which I only occasionally slept, I decided to fire back.

"I always envisioned Venusian women with antennae rather than ponderous breasts, but I'm a dreamer." I indicated with my hand that he should precede me to wherever we were going. I didn't trust him, regardless of his fluttering hands and pomposity.

After a long hallway vanished behind us, we arrived at a set of doors suited for a mansion. They swung inward silently. I admit it; the stench of wealth was everywhere, and I found the aroma agreeable.

"This is your personal shower room. You'll dress elsewhere, just through there" he glanced at a second door, equally as impressive, "to prepare for cocktail hour. Then, we'll dress you accordingly for dinner when Miss Delphine calls." He finished with a sniff that implied I would be fortunate to emerge from this room attired to be a ship's mechanic, let alone a companion of his mistress.

"That will be all, Joseph" a voice carried from behind us. There stood Delphine, in the flesh. She dismissed him with a squint, an expression that invited no discussion, but was clothed with a sweet smile that softened her tone—but only just. He inclined his head in a near bow and silently walked past me, closing the doors with a muffled thump. We were alone, and I felt myself being measured so thoroughly that any disguise on my part was futile. Delphine would know.

She was five feet three, or four, and her hair was waist-length blonde of a hue that hinted at short summers and rocky coastlines. A simple robe covered part of her womanly shape, the remainder of her toned body visible beneath the hem. Legs that were athletic but sculpted ended where the fabric began in a taunt that was impossible to ignore. She was bronzed, by what sun I couldn't guess, because there was not a flaw on her body that I could see. Full pink lips were drawn back in a smile that radiated predation and bubbling laughter, an unsettling blend of contrasts that many men had doubtless found endlessly thrilling. But her eyes, locked on to me with warmth and caring that was too intent to be feigned, the eyes were beyond anything I was prepared for. Blue, but shot with greys, and containing a depth that should have been frigid, drawing me to her just as she raised her fine-boned arms and offered me an embrace that I knew was the edge of a hole. A pit with a long, silent fall, full of pleasure and forgetting, crowded with the bones of men before me. Before I could muster a stand, I felt the heft of her breasts against my abdomen, and her smell crowded my senses in a short but decisive seduction. I willingly lost to her sensuality if I even fought at all. Her mouth was on mine, briefly, and she exhaled against my skin softly, a whispering caress. My body reacted so swiftly, I actually blushed. I was in deep water and tiring fast.

"To the shower. I'll wash you myself, and then we'll drink and eat, and you can have me in every way imaginable. And some you can't." Her honeyed voice was muffled in my shirt, but I felt every vibration of her mouth against me like a tuning fork wired to my libido.

I went with her. What else could I do?

58

I was disrobed slowly, expertly. Her awareness was keen, every touch or gesture measured. The consummate professional in a business that bridged pleasure and sexual power, she was even more erotic in the rising steam filling the cavernous shower. Stone walls surrounded us, a spatter of oranges and whites, with crystalline counterpoints that danced in the mist.

As I sat on a tiled bench, she knelt before me, removing my shoes and socks. I should have felt in command, but I didn't. Her subtle smile robbed me of even the hint of control. *Down, boy. You've got all night.*

"What are these walls? It looks like a meteor was cut into slices and mortared in place." I was frankly admiring.

She looked up with pleasure at my cognition of her tastes. "It's a base stone from the opal mines of Coober Pedy, Australia. Dreadfully hot there, I'm told. I had it shipped in and cut on site. I rather enjoy the irregularities; they frame the remaining opal quite nicely." Gems as tile. The mark of truly limitless money.

Rising, I shrugged out of my button-down shirt before she could continue with her exploration of my body. My knife made no sound, safely wrapped in the cotton fabric as it dropped to the floor. Thankfully, Delphine made no move to retrieve it. I hoped Joseph wouldn't be acting as my valet, at least until I could attempt to secret the blade somewhere else. I had had the foresight to wear slacks that she unzipped and dropped without ever taking her eyes from mine. Her robe slid from her shoulders, revealing round breasts with pink aureoles, attendant to my presence. Those shadowed a flat stomach ending in a secretive mound of soft curls, shy as a maiden's smile. We stepped into the spray together.

"The necklace is beautiful. Alive. Let me ask, Ring, do you think that I am worth the price?" Her fingers traced the line of my arm as she spoke.

"Yes. I think that you would be worth as much gold as I could carry here on my back, if need be, but I don't think you care." Her touch had unleashed the philosopher in me, which was incongruous with my erection. She didn't seem to mind.

"Quite right. I don't care about how much. Quantity over quality is rarely satisfying, unless every . . . single . . . experience is flawless." She punctuated the words with her hands, pulling me to her in an invitation that was not to be denied. I lifted her small frame and drove upward into flesh and heat, her shoulders slapping against the tile brought all the way from Australia to act as the backstop for my fuck of the century. I could not do anything she had not seen before, nor would I try. I checked my ego at the door and concentrated on the incredibly close quarters of her, wrapped against my length while her heels dug into my thighs with complete disregard for my health. The abandon was total. I ignored her needs with each lunge higher, higher into her, higher into the confusion and distant betrayal that I felt, but that fleeting second was a lie, driven away when she clenched down on me and I released, her tongue in my mouth without mercy. We sank against the wall into a sitting position, me still pulsing in her with the memories of every woman I had ever know, discarded now after wilting under her sun.

"Yesss. Shhhh. Again, in a moment, you'll be ready." Her optimism was accompanied with a kiss that drew me out and reignited my want, even though I was already in her to the hilt. It wasn't far enough.

"What about dinner?" I was only halfhearted in my hunger. I knew she had drawn from me, ever the predator, even as I took my pleasure, but it had not been much because I was alert. I began moving her up and down slowly, no part of me leaving her warmth.

"Dessert first." She held my face with her hands, kissing me with lips that seared and cooled. I did not argue.

To me, Delphine was a teacher, her disciplines being Flesh and Want. The next hours were a catharsis in which I was given lessons in craving and how to act upon that desire with her endlessly inventive sexuality. Her brand of intimacy stretched my definition of the word. Pervasive eroticism in her every move turned the mundane into acts of secrecy and lust from the completion of our shower. I saw, up close, exactly what real power could do.

"Joseph, my things. I will ready here for dinner" she said to the air, her voice even and pleasant. I heard footfalls before her order was complete, and, a moment later, a bustling Joseph knocked and entered the sauna-like conditions of my bathroom with two leather cases, which he began to distribute with robotic efficiency. Makeup, a hand mirror, perfume. A fine powder in a lapis lazuli crock, smelling of delicacy and summer. She looked at Joseph not once as he finished his work and exited. Delphine presented her back to me, a gift for my hands.

"Dry me, Ring?" It was less than an order, but more than a suggestion. I began to towel her, working towards her breasts and stomach as she purred, stretching her arms skyward with childish joy. "Very nice. You can be quite gentle when asked."

She watched me in the mirror, which had cleared enough for me to savor her form. "Tell me, lover, will you be as gentle when you use the knife you wrapped in your shirt? It's quite an unusual blade, very old. Knives are so personal. You must be made of sterner stuff than the average suitor who has sought me out through the years."

Despite my surprise, I kept both hands moving. I was inwardly impressed with her staff, her awareness. Her savvy. After her performance in the shower, I should not have been. This was a woman with few weaknesses, least of all being threatened by my cumbersome attempt to smuggle a threat on my person.

"I promise to leave the knife on the floor if you'll still have me. For dinner." Her discovery was an opening gambit, nothing more. I was determined to stay, if not for the sex, than at least for any chance to glean something of use from our experiences. At least that's what I would tell the girls.

"Hm. Dinner. Of course. Powder me?" She turned to face me, handing over a small carved brush, electric blue. It was smoothed by time and small hands. Tilting her head back slightly, she guided my hand in long, shallow strokes across her breasts, her neck, and one playful swipe circling her navel. I began to see the value in her approach, as the intimacy of our moment was overwhelming. It was humanizing her without my consent, binding me tighter to her after only two short hours. We were pairing off, becoming bonded not just from the physical contact but from the view into her feminine sanctum, where she rebuilt herself from a post-coital glow into the polished beauty she presented to the world. I was transfixed. When we left my dressing room, I was clothed in more than her choice of wardrobe. I wore the possessiveness of a mate, with discomfort, although her arm through mine quieted my tongue. In a moment, we were seated at a table overlooking the deck and the bustle of the waterway. That place on the other side of the smoked glass seemed a different planet. I was glad for the feeling and reveled in the proximity of her aura.

"Have you an appetite?" Delphine was again the gracious hostess, no hint of my transgression to be found in her tone. Wine awaited us upon our arrival, which I sipped and found its quality confusing to my pedestrian palate. I tasted sunshine, grass, and even Delphine. Her presence was light on my tongue.

"I could eat something small. I don't want to be lethargic. Just in case." I kept my voice neutral. Coquetry was not my forte with an immortal whose skill was my undoing. She snapped her fingers once, and a waiter I had not seen before delivered two small tureens of soup, ladling a thin bone china bowl to the brim with the steaming liquid. Brown kelp swam in the clear broth, along with slivers of field onions. Small snails, pulled from their yellow and black shells, lay poached in the bowl, their former homes used as decorative flourishes along the rim. It smelled like the sea and earth all at once.

She saw my question as I studied the soup. "It's a restorative, particularly for men. A recipe I reconstructed from my childhood. I spent many days prizing those snails from the rocks, dodging the waves that threw cold spume over my head." Her wistfulness told me that such days had been a long time ago. The soup told me that she remembered, perhaps painfully, and carried the river of time with her as a burden that was not entirely without regret.

She sipped the soup directly from the bowl, delicately inhaling with each venture close to the rim.

"I was born on an island, isolated. Not even a sail on the horizon, unending waves of cobalt rolling past the limits of my vision. Turf greener than any I've seen since, crying seabirds and the ceaseless bass drum of the waves, eating my home away one grain of sand at a time. I learned patience there, Ring. I learned about how beauty in a confined space can be a powerful weapon, and how the consumption of a lesser was not just survival, but delicious." She popped a snail in her mouth and rolled it sensually once on a very pink tongue, swallowing and winking at me lasciviously. So, she could still be playful. That was good. For now.

We ate and drank in reasonable peace, although the sexual tension remained thick. *As if it could dissipate around this creature*, I thought as she dabbed her mouth and rose. Pushing my chair back, she deposited herself on my lap and held my glass up for me to sip. Her eyes were very bright.

She drained my remaining wine and asked, "What do you see when you look at me? At all of this?" She pointed with a glance at the opulence of the yacht. Her palms were flat on my chest, and she swung a leg over to straddle me like a lover.

"I see garishness that isn't you. Not really your style. I see people who obey you because of what I *haven't* seen, the other you that begins when the fucking ends and it's time for business. Whatever that might be." I was close enough to see the fine golden hairs on her neck, strayed from her body and waving in disobedience.

"Very observant. This glorified rowboat was owned by a filthy pig who achieved sexual pleasure from rape. Of course, he won't be doing that any more, but I couldn't pass up the chance to undo his ghastly taste. So industrial, masculine, yet cheap. I can look at this holding or any of my other baubles and think that I'm rather secure for a former Pictish camp whore. No more being savaged from behind by stinking fighters, no more staring at the stars as they pounded away around the fire at night. I loved thinking that the black mask of the swan in the sky was flirting with me, telling me that soon, soon, he would spill in me or on my leg, and it would be over. Until the next time. No more squabbling over scraps like a dog, with my thighs covered in blood and wondering *how soon do*

I have to eat before I feel hands on my neck again. Now, Ring, I am the ruler. I am the force, the hammer, and I do it all wrapped within a touch that drives men to their graves willingly. I know who you are. I looked at you and sensed your lethality, your odd sense of commitment to those girls you pretend not to love. I know your type, Ring. I know *every* type of man; it's my business, because if I find a man I don't understand, it means that I am losing control of my flock. And that is something I cannot afford."

She leaned forward and brushed my lips with her fingers. "I know that your augmentations will let you survive me. I'm not even certain I can kill you. I know I don't want to. You have things I want. Or access to them, anyway. The necklace is a wedge, a fulcrum for me to build my access to power. And *that* is something that I want badly enough to give you that which you cannot live without, if only you taste them once. Starting with this."

She knelt before me and freed me from my pants. I was instantly erect when my eyes connected her destination with the potential pleasure she would bring me. I was not wrong. Warm silken sheets dragged along my length as her lips closed over me, her head moving up and down, varying speed, direction, and pressure. I could feel each whirling moment of her tongue as she rested at the end of each stroke. Only her eyes remained unchanged, never leaving mine, the corners wrinkling with mirth as she fed her ego from the wanton submission on my face. I could have feigned resistance, but it was a lie, and a weak one at that. In a moment, I began to pull away, but she placed both hands against my stomach, seizing the initiative against my flagging will. It was too much. I gave in and bucked, thinking that, even in that second, she was in command as her throat worked once, then twice, my muscles going dead slack in seconds from the aftermath of my orgasm. I felt her pulling spirit from me and I gave it willingly, just as I had given in to her mouth. Marcus had been the fortunate one. He was dead. He couldn't know the pangs of living without possessing Delphine, but I would, and as she rose from the floor to pour more wine, I realized that nothing I would do from that point forward would be without her permission. Just as she had planned, all along.

I spoke, my throat grating with dust after her attentions. "I know I must sleep to recover, but, before I do, why am I here? If you know the truth about the necklace, why this charade? Why give yourself to me when you don't have to?"

She laid a hand at her throat, charmed by my stupor. "You're not asking the right question, sweetheart. I know where you got the necklace. I know about the Baron, it's his work as surely as if his signature were upon it. I don't want the jewelry. I want the victory. I want you. I want anything and everything that secures my place. Hell is an upwardly mobile social club, you might say, and I'm not going to stop in the middle. I want to sit at the top. And, Ring, you really are selling yourself short. What if I just enjoy fucking you? Surely you cannot argue with such a simple pleasure? Or is there guilt? Guilt for your betrayal to both lovers? Guilt at lying down with the enemy? I assure you, I am not your enemy. Would an enemy treat you as I have? Especially knowing that time with me would not kill you? Look at this, Ring" she caressed herself lazily "it's all yours. For the night, and the morning, and again, in the future. Think about it. Limitless pleasure. A full exploration of these skills, and my singular attention. My hands will bring you to readiness in an instant, my mouth can finish you and you will be in me at your whim. Tell me, does that sound like a threat?"

"No." My lids were getting heavy. She was lethal, but not to me. She was just psychotically addictive and gifted beyond words at her tasks, all of which had driven me to the brink of collapse in seconds. "What do you want?" I had no idea what to expect. She was completely opaque, despite her patina of lust.

"A good question, very good. The first time you've cut to the heart of the matter. Well done, pet." She beamed at me from her perch on the edge of the table. "Let's start with what I *don't* want. Jewelry, no matter who the maker. Money, things, or places to put them. I have it all. I want you to confirm your suspicions. About the Baron, that is, as well as Elizabeth. Find out what he really asked you to do, rather than bring a wayward daughter home to a lonely, glorified hunting lodge in a forgotten dale. What I really want is quite simple. Kill Elizabeth. Kill her and let me reign as I should, and you will have me in all of my forms for as long as you wish. All my things, all my power, all of my passion, all yours. And all you have to do is rid the world of a greater evil. Kill my mother, and let me reign in this hell as I was born to do." Her lips touched mine with the promise of a silken prison and pleasures yet to come.

"Mother? Where is hell? What does it look like?" I asked, coming to an understanding that this was a family fight, on our world, and all of us were at risk.

Delphine snapped her fingers again for more wine. "Yes, mother—an uppity, frigid bitch. And, right now, hell looks a lot like New Orleans."

I slept, dreamless and still, my will spent in Delphine, allowing my body to take the lead. Delphine did the same in the morning. I awoke to her riding me, a coy wave with one hand and the other behind her, fingers dragging along my thighs in a double sensation that made me thrust upward involuntarily. It was spellbinding, especially considering I hadn't brushed my teeth.

Her amusement was gently reproving. "What, no sailaway fuck until next time?"

I laughed aloud. Her brazen tongue clashed so with her tousled hair and angelic expression. She pouted even as she settled on me, her warmth constricting and bending my will with each rise and fall of her hips. "I was Army, not Navy. But I accept your kind offer." She bent forward to me, her work undone, and I wondered how lonely the ride home was going to be—and what awaited me there.

Crow Hop handed me my bag as he refused my tip. "Thank you, sir, but I'm well compensated." He was the model of discretion, carefully avoiding the door that opened, framing Risa and Wally, their distress visible even at a distance. My slavish behavior was fading with each moment away from Delphine's presence. I could not say if that was welcome because the memory of her touch was incandescent.

"A word of advice, Crow Hop, although you're a man grown. Get away from her. Get away and stay away." I shook his hand and he searched my face for anger, something. I'm not sure what. But I think, as he turned away, that I saw fleeting compassion for me, and that made me feel even more unclean as I trudged Hector's last walk to my awaiting lovers. The situation had changed, but they had not, and I had a great deal to explain.

I warily entered my silent home, but Risa broke the ice and put her arms around me. Wally waited and we embraced warmly. I was thankful and relieved. Until that moment, my tension had kept me subconsciously wired.

"Sit," Wally directed. I sat.

"Are you hurt?" When I shook my head no, she said, "Tell us. Everything."

So I did.

My report ranged from a tale of debauchery to a clinical analysis of internecine warfare between immortals for control of New Orleans, Miami, and points between. It was broken by occasional questions or clarifications between the three of us when I remembered a voice. Delphine's voice, whispering to me in the night. I felt her lips at my ear, telling me secrets and promises in a sultry drone that drenched my psyche with a latent desire to do her bidding. The memory was hypnotic.

Risa wondered aloud if I was imagining it as I fought to heal from her feeding.

"No, it makes too much sense. And the things she said to me, they bolster what I heard while I was awake. Her little girl lost bullshit, her offer to me. Her needs, her wants. It's all a lie. Look, I went there a sinner who was ignorant of his transgressions; I walked out riddled with guilt." I sought any indication of penance with the girls. I owed them that.

"What? Sins? You didn't *sin*, Ring. You fucked an immortal" Wally was incensed. "You did what you wanted, what we wanted you to do, I admit I do not like it, the knowing how good she was and all . . . ," she trailed off, the sexual challenge of Delphine fresh in her mind as a threat.

"You learned a great deal. At some risk. So you had fun, you came home to us, not her. We have no lease on one another's bodies, only our minds, and only that by agreement," Risa summed up our less than traditional household. "Was it productive? Do we even want to participate in the politics of Hell, whether it is a real place, or some distant mine under a cabin adorned with bones? Who gives a shit? Do we?"

I thought we did for several reasons. Suma. Boon. Pan. Their families. Our futures. I didn't have to spell it out for them; the girls reached the same conclusion. "When Delphine was telling her story, I noticed some very human things about her."

"Her tits?" Wally asked, archly.

"True, they were magnificent, but yours are better. And Risa has better legs, while you're both better lovers. Less consuming, more giving. Although the burping –" Wally kicked me, and laughed. We were okay for the moment. "No, I felt her insecurity through her sin. Pride, and plenty of it. No surprise there, but the self-pity was a shocker. I don't think that there will ever be enough of *anything* to take Delphine far enough from the mud and rape of those camps she told me about. And that, ladies, is why I think she is easier to manage than Elizabeth. The devil we know and all that."

Risa was doubtful. "Easier how? Because she can't kill you quickly? And Elizabeth can? How do we know Elizabeth is even truly immortal? We have flawed intelligence from dubious sources about women who may or may not have ever been human. How is that truly knowing anything?"

I presented my case. "Let's assume Cazimir is an immortal, and, somehow, his family has spilled into the wider world. We have daughters, sisters, all females, for some reason- running wild, fucking and eating and murdering people on three continents. He concocts a plausible crime of theft, finds us, and does what? Hopes for the best, that we remain mute through the search? That his brawling brood doesn't turn on each other and inform us of the shitstorm we're walking into? No. There are only two possibilities. He knows and doesn't think it matters because the fight is happening whether we get involved or not. Or something that scares me."

"Which is?" the girls asked in unison. Too many days together can lead to that type of speech.

"Cazimir isn't a father, brother, uncle, crazy cousin, whatever. He's a *rival*. And we are his brass knuckles. He doesn't want peace. He wants war. Not to expand his empire, but to sit right where he is and reign, just as he has done since we, as humans, began to call him by his true name: Satan."

59

Our problem had an expanding set of outcomes. I detest moving goal lines, so we agreed to thin the herd. We would start with our easiest target, and the current president of my fan club, Delphine. I had recovered from our twelve hour dinner, so I could safely assume she was at her best as well. Girding my loins for battle, I made a mental note. Keep her mouth away from my zipper, and I would remain the picture of steadfast control. Of course, that meant violating many of my personal principles regarding never looking a gift horse in the mouth, or, in this case, refusing a gift whore's mouth, neither of which sounded very mannerly but made my point, nonetheless. Delphine had used that term, not me— I was just going along with her ritualized self-empowerment, and- she actually scared the hell out of me in the same way a superb rollercoaster does. She did everything except turn upside down, and we simply hadn't gotten around to that position, I sensed.

Our plan seemed perfect, with one small exception: When I called her phone, the number was disconnected. All of her email accounts were invalid, and her site had gone dark. Joseph would not miss the chance to shame me like the peasant he knew me to be, so when his number bounced back as invalid, I knew that Delphine had gone under, most likely minutes after I left. Risa and Wally tried every possible means we had of contacting her, all to no avail. When a street view camera outside her primary home showed a property that had been boarded up, we knew she was long gone. All of this meant that *something* had convinced Delphine teaming with me was a losing ticket.

I respectfully disagreed. But we still had one grape to squeeze. Suma.

60

Risa is tenacious when she gets an idea, no matter how nascent. She had that ruminating look when I found her at the kitchen table after dinner. The cloud of stillness around her meant she had been thinking for some time.

"Hey." She emerged from her reverie slowly. "I put a few ideas together while you were otherwise occupied, you tramp." I leaned against her partly in apology. Partly because I missed her, and I craved her approval after my sojourn to slutville.

"I'm listening. My answers are a bit thin, and I'm getting tired of being out-thought by immortals who are glorified criminals. Even if that's actually what we are, but you get me." I grabbed an orange and sat, whittling the nubby rind, while she gathered her thoughts. Wally came in from the yard, Gyro in tow, and stole the wedges I had peeled. She stuffed the first one into her mouth with an accompanying glare. I wasn't out of the woods yet.

"Wally mentioned, as you were no doubt cavorting with that hag, that we are being taught a lesson." Risa tapped at the laptop in front of her, opening a file labeled *Names*. "This is a compilation of our recent contacts. Guess what they have in common, other than all of them being acquainted with your penis?"

"Very funny. None of them stole my fruit and held grudges?" I wasn't going down without a fight.

"Hah." Risa was not amused. "All female, but that's old ground, no reason to re-plow that furrow, unless you've a need?" She was really riding this whole unlimited pleasure with an immortal courtesan thing into the ground. I sighed and dipped my head in what I hoped was submission. "Okay, all kidding aside, Suma is our last, best rope still attached to the main fleet. She's also a female, just like all the others. Wally thinks that this is not accident. Cut through the list, find the lesson. Remember how we used to think *just follow the money*? Well, Delphine just torched that idea. We were stupid to apply human traits to immortals. We got soft. Ring is too fucking good at killing the low-level vermin who pick off tourists from Ontario– the newbie vamps who get careless and hungry and come out a minute too soon. He pops them, cool as a breeze."

I interjected. "Again, old ground. What of it?"

Risa went on. "No kidding, it's old. But, if we look at this list as two groups, well, that's a different idea entirely. How about this for a schism? Some have, some don't. And there is only one who has everything, the control, and the whip that will cow even the most aggressive immortal. We've been barraged with females over the last two years, three if you disregard those two warlocks who were operating in Palm Beach. Does that sound random to you? No. I don't believe in random, not now, not at this level of deception." She broke for a long drink of water, and gently closed her laptop. "Which brings us, or, more directly, you, Ring, back to Suma, and soon. Because, if we're starting to ask questions about who belongs to which side in this ugly little power struggle, the humans on the list will be the first to die. And I do *not* want to be the one to tell Boon her sister is dead at the hand of the devil."

"Not me, too sad." Wally distilled it quickly. Honestly.

I knew we were missing something, but it was probably someone instead. "I'm calling Suma for dinner. Tonight. I think it's time to mention some specific names around her, shake her up. See if she blinks."

My phone rang on my way to pick Suma up at the Center. "Hullo Ring, it's Blue" she began without preface. "They were here, the two women smoking, drinking like fish, guilty of being sort of European, but still watching. No Brandi, but the girls got a good look at them. Come by when you can, and the cocktail waitress can describe both of them to you, including the mystery woman."

"Got anything general?" I had to know.

"Late thirties. Black hair, pretty. Asian. That's all I've got for now. Gotta run, come by later." She clicked off without knowing that she had given me too much. The weight of her call sank in me like a dying fish. As I fought the logic, the idea of dinner with Suma became as unappealing as telling her family the truth.

"We'll eat on the water." I held Suma's arm as we were led by a suitably demure hostess to the abandoned deck of a discreet chop house on the Intracoastal. A Chicago theme was meant to lend gangster muscularity to the interior, but it ended up being wistful and a bit sad, clashing against the dark, briny water. Suma's heels thumped across the weathered deck as we were led to the furthest table, a lone pool of light cast by a rustic hurricane lamp. It was ruggedly beautiful, and the potential scene of a crime. I felt sicker with each tread.

Our server appeared, a white-shirted specter with a tired smile. "I'm Jenna, welcome. You're all lonely out here. Is it romantic?" she asked, hopeful that it might mean a lover's gratuity. Her hair was falling from her bun, indicating another long shift on her feet dealing with a mercurial public. I made a mental note that, no matter what happened, I was leaving her a hundred bucks.

Suma smiled, pleased to be included in our mythical couple. "Very. Thank you."

"We'd like a bottle of Pinot, any kind of bread, and surf and turf for two." I took the lead, hoping for as much privacy as possible. We'd need it. Jenna appreciated my brevity and left, disappearing into the darkness with the alacrity of a woman on a mission.

Gentle changes in the wind made the lamp sputter and dance. Suma looked regal, her hair nearly blue with the night clinging to her at the edge of the glow. She was awash in her infatuation, and her innocence of my intent. My anger gathered, like the shadows around us. I reached out and took her hand, desire for closeness and control overcoming my combat principles.

Pounding steps announced our wine and bread, while the wind brought a heavy aroma of tobacco. A waiter, wine bucket in one hand, clumped to the table, where he inelegantly deposited the basket of a sliced brown loaf before moving on to the wine service.

"I'm Finn; I hope you enjoy your wine. Shall I pour?" He was thrifty with his words and uncomfortable as a server. The bottle had been opened before coming to the table, which even I knew to be an offense to any oenophile. He held the glasses in his left hand, standing at the edge of the light and waiting my instructions.

"I'll pour, thank you. Finn, do you have a light in case we smoke?" I asked, taking the wine stems from him.

Before Suma could protest my sudden addiction, Finn produced a cheap lighter. "Keep it, sir. I'll check on you in a moment. Jenna isn't feeling well, so she went home. I'll take good care of you." He handed me the lighter and pulled his hand back as if burned.

I'll bet you will. "Some more butter, too, Finn? This bread is excellent." I smeared the last pat on a slice as he turned to the main area. "Oh, Finn? Could you bring me another knife, too?" I examined the blade with a critical frown.

"Certainly, sir. Is that one dirty?" He leaned into the light.

My arm shot forward, stabbing him dead center mass. He fell over the railing into the water, dissolving into a sinking rabble of blue bubbles that seemed far too cheery for their purpose. His shirt floated, empty save for a ring of ash around the collar, and then drifted out of sight. In sixty seconds, there was no evidence he had ever existed.

Suma sat speechless as I critiqued the knife again. "It is now."

We had an unusually awkward moment in the car, dead waiter notwithstanding, but then I asked her "Do you smoke? Ever?"

She shook her head vehemently. "I know it's the dirty secret of the health profession, but no. Never. I'm a *runner*. But what does that have to do with you killing our waiter? I mean, even if he was an immortal?"

"The breeze. And his walk. And his hand. Together, I knew who he was and where he had been before he appeared at our table." I was driving carefully. Suma was precious cargo now. The situation had changed.

"His hand? What? His walk? I don't get it." It was my fault for being curt.

"Jenna, the waitress? She walked across the deck, made normal noise. But Finn? He walked like he was in someone else's' shoes. Which he was, in a way. Blue called and said that two women we've been looking for, immortals, in all likelihood, were at her place. Smoking foreign cigarettes. Like the kind that made Finn smell like a dumpster fire. And his hand, the second finger had an extra knuckle, but just for a second. It was a problem area in his disguise, you see. He was a shape shifter and a woman. And he has been moving about for the past months dressed up like you." I told her with relief in every word. I felt lighter, like I could finally breathe deeply.

"So you thought I was an immortal?" Suma knew that was a death sentence around me, and it settled on her, slow and heavy.

I reached out and took her hand again. "Not just any immortal. One who was passing secrets to the Baron, or Elizabeth, or maybe whoever the highest bidder was on a day in their brushfire war for control of hell. Or New Orleans, if you believe Delphine."

Suma sat stunned. "I love my family. I—all this death—I'm a *healer*, Ring, not some spy who delivers people to those monsters."

"I know, and I'm sorry. Finn even knew you spoke French with an accent, so he or she has been watching you for some time. Closely," I added. She was even more violated by that simple fact.

"God in heaven. I feel like I've just cheated death." She slumped in her seat, adrenaline rush over.

"He may be in heaven, but we're here. And we're going to do the dirty work." I drove on, knowing that Finn had not come from a void. He had come with Elizabeth, and that meant that she would be meeting her pet for drinks. Soon.

61

"Did you notice anyone else who came in with them? Anyone on the edges, a bodyguard, maybe?" I was quizzing Blue about Elizabeth's trips to the Corral. She paused, thinking. I could hear a floor buffer in the background, meaning she was at the club early. It wasn't quite nine in the morning, an uncivilized hour to be holed up in a garish nudie bar, even if it was your primary source of income.

"I hire a lot of one-and-done girls, they'll work a shift and I don't see them again. There have been three who stood out, only because they were really fresh faced, model pretty . . . they seemed cut from a different cloth, you know? They all applied in the morning before we opened, sober, clean, friendly. It was hard to say no to them. I gave 'em a shot, all three vanished. Two of them were hired the day before Elizabeth showed. How's that for coincidence?" The floor buffer whined to a stop. The silence in the phone was jarring.

"I'll be right over. I have a present for you. Something you just can't do without." Blue chuckled low and told me to keep my shirt on. I would, but only because it was part of my plan, and I don't do nudity without proper enticement. I'm cheap, but not free.

I didn't wait long, considering. On the second day, with Wally and Risa watching through cameras in the Corral's office, a hopeful applicant walked in, paying me no attention and walking straight towards Blue, who sat at the bar, eating takeout and assembling the liquor order. My earpiece buzzed *is that her* in a small, tinny voice. I nodded once and bent back to my task as a young woman shook Blue's hand confidently before taking a seat. She was dressed in jeans and a white shirt, her honey-blonde hair pulled back from a face with high cheekbones, naturally beautiful and abuzz with confidence. She reminded me of a European version of Wally, although she seemed a bit less likely to point a gun at someone in traffic. Call it a hunch. After a few moments of quiet conversation, punctuated by mutual laughs, she stood, shook Blue's hand again, and walked past me without even acknowledging my presence, just as I had hoped. I continued mopping, even, long strokes, back and forth. Blue wasn't paying me, but I wanted her gift of free labor to be worth her while. Any task worth doing is worth doing well, especially if it's for the owner of a club crowded with nude women. I know who butters my bread.

Blue brandished a paper application at me. "Meet my newest employee, Petra. Lovely girl. I told her that she could start tonight, but, because my net is down for repair, I can't check references until Monday. She was kind enough to give me three. Fancy a peek?" She was triumphant and deserving of an award. She really knew how to think on her feet. I took the application as her office door opened and the girls came spilling out to join in our exposition.

"Well, looky, looky. A name we know and two we don't. Christmas is early." I handed the sheet to Risa, who held it up for Wally to see. *Stacia. Karolina. Elizabeth*. Three of the most beautiful names I'd ever seen put to paper.

"We must search these names this afternoon and be back here, ready, tonight. Flats, not heels. I think we are fighting." Wally relished a good brawl ,but only in proper footwear.

62

Restless and nervous, we hovered in each other's way throughout the afternoon, even to the point that Gyro went outside to seek a quiet place to nap. Our only diversion was a delivery from Jim, a heavy envelope brought by courier that could only be the results of his search for weapons to fit the girls' hands. For now, they could wait, because Wally stalked out into the living room clad only in her underwear. She was either confused or pissed, emotions which have an interchangeable role for her.

"After we handle that woman tonight, what about the Baron? Have we made plans for him, or his staff? What if they are human, after all? Are we putting them in the way of harm?" She had a point. We were waging a war on two continents. With immortals, there was no after, there was only an end. Humans, who might be innocent? It was a new consideration for us and a moral issue that we had not encountered.

Risa shook her head. "Cazimir is a ghost. His staff, unknown, beyond glimpses of Ilsa and . . . Sandor, is it? I think that's the name he used once. We don't really even know how many people are in his home. Short of visiting, which is insanity until this is over, I don't know how to help them. I'm open to suggestions. I don't want innocents to die, not after all the murder that has gone unchecked for so long." Her humanitarian side was well developed, and she took the ethical breach of murder seriously. "Let's consider the red flags here. Cazimir Byk, keeper of forest bulls, tinkerer, and possibly Satan. Am I on track so far?"

"His last name *does* mean bull or something like that" Wally explained. "It could be taken as he is the master of bulls, the master of the horned beasts of the forest. Or maybe this man *is* the horned beast in the forest, but I have a problem with that."

I agreed. And I was dubious about something so obvious in a tapestry of half-truths, lies, and partial answers. "We're thinking only in modern terms if we assume that Satan is some horned beast. The notion of an evil being goes far back before the Church arrived." I pointed at Risa. "No eye rolling, I know what I'm saying. You're not the only historian, and I'm at least as versed in Catholicism as you are, Wally, and I don't ogle the priest, either." They both looked slightly abashed, but only a bit. "This character, Satan—who can say if he has horns? Or is real? This isn't some cartoonish creation from the minds of puritanical apologists who were busy making women into crones to subvert their power in the early Church."

"I hate admitting you're right. And a feminist, apparently." Risa patted my arm patronizingly as Wally clapped. My depths are underappreciated, even by the loves of my life. "The Baron likes giant cows that live in the depths of a European forest. So what? It doesn't mean he's some evil warlord, does it? We know Delphine wants Elizabeth gone. We know that they think of their positions as fluid. Why not women? Why not one of them, trying to play on us, on Ring, and get us off balance, confused. But lethal to whomever they choose to direct us towards, by lies. False trails."

"The Prince of Lies may be the Princess of Lies, right?" I was open to it. After seeing what Sandrine could do, I was ready to believe anything.

Risa disagreed, I could tell before she spoke. "Let's stop thinking about an immortal as having gender. Think about their disguise as camouflage adapted to their situation. Ring, you're our muscle. The killer, the final step. What appeals to you?"

"You mean other than Delphine's tits?" I ducked Wally's punch, but Risa clipped me on the shoulder. I had it coming. "Okay, seriously. Anyone could look at us and see what I crave. I'm living a life anyone would be jealous of. I have the physical, the mental, emotional satisfaction, too. Leisure time, income. I have it easy, except for the whole immortals-trying-to-kill-me thing. But aren't you making the same assumption that we made about Satan, just applying it to me? That, because I'm an incredibly desirable, virile male, all I would want is physical pleasure in the form of beautiful women? Who is being predictable now?" I raised a brow at Risa.

Sighing, she got up from the table. "I'm not suggesting that immortals are always that subtle. Not at all. Let me ask you, what did you find intriguing about your flirtation with Suma? Or better still; tell us what made you so enthusiastic about engaging in play with Delphine? Other than her tits, of course." Wally snickered at my discomfiture, but I considered the question.

"The thrill? With Suma, the forbidden nature of it, maybe, because of Boon and Pan? Maybe the same reasons for Delphine. Like a sexual chess match where I knew I was badly outplayed before I sat down at the table, but I thought that there was more to it than just, I don't know, withstanding her onslaught, her experience? So that we would win?" There was more to this than I could articulate. I could feel it.

"What about us?" Wally asked. "Did thinking about us make it dangerous?"

Saying yes meant that I had considered far more than just their ire at my connection with Delphine or how I would react to Elizabeth or any other women connected with Cazimir. The truth was I had, and my face told of it.

Honesty first, I decided. "Of course I had. I couldn't deny that line of thinking. I mean, what if I didn't come home as the same man? Would we still have a home? I didn't want to admit my own weakness. Not fear, just uncertainty. I didn't know if I could be changed beyond recognition, and, if that happened and neither of you were there, would you be left behind? How could we turn back the clock?"

Wally was standing next to me now. I could feel her possessiveness like a firm grasp on my arm. "I do not think you understand how much we already have changed, Ring. We are closer, yes? So, how could you be pulled away from us if we are holding on that much tighter? I do not think that we need to worry about this Elizabeth or Delphine or even the Baron in his lonely outpost. I think that they need to start worrying about us."

Risa nodded, forcefully. "We've already taken the fight to them, and, now, we will meet Elizabeth. If she is not the end, then we find Karolina or Stacia. Maybe we visit the forest one day. But don't worry about losing us because we aren't worried about losing you, okay?"

It was just the right tonic for me. I knew we were on solid ground and that my risks were physical, not emotional. At heart, I am a soldier, and we always fight better knowing we can go home. It was time to go to the Corral. It was time to close the circle. We would leave with Elizabeth, or she would be leaving in a torrent of blue motes. The choice would be hers.

63

This time, my knife stays close. I was going into friendly ground, and I meant to be armed, in position, and ready. All on my own terms. Delphine taught me a valuable lesson about beautiful distractions. I would not repeat the mistake, no matter what manner of flesh drifted across my line of sight. We were collectively ensconced in the Corral before the post work throng began to fill every spare seat. And, occupy every girl. Petra emerged from the back, attired in a tuxedo vest that barely covered her small, high breasts. A thong hugged her bottom and displayed her legs for maximum effect. If she was trying to make money, she would need a dump truck to carry it away, but her purpose lay elsewhere. For an acting job, it wasn't bad, I decided, as I watched her navigate the sexual minefield of handsy mechanics, attorneys and other nameless men who reached for her with each pass. Her attention was split between her surroundings and the door, which meant that we were in the right place at the right time.

Elizabeth walked in like a wall of ice–beautiful, impenetrable, and frigid. I had sorely undersold her magnetism and beauty because, even in the dim light of the club, she glittered with the light of an approaching star. She was magnificent in the same way I can admire a sword, or a falcon, or a stalking cat. Her purpose, to anyone who would look closely, was clear, and her design, flawless. She flowed onto a stool and motioned once to the bartender, who was instantly at her service. The seat next to her was conveniently empty, and Petra had gone to the front, called by Blue upon seeing my movement towards the bar.

Risa and Wally watched from the office, silent save their breathing in my earpiece. There was no need for talking now, only me, and the decision before me. Kill her here, or elsewhere under a pretense I would create. I had little faith in my ability to charm the devil, so I took two steps across the carpet, negotiating an oblique path to her side.

Elizabeth then quelled any notion I had of being her equal in that moment. Turning to me, across the crowd, she patted the stool next to her and waved me over, playfully, without fear, totally aware of my intent before I had formed my plan in my own mind. Her prescience was disturbing, her mockery complete, but I went to her and took a seat next to the mistress who seemed to know entirely too much about my own thoughts.

I sat without greeting as she poured champagne for me and herself, tapping our glasses together in solidarity. I was too stunned to drink, but she smiled and implored me.

"Taste the wine, Ring. It's excellent. Not the usual fare for such a colorful purveyor as your friend, Blue." The layers of her knowledge seemed limitless after that simple invitation. I proceeded carefully.

"I won't insult you by reaching for my knife, but it is most certainly close enough for me to use if I feel pressured. You're visiting my friend's establishment, and, more importantly, my home. What can I do for you, Elizabeth?" I asked as I sipped. She was right; the wine was crisp.

She focused on me, turning in her seat. Her charisma was nearly oppressive, despite her cool reserve. She said, "You have to imagine my confusion over your predicament. On the one hand, you're helping a seemingly caring father who seeks to return his heir to her place at his side. And, along the way, you've been asked to bring his collection of baubles, which is scattered to the winds, but still manages to end up in your hands by some twist of fate. Then, there is the jealous sister, a jumped-up streetwalker whose accent and concept of taste are both, let's say, -recently acquired. Her framing of me as the penultimate evil is petty, but not unforeseen. She has quite a taste for men, doesn't she? *And* a truly dreadful collection of occupations over the centuries, but always returning to her roots as a camp whore, on her knees in smoky tents for bread and protection. You've been asked to kill me based on what evidence, may I ask?" Elizabeth was composed and in good humor, both of which made me nervous.

"I don't care about Delphine. She isn't new to me, just a different name, a different accent, but always the same greed accompanied by the same pride. No, I find myself having a difficult time not killing you because of three little acorns. The ones that you seeded me with, that nearly killed me? Those make me so much less forgiving. In fact, my good manners are nearly extinguished, just like you will be soon because of something as simple as a good, old-fashioned murder attempt on your part. Unfortunately for you, my resistance is quite high, even to such unusual methods as you used. So you see, Elizabeth, despite the fact that you've given me this truly lovely wine" and I saluted her with my glass, "I find that I'm not in the forgiving mood tonight."

Pouting was not her style. Her eyes took on a steelier shade, and she held out her phone to me, the image causing me to stop short of reaching for my knife.

Suma. She was spread-eagle on a table, nude, with livid red marks on her stomach and thighs. I could guess what from, and my stomach flipped, curdling with impotent rage. Bile hit my tongue, and I sat very still, waiting for the moment to stabilize until the floating motes in my sight drifted away and I could once again focus on Elizabeth's perfectly beautiful, evil face. I examined the picture again. On a chair next to Suma crowded two knives, their blades dull and smeared. An ashtray, with cigarette butts strewn about it, and a lighter. In the picture was a new player in our ugly drama–female, tall, thin, with long dark hair and intelligent eyes. She was waving shyly at the camera. *You caught me!* Her casual embarrassment was jarring, given the background of Suma.

Elizabeth tucked the phone in her purse, watching me for motion. It was the first reasonable thing she had done since arriving because I was on a knife edge and leaning towards killing her right there.

"Ring, I'm afraid we've started our discussion on a sour note. I apologize for inconveniencing your friend, but I had to guarantee that you would listen to reason."

"Reason?" I was apoplectic. I shook in my seat, my hands on the bar and the skin of my knuckles ghost-white. She was so close to her end.

"Let me say something once, and I want you to remember this when I leave here tonight-and I will leave, no matter your plans for my demise. I am *not* who, or what, you think I am. I am a woman who is surrounded with a family that diverged from this world long ago. I am made from their thread, but I am not of their cloth. Remember that when you try to kill me, won't you? Now, on to other matters. I can see by your reaction that I've misjudged your opinion about asserting my safety. When I am in my car, safe, I will make one call. One. Suma will be freed. She will call you immediately, and Karolina will help her to her vehicle, to come home to you and her family." She rose, brushed her lips over my stony face and patted my hand. "A good friend knows when to let pride lose a battle. Let's hope you are a true friend to Suma. Goodbye, Ring. Leave my family alone, or don't. The choice is yours, but know that, eventually, you are going to lose to an undying soul who will *not* kill you, and then you will begin to understand what real sacrifice can be."

Even in the clatter of the bar, her heels sounded like the nails in my coffin, pounding with mockery at my weakness as *Suma, Suma, I am sorry, forgive me* looped in my head, unending and without care for my shame.

We sat in my truck, mute. Risa and Wally waited for some sign from me that I was going to take action, but I was paralyzed with my failure. Watching Elizabeth leave the Corral unmolested was close to castration for me, but watch her I did, hating every step she took with a ferocity borne of fear. A moment later, my phone rang. *Elizabeth*.

"Ring, I'm sending you a picture. Pay attention to detail this time, and I'll see you soon, I'm sure. A storm is coming to your home, which means trouble for my family." She delivered this news as fact.

"Does this picture have anything to do with Suma's freedom? Because if it doesn't . . . ," I let the threat hang, no matter how empty.

Elizabeth laughed, patronizing and cold. "You fear someone who you have already dispatched. A slip on your part, to be sure, but understandable, given your excitability. I may choose to travel soon, since it will shortly become very unpleasant here. Or don't you pay attention to the weather? I would think a mariner like you would at least be aware of an oncoming hurricane, which causes such problems with my family's dinner plans. So many tourists taking wing, it makes other venues seem more attractive. Batten your hatches, Ring. Perhaps we'll talk before I leave."

With a click, she was gone. I looked at the image she sent to my phone, closely. It was the same scene as she had shown me in the Corral. Suma, a victim. Karolina, the torturer. There were two small differences. My stomach fell a thousand yards, crushed by the deception of the picture.

"What is it?" Risa asked, as Wally leaned in from the back seat.

"Suma. Her hand. I'm such a fucking idiot, look at her hand! Elizabeth won, and I didn't even fight her." I handed my phone to Risa, burying my head in my hands, awash with relief and anger. Suma was fine. Safe, and had been all along. The picture showed a woman with a hand that was slightly deformed, cast in shadow, a single extra knuckle pushing outward due to a momentary loss of control. It was not Suma in the image. *Finn*, who was now ashes in the water, dead by my hand. The scene was staged by Elizabeth, no doubt days before I discovered Finn's true nature. She used the picture as a trump card, knowing that we would tighten our noose around her neck, but fear for Suma's life would cut the rope clean.

And I let Elizabeth walk past me to safety, freed by a lie.

64

A storm was, in fact, coming. Beaches emptied of tourists, just as Elizabeth had predicted in her damnably reasonable voice. Our previous concerns let a monstrous weather event sneak upon us, so, in a harried afternoon, Wally and I attached plywood to every window on our house, while Risa lowered the metal shutters at the Hardigan Center. This routine was old hat to us, and we performed like a somewhat oiled machine, with only minor scrapes to show for our efforts at circumventing the fury of nature. I sensed that Elizabeth would not have mentioned the storm had she thought it would turn elsewhere.

I was unfortunately correct in my assessment of her value as a weathervane. Boon, Pan, Suma and the kids came to stay with us; the remainder of our center friends went inland with relatives, or in the case of Angel, to an armory where his church group volunteered. We were collectively as safe as could be, watching the angry bulk of the cheerily named hurricane Jenny bearing down on the coast. Landfall, if it hit Hollywood, would be at dusk, nearing full tide, and when the city was most vulnerable. The situation did not look good, but, with our family safe, riding it out together seemed to be the best possible plan. Vengeance was far from my mind, but that is an emotion with brawn, and, before I would give control of my rage to the cause of Elizabeth's demise, I had a call to make—to the forest, for one last warning, a *mea culpa* of sorts. For, even if Cazimir was an immortal, he deserved to know that Elizabeth had well and truly slipped the leash, and even he could not consider himself safe in behind his barricade of trees.

"Risa, time for one call to the Baron before the storm takes down the 'net." She opened her laptop, only to find the icon for the Baron's call already pulsing in the corner of the screen. He had an open connection to us. She clicked, and the lodge flooded the screen, along with a scene of unmitigated death.

Sandor and Ilsa's feet twitched in unison, their bodies hanging from the beam that held the aurochs horns up for admiration. A wet stain colored Sandor's pants, one last insult to his body as his bowels loosed in a heave. His tongue began to protrude from a mouth quickly mottling with anoxia. Next to him, Ilsa's beautiful features were contorted in an ocean of agony. Her eyes locked on the camera for a fleeting second of recognition, then went dull as the weight of her muscular frame pulled vertebra apart with a dull snap. She died in seconds, tears and saliva streaking her face in a last baptism of pain.

A hand slapped on the work table, the fingers turning white with effort. *Cazimir*. Rising, he dragged himself into camera height. His shirt was crimson, and he held one arm across the breadth of his stomach, a soft pink coil peeked from the side of his bloodied forearm.

"She can be anywhere, Ring. Out of her mouth, only lies. Oh, that I ever fathered her, to visit such sin on the world." His voice was reedy, failing. Looking past us at something unknowable, he slid from the table and our view, and the connection went dark, just as the last breath of life left the haunted lodge in the forest of giants.

65

Rain began to hammer the plywood over the picture window in savage, slashing blows, while the wind rose and fell in a bass moan that crept upward in volume with each blast. After a meandering path pulling massive heat energy from the fertile Gulf Stream, Jenny had arrived. The canal was a crashing tub of violence, with whitecap foam blowing off waves that were already topping the seawall and punching at the dock erratically. Aluminum caps from each mooring post were ripped off and flung into the dark, speeding discs of wobbling metal. The entire dock swayed slightly and trees were bent, released, and bent again by the muscular gusts that ebbed but never relented. The water was gunmetal grey, and it was hard to discern where the saltwater ended and the rain began.

A palm frond banged against the kitchen window and was swept past instantly into the twilight. Awnings and street signs sang in metallic vibrato as the wind lashed them side to side. Risa and Wally sat silently, Gyro panting between them, on the couch. They both looked at their phones, watching weather radar.

"It's a direct hit." Risa was calm, but there was an undertone of worry. I understood. I checked on the kids again, only to find Boon smoothing their hair and whispering to them as they lay curled under blankets alongside the bed, their fear keeping them from the window. Pan was leaning against the wall on his haunches, his hands clenched with frustration and worry. I stood looking out into the false twilight, where shadows blew by in a torrent.

My phone rang, startling me from watching the storm. I looked at the screen, surprised that a call could connect in the savagery outside. *Elizabeth*. I looked pointedly at the girls and answered.

"Ring, I have a problem" she began. The clarity of her voice was shocking. I heard the snap of her lighter and the clink of glass. She sounded like she was in the next room. It was disconcerting, but so was her tone. She spoke in a friendly, conversational way.

"Inclement weather aside, this is the time to meet. I need to speak to you, and the only place that was open on a day like this hasn't been open for thirty years, but it's quiet, and we can chat. This pursuit grows tiresome. You and your friends harried me like a fox these past few months, and for what? Because you think my children have been misbehaving? I assure you, Ring, I have never given birth, but I expect you'll wish to meet, regardless. It's getting dark now, nearly time for dinner. Dress appropriately. And do be a dear and bring wine. I'm afraid I've finished mine, and we have a great deal to discuss. The eye of the storm will come ashore soon. Stop by then."

The connection cut, I told the girls "She's at my uncle's, in the Center. Alone, I think. She asked me to bring wine, like a date. Let's make it a foursome, shall we?" I asked, handing the package from Jim Broward to Wally. "We leave when the eye wall is here. That means time for sleep. And then, time for Elizabeth to sleep. Permanently."

66

In the Wagoneer, I turned the heavy envelope up. A musical clank came from within, and I tore the top away in one motion. Inside were two beautifully made British trench knives, fine examples a century old, built for close fighting in World War I. I handed one each to the girls, who slipped their hands around them at once. They fit perfectly, filling their hands with deadly metal. A long blade finished in a wicked point, designed to be thrust forward or down. There was no time to sharpen them, but they would wreak havoc with contact and aggression. We would supply both of those needs.

"They're inscribed", Risa announced after holding the blade up to the overhead light. "Trevor and William Bruton, of Warwick, England. Brothers who fought together in the infantry. These knives have seen a lot of fighting, I bet. Especially since they were British. They never played defense."

"What does that mean?" I asked, and backed up into the hammerfall of rain. The noise was deafening and the wind moved the heavy vehicle playfully as I edged down our street. I would have to go very slowly, picking my way through the limbs and errant lawn furniture that dotted the road. Risa leaned forward to get closer. Wally turned halfway as the bullets of water drummed the metal roof and then in seconds, the rain began to slow. The clouds were parting, quickly. It was unsettling after the howling of the past hours.

"The British had a simple doctrine in war. At Gallipoli, they attacked. At the Somme. Ypres, twice. In Palestine. They always went on the offensive. It was simple but it took incredible discipline." When Risa spoke of history, it was as if she lived it.

Wally was testing the heft of her knife, listening and peering upward as the eye of the storm began to pass over, revealing an astounding column of clear, velvety night sky. She pointed to a single, bright star shining in defiance of the storm that curled around it. "So what does that mean to us when we meet Elizabeth?"

Risa didn't hesitate. "Simple. As soon as possible, we attack."

After a rocky ride over, my lights hit the Center, and we parked close. I knew the storm would return soon, and I respected the coming violence, both in and out of the building. Getting out, we were surrounded by unnatural calm. Where wind had been screaming minutes before I could now hear the drip of water. It was unsettling. I pulled on the door without any attempt at stealth, and the glass swung wide, groaning slightly from years of disuse.

"She's here." My voice sounded thunderous in the uneasy quiet. The back of the shop was hidden by a shabby paneled wall. Behind was a long, open space with threadbare carpet and plain walls. I knew that only a card table and chairs lay beyond the flimsy barrier. A single fluorescent fixture popped and hummed, casting a flickering light from beyond the door. Both bulbs pulsed with shadows and glare in alternating moments. The rhythm was disquieting.

"Come in, Ring." Elizabeth's voice floated through the sanctuary of the shop. "Tell the blonde to leave her crucifix on the counter. I can only tolerate so much heresy at once." She laughed to herself, amused by our silent discomfort. It was palpable. We stood, dripping slightly. Waiting.

"Before you cross the Rubicon and come through that door, why are you here? I haven't had the chance to ask you. Is it pride? Vengeance? I won't patronize you with talk of *détente*. So, please, come in. But done is done, and you cannot bring back the dead, no matter how intense your anger, and you will find me unwilling to go quietly to your particular kind of justice." With that, she fell silent. We moved through the door, instantly fanning out. Wally was to my right, Risa on my left, slightly back, tense. We were all silent now, but the wind began to rise outside, wheezing and then slamming the outer door shut with a violence that shook the building.

"The storm will return soon. So loud." Elizabeth's voice was full of a secret longing . "Could you see any stars? I've always found that to be unnerving, with such violence close at hand." I wasn't sure if she was speaking of the storm or us.

Wally spoke, cautiously. "There was a bright one, by itself." Elizabeth seemed pleased by that, for some arcane reason. "Well, now, you've seen two." " She bowed from the neck, smirking. "An unusual occurrence, given the situation at hand."

With a moan and a bang, instantly, Jenny returned, as the rains began to pummel the building like a demonic snare drum.

There is a moment of balance before a fight begins, where I stand on the edge of motion, my body screaming for purpose, but my mind holds me fast. Blood roars in my head and the delicious chill of anticipation runs the length of my spine, like an angry secret I cannot contain. We were standing, knives out. There, framed in the weak light, sat Elizabeth, leaning carelessly in a creaking plastic chair. An empty wine bottle, her high-heeled shoes, and a single cup crowned the tabletop. She wore a simple dress of navy silk, her hair unbound over her shoulders. She was erotic and frightening in the same glance. She had been smoking, and the plumes curled lazily in the harsh interior light.

"A Jew and a Catholic who kneel together in church. And, in supplication to you, Ring, leaving you squarely in the fleshy, sinful middle" Elizabeth laughed, richly. "Just as you want, although your cowardice will hold you from admitting the truth. Risa's hungry mouth. Wally, looking back in lust, urging you to ride harder. Such dutiful sinners, beholden to each other as much as your own pleasure. I'm glad you brought your whores. Admitting you want them with you is the first honest thing you've ever done in your vapid life." She rolled her head on her shoulders, slowly, like an athlete limbering for an event.

"No wine? I had hoped that manners would win out, Ring, but you've regressed to a rather brutish state. Killing women. Harrying me about the coast. How distasteful."

Cat quick, she was standing, bottle in hand, broken on the exposed concrete wall behind in one seamless motion. She moved like angry water. I nodded imperceptibly to Risa. In moments, there would be no chance to talk, as the winds and rain began to rake the building again with mounting ferocity.

"Wally. Risa. Stay in your lanes, and just like the British, right?" They both hissed in agreement.

We attacked.

I feinted low and straightened, blade whistling at Elizabeth, who turned to the right and pulled the table in front of her with a crash. Her heel leapt out and crunched into Wally's midsection as the wine bottle caromed off her ear, slicing deeply behind her jawline. Risa stepped over the table and calmly lunged forward with her knife hand only to have it turned by Elizabeth's hand. There could be only one ending, and Wally tried to make it happen with one vicious, loping sweep of her weapon. Elizabeth dodged back, her shoulders thudding into the wall, and then flicked the bottle out to cut my lead arm.

It was a wound I was willing to take to get closer. The wound burned, blood roping off into the air as I rolled my body sideways and closed the gap. The storm was in full fury now, adding to our curses and grunts as we closed on Elizabeth. Wally hesitated and was struck again, a long, shallow cut that glistened sickly down her side, her shirt parting to reveal her ribs. In a decisive flash, Elizabeth spun and pounded the bottle neck into Wally's temple, dropping her instantly to the concrete, groaning, as Risa rolled under me and came up swinging, naked rage on her face. Risa's trench knife slammed forward but was brought up short as Elizabeth's elbow rushed down like an anvil. With a muffled thump, the bone connected with Risa's forehead, her skull cracking against the floor. Risa was dizzied by the blow, but still conscious. It was the opening I needed.

I was in arm's reach of Elizabeth, who began to wheel the bottle up in a slash that would have cut me from navel to neck, but I drifted right, and then spun under her angled attack to rise nearly chest to chest with her. I headbutted her between the eyes and buried my knife in her ribs, the blade slipping between bone and sinew until it struck her shoulder blade and stopped. She bellowed, an unearthly, chorded shriek of tenor and bass voices, all crying to the violation of my blade.

I held her, blood streaming from the lurid cut on her beautiful face, now frozen in a rictus of pain. She splashed wetly against me, her breath trickling out in a long, mournful whisper. Dropping her body to the floor with a thud, I turned to the girls. Risa waived me off as I kneeled before Wally, her hair a caked mass of blood. One ear was nearly severed, and her ribs showed through the longer wound. I found a pulse, weak but present. She would live.

"I'll get the car. We need help *now*. We can say she was hurt in the storm." Tearing open the front door, I stepped into the frigid rain and howling winds to back the Wagoneer closer. My hands were shaking from the adrenaline, and it took me three tries to get the damned key in the ignition. I needed the hospital and a dry bed, far from the killing ground. After laying Wally in the back seat, Risa held her head, talking quietly to her as the rain pounding the metal roof drowned her words into mere sounds of comfort. It was enough. One look into the rearview mirror revealed Risa's face, blanched in fear and sudden recognition.

"What? Is she okay?" I panicked, my hands fighting to hold the wheel steady. The wind pushed us like a toy from one lane to the other. We had six dangerous blocks to go.

"Elizabeth. Her body. It was still there!" Risa looked sick, and not just from the fight. It was true. Her corpse had lain there, rent. Bloody. Broken.

And very, very human.

67

It took too many minutes to get to the ambulance entrance to Hollywood Memorial, and the staff rushed out even as I rolled to a stop. A whirlwind ensued as Risa and Wally were bustled in through the doors with hectic efficiency. Nurses and doctors fired questions at me and the girls as the triage progressed. No one assumed any dark cause for the wounds; the hurricane raging around us assured that line of questioning would be overlooked. In a matter of seconds, I became superfluous, to be left standing, soaking wet, exhausted, and angry. The white floor was spattered with blood and rainwater, leaving the room in four lines where the gurneys rolled. I was alone in the waiting room. Three televisions overhead showed beautiful newscasters grimly urging residents to stay cowering inside, their practiced tones of concern repeating the same mantra, *get down, get down, get down.* A backdrop of weather radar outlined an enormous pinwheel of colorful violence spinning west over the city. It wobbled like a dizzy child and slowly surged to the edge of the screen.

I sat on a frigid plastic chair and hung my head. A murderer, not an avenger. I had become Wrath and I felt the weight of sin's fingers squeezing me tighter with each gusty sigh.

68

Light, blazing and painful, hit my face from the window of the girls' hospital room. My beard itched abominably, four days of growth that had seen neither water nor soap. I could smell my own breath, never a good sign. Risa lay supine on the left in her bed, Wally on the right. I had curled like a junkyard dog between them, threatening anyone who even looked in the room without my personal invitation. A rotation of visitors had spelled me for a few moments as I wandered to the cafeteria for a listless bite of food twice each day. Suma, Boon, Pan, even Glen, accompanied by his nearly identical brother Gabriel, who inexplicably sported a British accent, had each done a turn. Angel had visited, too, a glowering hulk who watched every hospital employee with suspicion, only to be spelled often by Liz, who adopted a cracking tone of authority and ordered anyone in scrubs about without a moment to breathe.

Slowly, they healed. Risa was the first to sit up, the first to walk. Wally floated in and out of consciousness, her body working hard to throw of the grave slashes that were healing at a rate which puzzled the doctors. I did not invite questions, and, after a day, they stopped asking. When Wally was smiling at me, a sweet, kind look on her face, I knew that I had not lost my family, my partners. I sat on the edge of Risa's bed, one hand holding hers and the other laying on Wally's leg. I could breathe again, and that meant I had an errand to run.

I kissed Risa lightly, then Wally, and told Boon "No one in or out. And then, the same when they are home. Spare no expense, no feelings, and no chances. I'll be back in two days."

Risa's sadness was too great to address. I could not look at her directly. To do so would be to lose my nerve. It was hard enough finding the strength to leave them at all.

"Ring? Where are you going?" Wally asked, sleepily, although she knew.

I walked to the door, and, without looking back, said "I'm going to return some jewelry." And, without another word, I left to hail a cab, fat hot tears on my face at what felt like the last betrayal of my life.

69

I have with me two gods, Persuasion and Compulsion - Themistocles
The Forest

Tadeusz drove without fear. He also drove without brakes because the autumnal scenery blew by in a smear of browns and yellows as his ancient rust bucket of a car banged along a rutted track in a spine-crushing series of skids, stops, and wild accelerations. I had found him by searching on my phone while in a cab to the Fort Lauderdale/Hollywood airport. My simple search of *Guides: Bialowicza: English Speaking* led to a phone call, a hurried negotiation while I purchased my ticket and, thirteen hours later, a hale greeting at the airport before he whisked me, jet lagged and bewildered, towards the looming green of the forest.

"This I think is far enough, Ring" Tadeusz told me, pointing with emphasis at a double row of odd mounds on either side of the track. "That is the edge of the estate. No one will go here, so I will not go here, but if you must be a stupid hero American, then you will go alone, and I will be here, drinking the delicious *Nalewka* my wife has given me for this trip." He brandished the bottle of herbed liqueur and pointed to the growing gloom. "Not much light left for your walk. You must go."

I looked meaningfully into the backseat, where a well-cared-for rifle lay under a blanket. Gleaning my intent, he shook his head. "I cannot let you have that. But this, this is okay." He handed me a savage-looking hunting knife, honed to a mirror edge. It looked brutal and functional, a mankiller. I took it and thanked him. Its weight comforted me.

The door creaked and closed with a bang, and I was surrounded by a forest of such depth and silence that I could not tell I had been caroming through it seconds earlier. No birds called, no wind. Nothing. Just the crunch of my boots over inert leaves as I walked to a paired row of hulking shapes, nearly covered with mosses and grime.

Cars. Two rows of cars, cast aside, forgotten, rusting into the soil. Like cedars lining a levy, they sat, immobile, their state of decay greater as I moved forward towards the location of the lodge, according to Tadeusz' directions. Here a *Syrena*, tiny and globular, sitting next to a Polish *Kredens*, its entire side stove in from some mysterious disaster. Further along, I passed not two but three of the once-feared Crows, their government plates ripped off by some unseen collector. The majestic remains of a Zil limousine lazed on an embankment, state flags that were once brilliantly colored now a faint, bloody pink. It was a parking lot made by something incredibly lethal, filled with the remains of the greedy or the stupid. I was choosing freely to walk towards this unknown killer, but, a knife was in my hand and in the dying light of the primal, filtered sun, I stalked with supreme confidence. The Baron, whether he wished it or not, was about to have a houseguest.

A slight incline announced the manor proper, where three oaks large enough to hide a small home squatted imperiously before me. I lay against the nearest, bark as old as time rough against my face, and peered around the massive trunk to select my path.

There was no need for stealth. Only then did a bird call, a laughing, raucous jay, piercing the quiet in the growing dusk. The ruin had once been magnificent. Even looking at the bones of the home, it was easy to see what was lost. Logs tumbled in upon one another in a jackstraw of abandonment and the ravages of time. Jewel green mosses slowly pulled the remaining height of the structure toward the soft earth, with mushrooms quietly breaking the wood into soil, while spilled slate announced the former shapes of walls, and a wood pen, and perhaps a fire pit.

Gone, and long ago, perhaps centuries. Another fallen house of lies, slowly slipping beneath the verdant waters of the forest, one wavelike season at a time. I walked forward to where the massive doors had once hung, now only collapsed hints of a stone arch left among the jumble of relics. *Lies. What else did I expect?* Blackness yawned to my left, tucked under the angular remnants of a roof joist made of waist-thick beams, dissolving under the attentions of the weather. I stepped carefully over the fallen majesty of the ceilings that had held the aurochs horns aloft. The hole was lit by the last rays of the weakened fall sunshine, a last hurrah of joy to let my eyes see into the seductively open stairway. Carved from stone, each step angled slightly down and away, a curling invitation glistening with dew and uncertainty. I stepped forward once more as the sun spangled off the jeweled eye of a silver horse, spinning gently in the moist air pushing lightly from the unknown pit. The necklace hung just out of reach. To secure it would mean taking several steps into the dark. *Clever girl, oh very clever, indeed.* I stood erect, backing away silently. The breeze from below carried such a wealth of scents—mosses, time, mystery. And perfume. One perfume I have smelled before and will always remember—and not worn by any human. Stepping away, I thought I heard her laughter welling up from the depths, mocking me.

    Inviting me.

Epilogue I

One Month Later

We healed. We stayed close, fighting the urge to slash at shadows; we learned to sleep again, to live, to find solace in the comfort of one another. We became more of a family and emerged, like a ship fighting through a rogue wave, battered but whole, cleared to go forward.

I was hot, and that meant that the girls were scorched, so I found myself walking to get the car after a recuperative day at the zoo, where we had walked and eaten and circled about, while pretending that we had chased every spirit and echo from the corners of our minds. The parking lot blazed like an airport tarmac, nearly empty during the peak heat of the day. A lone grandmother braved the heat, fruitlessly waving a brochure at her florid face, sweat beaded on every inch of her skin. She smiled at me in commiseration, the unspoken, *scorcher, ain't it* unsaid between us, but understood.

It was a small hole in the concrete, not more than the size of a tennis ball, but it caught her birdlike, ancient ankle perfectly, snapping the bone in a sickening crack that sent her chin first into a graceless arc. The impact made her breath leave in a surprised *oof* as she rolled over, laughing, before I could get to her.

She spit two teeth at my feet, connected with a stringy gobbet of flesh that sent them into a bolo spin to land on my shoe. I moved quickly to her, reaching for her to help. She slapped my hand, hard and pulled herself to her feet, leaning on her ruined ankle without notice.

"That will be enough touching from you, Ring. You save those hands for your whores." She smiled, gap toothed and bleeding. I knew. This was no grandmother, not at that second. "My mistress wants to tell you to stop being so fucking *jumpy*. *Y*ou're going to ruin the surprise!" She put her hands on her hips, chastising me. "She will call on you soon enough. It's just that she's been so *busy* with you and your common-law sluts being laid up and all. Can't have you out and about when she had business to attend to, right, lover?" She cackled once and spat again, spotting my sock with her bloody saliva. With a series of grotesque cracklings, she walked away, each step making her lean in more pronounced fashion until her shoe ran red from the bone shearing through the remaining papery skin.

I turned to the gates, where the girls would be waiting. I felt the heat of the macadam, the glare on my face. I thought of the blackness. The laughter.

I thought of revenge.

Epilogue II

Two Months Later

Herr Kreiger was thrilled to have the collection back in its rightful place, although his professionalism was such that he betrayed nothing to the client. Lovingly, he placed each piece on the velveteen lining of the deposit box, tucked in a specific order according to usefulness, size, gem quality . . . oh, so many variables in the three hundred tiny works of art. Occasionally, he polished an item before returning it to the box, even removing the odd spatter of blood, which hinted at a less than forthright retrieval. The owner was not known as forgiving, and who was he to question the gathering of something so unique? So valuable, in so many ways?

There, the last one. I have always loved that horse, even when I was a boy. How it prances in the silver, its eye daring you to look away!

He cleared his throat in an unobtrusive manner, gesturing respectfully at the heavy lid.

"May I close the box at this time?" His voice was laden with respect, fear. Even awe and love.

A single nod from the client, who picked up gloves made of buttery leather, pulled them on, and then gathered her things. She was close enough to kiss him, and she did, chastely, on the cheek.

"'You have served me very well through both wars, Dieter. I am not ungrateful. You should be proud of this. So few have met my exacting standards through the years." She patted his cheek once, the leather faintly touching him and trailing to his neck with an intimacy few people knew he was capable of.

"It is my honor and my pleasure to serve you in any way that I may, Mother. You need only call, and I am at your service instantly." He radiated with pride at her compliment and the opportunity to serve at her feet. It was his mission, his instinct, becoming reality, here and now.

"Such a good boy. Yes, I think you shall be rewarded with a position in my next little endeavor. It will require some preparation on your part. You have, I think, until the summer to be fluent in Creole. Be ready for a move, and have all the resources necessary for the acquisition of property and quiet spaces. If you are not properly ready, I shall be-how did I tell your father after the first war-vexed? Yes, vexed."

Herr Kreiger paled. His father had died screaming in a rocky room beneath a café, his dying voice saturating the walls even as his blood ran rivulets into a stone trough. It had not been a swift death, either. Dieter tried, every day, to forget what disappointing his mother could bring to his doorstep.

"I shall be ready, Mother. I promise." He was earnest, and riddled with horror.

"There's a good lad. Until we visit New Orleans, then". Elizabeth walked from the vault, her heels on the carpet leaving no trace of her, save the spindrift of her perfume.

Made in the USA
Charleston, SC
20 March 2014